To Move the Farthest Star

Joachim Gordon

I0554101

Spytech Publishing, Toronto, Ontario

Printed by Spytech Publishing., in Canada.
First printing, 2019.
ISBN 978-1-9992163-0-6

Spytech Publishing
2005 Yonge St,
Toronto, ON, M4S 1Z8
Canada

Table of Contents

Chapter 1 - Death

"Nobody will ever read this." Sophia predicted as she hit the publish icon on the article she just finished writing for her blog. The name of her blog, "The World's Greatest Historian", alluded to the passion for history she shared with nobody else she knew. Unfortunately passion was her only motivation. You could find no better way to repel readers than a well researched, fact filled, long form article about a non-celebrity. She anticipated almost nobody would be clicking on her newest article about the life of Queen Anne of England. Of course the royalty and legendary historical figures she wrote about could technically considered celebrities, at least they were during their own eras, but in today's fickle society, they did not meet the most universal requirement of that status, which was having their butt-selfies go viral. Maybe she just needed to do some more research, and perhaps she could dig up some secret historical thong pictures, she mused to herself as she finally stood up from her desk.

A sudden increased level of shouting and honking from down in the streets, ended this daydream of e-glory, and reminded Sophia that the time had come to push herself into real-life mode. She had been slogging away all day long at her keyboard. That way she would have no "must do" tasks hanging over her head, and thus she could enjoy some time to herself. Today this meant finishing up a few pages of copy she wrote for several different corporate websites and her self-imposed deadline of keeping her own history blog up to date. Writing inane promotional announcements and newsletters did pay the rent, but her blog kept her sane, so she valued her hobby as much as her job.

There was no time to investigate what was causing all the excitement a dozen stories beneath her window, although it sounded a bit more chaotic than the usual Manhattan traffic drama, maybe there was serious road rage going on out there. Instead of gawking, she decided to prepare for her big date. Hyping the night up as her "big date" was Sophia's way of challenging herself to make a final decision about this relationship one way or the other, because this being their third date, she would be meeting her self imposed quota for deciding what to do next. If you can't decide about a relationship at this point, by the end of the third date, you never will. That was her philosophy and it seldom allowed for a fourth date.

As she contemplated the effectiveness of this life plan, she multitasked a quick tidy up of her bachelor pad, while doing likewise with her physical appearance. Windex in one hand and lipstick in the other. Easy enough to do, since everything in her typical Manhattan apartment was practically within arm's reach. Of course, living in a tiny home, not owning a car, nor having a yard, were the types of sacrifices you made to be located in the center of the universe, or as New York City was also known, the "Capital of the World". Sophia just wished she could enjoy the place a bit more. It's not like she was agoraphobic, but sometimes that swarm of human egos, and emotions, and agendas, and odors could be overwhelming. It did make her value her alone time, that's for sure.

Speaking of human swarms, was that racket of sirens, shouting and horns indicating that something really dangerous was happening outside her building?

Well, no need to speculate any more, it was time to go out and see for herself. Sophia was intent on being punctual in order to make her own contribution to the date as impressive as possible. She checked if she had her phone, keys, credit card, all there, and hurried out the door and to the elevator. Nice and quiet in the hallway at least.

She had no idea what the night promised but she did intend to keep an open mind about 'Ordinary Gus'. Sophia and her friends dubbed him 'ordinary' because after her first two dates, her only conclusion about him was that he was mentally stable, respectfully employed and not married, as far as she could tell. The nickname was actually a compliment. Now that their 20s were at an end, she and her friends came to a consensus that dating extraordinary people usually went along with extraordinary baggage. Sadly this statement even included a few bachelors she had dated herself, who could strut shirtless among all the Hollywood Chrises, and would not look out of place. Ordinary Gus looked more like a guy who collected action figures of the Hollywood Chrises. On the plus side, he listened to her when she talked, he was very intelligent, and he didn't immediately try to grope her boobs, all of which actually put him right near the top candidates of her dating experiences.

On their previous date, Gus had been polite enough to take her to her favorite Italian restaurant in the neighbourhood. Over angel hair pasta, he brought up such seductive topics of conversation as quantum entanglement, delayed choice experiments and his theories about self learning artificial intelligence. What a silver tongue this guy had. Yeah the conversation was a bit dry, and perhaps even over her head, but it was still an improvement on the usual favorite topic her dates would ramble on about, which was themselves. She figured that Ordinary Gus would have to be a real jackass tonight to make her lose all her positive vibes about him.

She entered the elevator and pushed the "Lobby" button that meant it was time for her next adventure to begin. Every outing into the streets of New York could be an adventure of course, but this time she was putting herself on the line. Her life goals, passion, love, success, happiness... heck, her very future was at stake! *Shit calm down girl.* She chilled herself out by spending the ride to the lobby eating an edible 50mg THC infused peanut butter cookie, just to get in a calmer mindset. She resolved to just go out, have a beer, and let the universe decide her fate, for better or worse. *No matter what you do the universe always wins!*

She exited the elevator.

A catastrophe welcomed her. The lobby was filled with people weeping, rambling incoherently and cowering in corners. Even for New York, this was unusual. Several others were staring outside the front windows in horror, while some were looking around like cornered cats, for a way to escape... but from what?

"What the fuck?" Sophia inquired as she took in the scene before her. Nobody noticed her.

"What the FUCK!" this time she used a tone only other New Yorkers could translate into a much longer message, something like, "We are all New Yorkers here, so we see crazy shit every day, and we have been through all kinds of chaos and terrorist attacks, and therefore nothing can shock us anymore. Now someone please explain why you are all shaken up!"

"It's Thanos," a cowering man finally mumbled while hiding in a corner.

Sophia understood. Someone a bit older might have referenced War of the Worlds, or Mars Attacks, but any of these examples promised a bad outcome. Apparently something really destructive was going on. The way this guy implied an alien invasion, however, she would just write that off to hysterics. Everyone knows witnesses of traumatic events are unreliable.

"No. It's the end of days," an old lady gushed, drunk with a religious awe that didn't originate from comic books, but sounded just as delusional. She stood by the window and never wavered from staring up at the sky, searching for some handsome TV Jesus to come down, and take her away from all the danger.

Sophia realized she was either at ground zero for some kind of major terror attack or some kind of alien invasion. Both of these possibilities were actually events that she often played out in her mind, when she would read about various historical catastrophes during her research, or just when she saw any big budget summer movies. Not that she thought it would ever happen to her but the people in those stories never thought so either. During any major catastrophic situation, she always figured the best course of action would be to assess the scale of the attack, and if it was large enough to destroy actual buildings, she would choose a direction that looked the safest, and run that way as fast as possible. Conversely, if the attack was smaller scale, she always liked to think that she would be brave enough to help people, because everyone else would be too busy standing around, filming with their phones.

She stepped outside into the street and immediately concluded that this was clearly the "run-away" type of situation. Buildings in the next block were already crumbling, while she noticed many people had come to the same conclusion as her, and were running away, passing through her own block at full speed. Smoke was obscuring her vision and filling her nose, but Sophia could still see a few people wearing various uniforms, NYPD, homeland security, postal workers, all shooting hastily up into the sky without any coordination between them. These people with firearms didn't look like they were very happy with the results of their shooting. Her ears were filled with the noise of human panic, car horns, gunshots and large objects crashing onto other large objects. Several people were lying on the ground and not moving. She couldn't tell who was dead or who was unconscious or who was simply paralyzed with fear. Many other people were injured and crying, or maybe just crying because they had no idea what else to do. The scene was one of overwhelming despair.

Most alarming of all, there was a massive alien ship hovering just above the height of the buildings. It was in the shape of a hockey puck and looked like it could easily engulf a small town inside it. There was no logical means for this behemoth to stay airborne that she could comprehend. Flashing lights and moving parts were all over the thing, but it didn't seem to be firing off any type of weapons at the moment. Instead it was pulling chunks of the city up into some chamber inside itself. Sophia looked closer as the debris floated up by some invisible force. She could see parts of buildings rising, including a lot of the furnishings and appliances from inside the buildings, but most of all, she saw a lot of people were being pulled up towards the spacecraft.

At the same time she noticed that the aliens were harvesting humans, she also realized that she had been standing in one place and ignoring the important "running away" phase of her plan! *Great timing getting high on edibles, Sophia, you dumbass stoner.* Just as She pivoted around from the direction of all this action, she froze. A large chunk of her own building - perhaps even her own floor - landed on the street exactly in the spot she was about to run to. *Awe shit.* The thud was so loud it caused her ears to start ringing, but luckily none of the rubble ended up hitting her, because she certainly didn't have the reflexes to dodge it. She wiped the thick disaster soot out of her eyes in order to immediately search for a new escape route.

As she scanned her block, she saw even more people were now lying on the ground, probably others were buried under the fallen debris, and more of the inevitable walking wounded still passed by her. Nobody was shooting up at the sky any more. Nobody even appeared to be yelling any more, although she wouldn't be able to hear them, much less help them, if they were. Sophia was startled by the sight of several dogs and cats and rats emerging into the middle of the street, all with a very calm demeanor, even though the most natural animal instinct should be to flee from so much chaos. This rapidly growing assembly of pets and the pests stood motionless and stared up at the slowly approaching craft high above them, the way she would see tourists stare up at the Empire State Building the first time they saw it. Within seconds she observed with some dismay that the nearby humans were also beginning to imitate the exact same routine she had just seen the critters perform. This was senseless.

Mind control!

Sophia reckoned that these aliens must have vastly superior technology to anything humans could easily comprehend. She assumed that even with Earth's most powerful weapons, we would essentially be as threatening to these aliens, as apes throwing sticks at an Apache Helicopter. Resistance was futile. Putting the technology disadvantage aside for a moment, she had seen enough movies and played enough video games, to figure out how this was going to play out. Somehow the space travelers were stealing humans (specifically living people not corpses) so the easiest way to keep their trophies from fighting back, hurting themselves or even pooping their pants in fear , would be to immobilize them somehow. If she was right about this theory, then she could also figure out a way to avoid it... Maybe. She squeezed her eyes shut so nothing could influence her mind visually, and she conveniently couldn't hear much of anything, as her ears were still ringing. She also tried to lock up her mind by concentrating only on her next blog topic. *Should I write something about Rome?   I never wrote about Rome before.   Which emperor would be fun to write about?   Is this even working?   Shut up and concentrate on Rome!*

She eventually decided to take a quick peek and was alarmed to see the ground now descending far below her feet. She did not feel like she was in motion. Looking up was out of the question in case that mind control tech would zap her brain through the eyes. Sophia wasn't sure how she managed to avoid whatever was effecting all the other humans and animals. Perhaps it was her diminished hearing, her heroic mental determination, or was it just that the high level of THC in her brain was acting as a countermeasure? Whatever the reason was, it was working! *You're Jedi Mind Trick won't work on me, you fuckers!* She was feeling pretty confident for someone suspended some 20 stories above the ground by unknown means. The mysterious energy that was lifting her did not feel like it was pulling, or even touching her at all, but rather she felt like she was still just standing on solid ground, and the ground was moving. The only way she knew she was still rising was the increased breeze on her face as she cleared the surrounding buildings. Then the wind stopped.

She opened her eyes and looked around for what to do next. Her location resembled a large warehouse space filled with all the other people that had been abducted along with her. She couldn't spot any superheroes, unfortunately, except for one fake Spider Man from Times Square, but he did not look like he could hustle tourists for cash selfies right now, never mind save the world! Of course she knew that there were no super powered humans in the real world and she had read enough about history to conclude that there probably never were any. However, a hero doesn't have to have powers. She wondered why some billionaire didn't build elaborate super gadgets to fight for justice, like a Bruce Wayne, or a Tony Stark. All those super rich and powerful people in the world and not one is coming to save us now? So all those billionaires just bought themselves useless crap like everyone else? This would have been the perfect situation for a hero to show up!

13

So it goes. Even though her actual circumstances eluded her, she was decidedly on her own, like it or not. Nobody else was even looking around the room the way she was. Could she yell and wake them all up to fight? Not likely. If they didn't even notice they were flying just minutes earlier, nothing she could say would wake them.

None of those dazed critters from the street were up there. Somehow this enraged Sophia. She pictured all the rats devouring all the humans' pizzas, and hot dogs, in a completely undeserved victory party. This was the ultimate insult to a New Yorker. She truly hoped that the homeless dogs and cats would spoil the rat tailgate party on behalf of their fallen masters. Let those rats go back to solving mazes and spreading plagues.

She also couldn't locate any of the junk that she had seen levitating up from the buildings. Maybe, if she could just get into a pile of that crap, she would be able to find some useful tool to help her escape? It was probably over in some separate cargo space, far out of reach, which eliminated any chance of finding weapons, or hiding places, or best of all right now would be a parachute. *Don't get discouraged, just think!* She was trying to snap out of the panic that had caused her to stand in one spot, like a deer in the headlights, ever since she exited her building.

A few dozen bodies ahead of her, she could see that people were being zipped off in various directions, towards what she assumed were their designated long term human storage facilities . This is where she finally saw one of THEM. An alien was supervising the sorting and transfer operation of each human in the line, and gradually making its way towards her. The thing was shaped like a fifteen foot long worm-slug, but with a few dozen limbs, and each of these ending in a claw. Two antennae protruded from its head just above what looked like eyes and two rows of spikes stuck out of its back and resembled another set of legs. The thing looked like a monster from a nightmare she never had. The creature had a thick skin, probably pretty tough, but it did look like it was some kind of organic living animal, which meant to Sophia, it had to be possible to kill it.

With only seconds left before her turn would come, Sophia spotted a man in a NYPD uniform, including his service weapon still holstered on his belt. It was only a few steps to reach the officer, and she already had her target, so no more planning needed. Quickly she lunged for past the person on her right. Until the moment she took those five steps to close the distance between herself and the weapon, she didn't know if she would actually be able to move, since she had been acting as if she was paralyzed for a while now. She pulled the handgun out of the holster and the cop didn't even flinch. The extraterrestrial being, who was only three rows ahead of her by now, stopped its work routine and remained motionless. *Hopefully I caught him off guard...*

"You think you can just come here and Bill Cosby me right off of my own planet? Eh you bastard?" Sophia yelled in a tone that she intended to communicate her anger to this alien who would neither understand her language, nor her weapons. She was under no illusion that raising her voice would accomplish much, since it never did with her fellow New Yorkers either, but she was willing to try anything before ending up in a shootout against whatever the hell these aliens used as weapons.

She yelled one final command as she raised the gun and aimed, "Return us all to the ground or I'm gonna put you under it!"

Obviously, the critter had no idea how to react to this ultimatum, and it was pointless to continue with her demands. She decided that the only appropriate end to Mankind's first encounter with intelligent alien life was a hail of bullets! She closed her eyes, prepared for the recoil and pulled the trigger, but "click click click," is all that the gun would say. Of course it all made sense. That cop would have unloaded everything he had, as soon as he saw a space ship coming towards him, so he probably ran out of ammo within the first ten seconds of this event.

Fuck it! Strike first, strike hard, no mercy.

With a sudden burst of Karate Kid nostalgia guiding her movements, Sophia sprinted the few steps remaining between them, and lunged directly at the huge monster. It remained still. She raised the gun as she ran, and swung it down with all her weight behind it, onto what she considered the creature's head, just at the instant that she landed on top of it. The space traveler let out a noise that sounded like the beginning of the song White Room and she felt its body collapse beneath her from the blow. The sound made her panic because she only now realized her hearing was returning. Her fear of being stunned by a mind control weapon at any moment inspired her to unleash a furious beating on the helpless alien. She was not a trained fighter in any way, but neither was her opponent, it seemed. With all the strength she could gather, Sophia pounded on that creature, using both of her fists as hammers.

Freelance writer, history blogger, serial dater, and in the span of merely a few minutes, earth's only alien slayer! Sophia ran out of breath and finally stopped raining blows upon the monster. Since she expected to be killed way before this point she had to look around to gather her thoughts. The handful of people that were still standing in the same room were all staring at her and yelling the type of vulgar affection New Yorkers reserved for their most beloved Yankee players. She had somehow released these people from their trances with her violent actions. Based on this outcome, what could be a better choice, than more violence?

"Alright lets fuck up these aliens and take their ship!" Sophia addressed the adoring crowd. If she had more time she would have quoted some of her favorite lines from Henry V, in order to rally this mob with more grace, but she was pretty sure the aliens were about to act. Sure enough electronic beeps and mechanical movements filled the room.

The people before her were in the middle of shouting, "YEAH!" when the cheer suddenly changed to screams of terror, as they dropped down through the floor and into the sky below the space craft. So much for that uprising.

She turned to see the same many-armed-worm she thought she had beaten to death, standing up on just the last few back legs, so it could effectively tower high above her. It did not look injured except for the disgusting fluid that it was leaking on her. But the fluid was not

16

alien blood, or alien vomit, it was glue! A few big drops landed on her arms and when she tried to wipe them off her arms became stuck to her body.

The alien made some sort of noise that she assumed was a condescending lecture about how she barely even hurt it when she attacked, and probably something else about how humans were such harmless dopes compared to these advanced space traveling worms. If she could have raised her arm she would have flipped it off. When the creature finally decided to drop the mic, she saw it flick its right antenna, and she immediately went flying out of the space craft and into the sky.

As Sophia was falling towards the ground she thought about the date she would never have, the ordinary man she would never get to fall in love with, the places she would never go, the movie franchise sequels she would never see. Every little pleasure in life seemed so extra precious now that it was only seconds away from disappearing. She felt a little satisfaction in the way she would go out, on her own badass terms, but her goal all along was to save herself, not to become a martyr. In about half a second Sophia would hit the pavement at 120mph and die instantly.

No matter what you do the universe always wins.

Chapter 2 - Life

"... and that is why you have been chosen to save the universe," God was in the middle of explaining something to Sophia, something she could hear, but her mind did not process the words properly.

"Um... what?" she had been fading in and out of consciousness throughout the conversation.

"Of course. Take your time. It makes sense that you would be confused right now," God sighed and stroked his big white beard patiently to give Sophia a moment to get her bearings.

The two of them were standing face to face in a large empty room. There was nothing visible to indicate where that room was. Some kind of afterlife meet and greet? Sophia didn't think so. She could feel gravity pulling her to the ground, hear the breeze outside the room, and sense the aches and pains of her flesh and bones. She was breathing heavily, almost as if she was exercising, because the air seemed quite thin where she was. All of this evidence suggested she was not dead at all.

"Where am I... No wait, how am I alive?" Sophia could barely spit out one question because she had so many.

"You are correct about being alive... right now at least. However you were quite dead just a few minutes ago," the elderly gentleman explained to her. "In fact, you died many centuries ago, but you have just been reborn."

"Well, thanks for the resurrection," Sophia didn't know the proper etiquette for an audience with the Lord Almighty. She bowed as if she was greeting a respected Japanese businessman. "Are You THE God... or are you a... cosplay God?"

"Ah yes 'God' is the way someone from your time would address me. I am known by most as 'The Creator' and I am called by many names though I do not have a name," he said with a hint of nostalgia.

His answer made it seem to Sophia that He had not heard her common 21st centurey Christian lingo, for quite a while now. If she had been absent for several centuries, there must have been some major changes in the human culture as she knew it. Of course the final event of her life must have had a major effect on religious views, along with science, and pretty much every other type of attitude in the world at that time. Obviously humans finally had confirmation that they were not alone in the universe. It was a huge concept for all of humanity to rationalize, but on top of that, they also had to come to terms with being the far more primitive life form, certainly in comparison to the only other life form they had contact with. Too bad she was not around for all those confusing times. As an amateur historian, it would have been fascinating to witness a period of unprecedented upheaval and self reflection, all around the world.

"I'm surprised that you look just like the God I used to see in movies and paintings," Sophia was pleased that it wasn't a burning bush she was addressing.

"I have no form, at least none that you could possibly see, so your reality is formed by your perception. And perception is reality," said the Creator , "I look the way I do because that is how you expect me to look."

"Well that makes sense," she now understood why God had a white beard and why they both wore robes in the style of Middle Earth Wizards, "May I ask you, Lord Almighty, Oh Holy One, Creator of the Earth and the Stars, Ruler of the Kingdom of Heaven, what do you want with me?"

"I have summoned you to save the universe. There have been a lot of changes since you were last alive. The age of man has ended. The world you once knew is now ruled by the Fallen One whom you would know as Satan. His strength has increased over the centuries and now He is so powerful that he can even threaten My own existence!

"After many millennia of competing with each other, we have both learned that our battles would only sustain an endless stalemate, as nobody could ever decisively win. In fact, it would only be a stalemate until our battles grew so large that we would one day cause the destruction of the whole universe. This would also destroy both of us as well so there is no reason for either of us to pursue that end. However the Fallen One is the expert in destruction and he has recently found a way to spare himself from such a fate. Even now he is gathering his armies and preparing to destroy the universe and put an end to everything, except of course, Himself."

"That really sucks," Sophia lamented, interrupting God's narrative, "I didn't even know there was a Satan, or a God until now, and here You are telling me all of existence is about to be finished! Can't You do something? The bible says that You sometimes cause catastrophic..."

"Bible?" God spat the word, "I did not write that book! Man has always had a bad habit of speaking on My behalf. How could a mere human author presume to interpret the thoughts of an infinitely superior mind, or attempt to describe such divine actions as the creation of man? Such arrogance!"

"Yes that sure is the way it has been throughout history, and during my time as well," Sophia agreed, "But I never knew of you appearing in person like you are now! Why not dispute the actions mankind has done in your name?"

"As I told you I am the Creator. That is why I never directly interfered with your history. That is why I do not directly interfere, even now. If I ever stop creating and start destroying, then destruction will be the only force left in the universe, and everything will vanish. You may not understand it but In many ways I am the most powerless of all beings. The Fallen One is also powerless in His own way, as he is unable to create, much like I am unable to destroy.

"The only means I have to stop Him is through the use of creation, which is why I have created you. You have something that neither He nor I have: Free Will. You should know about this dangerous gift even more than most humans. I chose to resurrect you, Sophia, for two reasons. One is that you were among the very last of the First Men. The second reason is that you are the 'World's Greatest Historian.' Your knowledge about all of human history, and the ways your kind has used your power of free will over thousands of years, will be essential in saving us all."

Sophia pondered the logic in this explanation. According to the mainstream science she learned, from science fiction movies and television, she understood that the universe was forever expanding, ever since its creation. Could it be that this creator was somehow maintaining that expansion? If he stopped what he was doing, would the universe implode into itself, and maybe reboot itself with a new Big Bang? Who knows? Unfortunately, Sophia was not an expert in omnipotent beings, or advanced physics. She decided to take the Elderly Gentleman's reasoning at face value instead of challenging Him to provide scientific evidence. A bit of good manners was the least she could offer, after he had chosen to resurrect her out of billions of people, and it seemed mainly because of her ironically exaggerated blog title. At least that title made in impression with Someone. She decided not to bring up the fact that God was mistaking her for some kind of PHD-level academic historian, when in fact, she had PH nothing.

"Last of the First Men? What does that mean?" Sophia inquired nervously.

"Before that catastrophic event that caused your death, you knew mankind as the descendents directly from the first man, whom I created in My own image. However, after your encounter with the non-humans, man's soul became corrupted by new perilous kinds of knowledge. Man embraced the impure ways of the non-human visitors and was easily seduced into defacing his own flesh. The beings you knew as 'people' quickly became some new breed of animal of their own design. Over time, the remaining First Men became fewer and fewer, and have since perished.

"But that is just a brief update. There are many centuries of history you have missed and it is not in my nature to impart such knowledge. You will have much time to learn it all for yourself as you journey back to your home. My nature is to go back to the business of creation."

"Holy shit!" Sophia's head was spinning at all these revelations. "Where are we?"

"I mentioned that the world you knew was gone. Today we are standing on a nameless world far from searching eyes. It is empty and cold. I have already begun to create the beginnings of life upon this world but you are the first of your kind here," as he spoke, he waved his arms theatrically for Sophia's benefit, and the room they were in disappeared.

They now stood outside on a hilltop. Sophia could feel a strong wind blowing through her new hair. No wonder, there was not a tree higher than her waist in sight, and she did not see any buildings either. It looked like a landscape that had been devastated by a forest fire, to only recently start growing back. She noticed that any vegetation she could see was unfamiliar to her. Looking up, she could see some thin clouds speed past, and beyond that there were two large moons illuminating the night sky, one yellow and one white. The planet's local sun was hidden beneath the horizon for now.

This is fucked up - I'm on another planet!

God explained to her, "This place is safe for now. Food and drink will soon be plentiful. You will not be alone much longer. I have the resources and the time to create only 10 more humans like yourself. I can already tell you that this process, the one that created you, will draw the attention of other beings in the universe. Once that happens, the Fallen One will quickly end this place like He has ended so many others, and therefore, I will send you and your fellow travelers away as soon as I have finished creating them. That is the only way to prevent your destruction."

Sophia had millions of questions to ask but she could see that God was not used to explaining Himself. She decided that she would wait for more information to be revealed. What was she supposed to do to stop a supernatural being? How was she going to reach earth from here? Who were these 10 other people that were being resurrected?

"Sophia you go and rest now. I must continue my work or I will not have enough time. Go forth in that direction and you will find shelter and nourishment," He indicated she should walk in the direction behind her, "From any of this garden you may eat freely."

"But not from the tree of the knowledge of good and evil?" she wondered out loud.

"There is no such tree here, and besides, you will find enough knowledge of good and evil, in your shelter. Use your skills as a historian to learn about what happened to your world. But first, use your knowledge to give me 10 of your greatest Earth men of the past to resurrect. These names must be from before your time, so that they are pure human souls, and not corrupted like the generations after yours. Choose men of courage and wisdom and skill. They should also be strong willed, so that they do not bend under the temptations of the Fallen One, reliable in difficult times, and loyal to you."

"Very well. I will give you 10 names very soon." Sophia was already brainstorming.

"Before you leave me, just give me one name, with a description. Who is the first person you would surely want by your side? Then I may begin the next creation process as you rest and think of the other names," God was certainly in a hurry to begin.

Sophia didn't hesitate,"Any person in history? Well, that's an easy one..."

Chapter 3 - Fire

It was a warm spring day as thousands of people crowded into the market in Rouen. A festive atmosphere grew throughout the morning, since the one person they held responsible for all their problems was about to be put to death, before all their eyes. This was a day they would remember for the rest of their lives. Instead of the usual peasant routine of manual labour, pain and dirt, they would all be treated to a flaming spectacle of someone else's suffering. This day they would watch a nasty witch burn.

Sure enough the large crowd erupted with noise when the Maid of Orleans appeared before them and was roped to a post high atop a mountain of firewood. It was not pleasant to watch. The sight of this harmless teenage girl trying to keep her composure, despite obviously being terrified, was alarming to see for many of the people. Some cried, some laughed and some shouted with outrage. Their reactions were based on their own perceptions of this person before them.

"You killed my son! Witch!" shouted a filthy woman in rags.

This unruly peasant woman had traveled on foot for hours, before the sun rose, just to see the execution with her own eyes. It was the furthest distance she had traveled in many years. Of course, she could have stayed home and heard all about the event eventually, but there would always be a little bit of doubt in the back of her mind. Perhaps that girl would escape! After all, this woman, who's name was Oriane, had already heard stories about the Maid of Orleans speaking to spirits, predicting the future and winning impossible victories in battle. Those deeds were even more impressive than escaping an execution.

One day at church, the peasant Oriane had heard about the Battle of Jargeau, where the Maid fearlessly climbed up a ladder to scale the city's outer wall, only to be hit by a large rock thrown by one of the town's defenders above. The Maid fell to the ground surely never to

24

rise again. But rise she did! The attack on Jargeau continued on with more vigor than ever, and the English, along with their French Burgundy allies, were massacred within hours. That notorious rock did not survive the encounter with the Maid of Orleans and neither did Oriane's only son. The woman was told by her priest, after the service, that her son had been crushed by one of the buildings that fell as a result of a brutal cannon barrage. Almost the very same death that the witch herself had cheated! If the rock had split the Maid's skull, just a few hours earlier, the battle would have ended before the young boy was killed.

Before her young soldier boy ever went off to join the war, the woman was confident that he would find his way into a favorable rank, and perhaps become a famous war hero one day. Then one day, the whole family would celebrate the boy's victory when France and England were finally united under one King. Why shouldn't they? They were all French - even the English royalty were from French families - and they were all God fearing Christians. There was no reason for this war among such close brothers. The one and only thing stopping all this potential peace and unity from progressing, was that pretender to the throne, Charles the treacherous Dauphin, forever cowering in some village far from battle. All the while some little girl fought his war for him!

That same little girl was somehow able to stop the endless succession of English victories when she appeared at Orleans just a few months ago. How was it possible? The English had not tasted defeat in a generation and still they fled the battlefield before a woman who could barely even swing a sword. Then more battles followed with the same catastrophic result. The universe appeared to have taken the side of the Maid of Orleans, both from her allies' point of view, and her enemies' as well. That was when she was finally captured.

The English army was almost wiped out by then, and the only thing the Duke of Burgundy could do was try to discredit the girl who had cost him his claim on France. He organized a public trial to humiliate the idol of the French people, but even in this battle of wits, she still defeated him. The girl would not even speak ill of the villainous Dauphin who was content to let her rot in prison without sending a single sword or coin to save her.

What evil magic did this girl conjure to destroy of the dream of a United Kingdom of France and England? How could this witch be just a normal peasant girl from a small French village? The old woman had lived the same life as the Maid had. The only difference between them was that she learned, over so many hard years, that there was no way for someone like her to change the world. So it was only logical that some unholy forces had to be involved, and neither peasants, nor soldiers, nor Kings had the power to stop them. With that in mind, many in the crowd were still speculating about how the supernatural girl would escape her execution. Let them have their fantasies. The old bitter peasant woman was going to watch the witch burn alright, and just to put her mind at ease, she was going to watch until the very end.

"Do not burn her! You will curse this town!" one man screamed louder than most.

The man was a local merchant named Roul. He could see no positive outcome from this execution. The trial was a sham, even by 1430s standards, and everybody knew it. But it was not the stigma of injustice he feared. There were rumors in the crowd that the notorious brute, La Hire, was rampaging through the countryside in search of his former colleague. What would the man with the famous bad temper do to this town that allowed the execution of his most legendary friend? Any moment he expected to see La Hire's cavalry charge into the market and start slaughtering the people in a last second rescue attempt. The merchant looked to the heavens in despair. Yet, even as he looked at the sky above he realized praying was pointless in this situation.

For one thing, this merchant understood the logic of being a "Good Christian". Simply put, if there was actually a God, as Christians are taught, then a good person would be rewarded, and a bad person would be punished in the afterlife. If there was no God, that didn't matter, because you still had nothing to lose by being good. So why

26

not wager everything on that rewarding afterlife? It was a beneficial transaction. Being a merchant, it seemed like the obvious way to live, and the most profitable. Likewise, the merchant reasoned that leaving this Maid of Orleans alive was the obvious choice. What if her visions were real? God would surely punish the ones who declared His own messenger a heretic! What are they gaining by this execution? Some petty revenge? That was such a tiny reward, compared to being punished by the wrath of God, if they were wrong about her!

But what could be done about it? Another lesson the merchant had learned long ago, is that the rational way, was rarely the popular way. The people, the crowds, the markets, they always followed an unpredictable path, even when it went against their own interest. It was frustrating for the reasonable merchant to observe, but to succeed in his trade, he had to study all the illogical notions of the masses, for they were his customers. Right now he could observe that his customers were in the market for blood. These people would happily burn this woman even if she grew angel's wings and a halo right before their eyes! He gave up on trying to warn them. Alas, all he could do was hope that La Hire would seek revenge against the Duke of Burgundy, instead of him, and that this girl was indeed just another false prophet, so God would not be angry.

"Hold the cross high so I may see it through the flames," said the young Maid of Orleans to a monk standing nearby while someone out of her sight line was lighting the fire beneath her platform.

The 19 year old warrior maiden, who would in later years be known as Joan of Arc, spoke a few words to her favorite saints as the flames began to rise. She even asked God to spare the city of Rouen and forgive all those who had sinned against her. The fear she had felt earlier that day was now replaced by pity. All these people watching her today, did not know what she knew about the world, nor would they ever accomplish half the deeds she had done. None of them had heard messages from God. None of them had driven the English invaders out of France. If they all lived to be 100 years old none of them would live the life she had lived in her few short years.

To ease her mind, she reflected on her glorious moments. There were the battles where she rode at the head of her army, directly at the enemy forces, without a weapon. Somehow she knew she was protected by divine influence, though she did not understand why, and it gave her the courage to face any danger. The courage she displayed rubbed off on her own troops, and also struck genuine fear in her enemies. Most of her victories were simply the enemy army surrendering at the sight of her approach. These were the days she cherished the most, and remembering them comforted her, because nobody had to die on those occasions.

Then there were the battles that did have death.

Joan remembered watching her commanders prepare a siege at the town of Jargeau. As these career military officers discussed their different strategies, and made their plans to take the city, they still occasionally asked Joan if she had any divine premonitions about the coming battle. This treatment was similar to the humiliating days in the court of the Dauphin, when the noble men would endlessly question her about their wives' adultery, or the noble women would ask her about intrigues and scandals of the court. She cared nothing about such trifles. Her irritation at being treated like some curiosity inspired her to leave those military commanders to their own discussions.

So she decided, instead of listening to the minds that had engineered a generation of French military defeats, she went to visit the soldiers themselves, who were far too inferior to be any interest to the noble officers. The peasants, the servants, the foot soldiers; she grew up among their kind, not in the palaces among Dukes and Knights. To them, she was just a savior, not an oracle, not a noble, not even a general. They had already watched her stand in their midst under fire. Even before any of these soldiers knew her, they had watched her mount a horse, and without any of their commanders joining her, charge off towards the enemy lines. Of course the foot soldiers were right behind her, this mysterious girl that had no rank or title, and the army became her army that day. Now she could order them to follow her into any battle and they would not even wait for their commanders' orders. She could ban profanity and they would not complain. She banished the prostitutes and ordered the men to go to confession and they did. As long as she would ride among them on the battlefield, in her shiny white armor, they feared no enemy, and they accepted all her guidance.

During her time visiting among these people Joan learned about their morale. These young men understood that they were nothing more than pawns in the chess game of their aristocratic leaders. There was no will to win, because there was technically nothing to be won. It made no real difference to the average peasant whether he lived under a French King or an English King. In fact, nothing about his life would change. Nothing about Joan's life would change either. Yet here she was, fighting among them for a cause she believed in, not for her own self promotion, because her easiest path to social advancement she had left back at the palace. The men were inspired by her example. That inspiration, and the way it improved morale, caused the turning point of the French fortunes.

But inspiration could only convince men to march into battle. If there was no coordination, or strategy, the soldiers would merely be inspired to march to their deaths. Joan made an effort to learn about strategy. She was illiterate, inexperienced in the art of war, and could barely swing her own sword. But if there was one thing she understood well, it was the pompous arrogance of the nobles, and that they didn't have any better grasp on strategy than she did. Of course, the people who really knew what was working and what wasn't, were the soldiers.

With some more discussion, Joan learned about the many mistakes her commanders had been making. In the world she lived in, the noble class was in charge, and the peasants knew their place. It was not a normal procedure in the military for someone in her position to ask advice from an inferior. However, Joan learned much from the soldiers about tactics, weapons, armor, horses and most of all, cannons. The official commanders were set in their ways. They were superior in the class structure but not in military knowledge. Joan would be able to take all the information of the most innovative soldiers she talked to, use her rank to influence the commanders, and thereby impose new strategies that would have been ignored without her.

When she returned to the commanders, who were now standing on a hill overlooking the town's defenses, Joan yelled a warning at the Duke of Alencon, who was the so-called leader of her army. The Duke had spent years as a prisoner in this war, and had long ago lost his taste for danger, so he did not hesitate to move away from his location, even if he did not think he was in danger. Within an hour a cannon blast from inside the town hit the exact spot where the Duke had been standing. Poor Alencon was shaken by the fact that he had been standing directly in the line of fire. How could he protect the soldiers if he could not even protect himself? This event made Joan realize that, even without divine knowledge sending her orders, she intended to make the decisions for this army from now on.

The downside to this responsibility was that Joan now had blood on her hands. When she oversaw the artillery barrage into the town she directly caused the deaths of soldiers and even civilians. When she argued with the other commanders she always argued for the most direct and violent strategy. Whenever she was faced with the choice to run away, or to fight, she always chose to fight. It was all a strange paradox. She was the gentle girl who would not strike her enemies with her sword, and yet she was ruthless in her strategies, and so many died by her orders.

That is why she was facing execution. This is why a whole city full of fellow French peasants were there to watch, not to rescue her. She knew it was going to end this way when she started listening to the voices. Didn't it always end this way for people like her? Certainly it did for Saint Catherine, one of the spirits she had spoken to, which could only have been an omen of her own fate. She was never on a path to a long peaceful life.

As Joan drew her last breath of thick smoke, she thought to herself, would she would do it all again? Sure she would.

Chapter 4 - Friends

Several weeks had passed, and this strange planet was becoming somewhat familiar to Sophia, and even to its newest inhabitant, Joan of Arc. They spent all their time getting to know each other, learning about the vast amount of history they were not involved in, and exploring their new world. There were no more visits from God with his nice white beard. He was busy in some unknown location, creating the crew of the best humans Sophia could come up with, for her upcoming mission.

It was about two weeks after her arrival that Sophia had been awoken one night by their automated talking house. She was told to return to the same place she had arrived at, because a newcomer would be there. Someone that looked a lot like Joan of Arc was standing there in a state of confusion, so Sophia greeted her and answered her questions, trying to put her at ease. She also noticed that God apparently passed his greeter job on to her. This was probably a solid plan, since she was the one choosing the people that were being brought to this place.

After spending just a few days together, the two women became friends, as anyone would if they were the only two people in the world. They investigated the vegetation that was just starting to spread around their world. Together they would taste any plants that looked edible and sometimes experiment with cooking them in different ways. Gradually they decided that their favorite treat were some blue tennis ball looking fruits, that could be peeled like oranges, and tasted like Pina Coladas. They also had a more valuable effect of easing their stomachs whenever they tasted something that was not meant for human consumption.

The only competition they had for these fruits were some furry creatures that occasionally appeared from the bushes, but quickly scurried away when spotted, presumably to some nearby burrows.

Sophia had been interested in catching one of these creatures when she was alone because they reminded her of a real live Pokemon. But then Joan was never interested in hunting those things for food or entertainment, since they looked less like Pokemon and more like some kind of plague-filled monster, from her point of view. Sophia eventually gave up on the idea. Besides, she never hunted anything in her previous life, so why start now? Starvation, of course would be one good reason, but it was never an issue. The incredibly advanced house had the ability to generate all the food they could eat.

The whole point of their food gathering excursions was to go out and stretch their legs and explore. No humans, in either of their lifetimes had ever visited another planet, and their location was not lost on them. What they witnessed was the birth of a new world. Every day, they noticed the vegetation was increasing, the life forms were growing, and the air becoming slightly richer in oxygen. Yesterday's primordial soup became today's main course. Whatever process had been set in motion, it was rapidly improving the diversity of life, but how it worked was beyond human comprehension. Nevertheless, there was a wealth of information available to help the humans learn anything they wanted.

Sophia spent a lot of time researching everything she could think of, using the artificial intelligence embedded within their enormous house. This AI had the ability to display videos on the many big screens, generate holograms, play music recording, and even 3d print any object that Sophia could describe in enough detail. The AI had archives of millions of files including videos of movies Sophia knew, text news stories from older ages of history, and media files in futuristic formats like VR and holograms, that became common in the decades after her death. It was essentially the internet of the future. There was endless content to keep Sophia occupied when she had nobody else around.

When Joan eventually joined her, Sophia spent time telling Joan about the many years that separated their two lifetimes. She explained to Joan how her image was used to promote everything from freedom and liberty, to racism and violence, but she was never really forgotten. She gave Joan a brief history of France and Europe as well. The two of them spent a lot of their time looking at screens and reading research material, so it was a nice relief to go outside in the evenings, when the weather was not exceedingly hot, and explore the strange reality of the planet instead of the virtual media they looked at all day long.

As they wandered around one evening, the two of them tested their physical conditions, by running full speed, and leaping as far as possible. It seemed to Sophia that they were able to run much faster and jump much further than she remembered being able to before. It was very likely that the atmosphere, the gravity or the environment were influencing the results, but Sophia did feel that her new body was clearly far stronger and healthier than her previous one.

"I am alarmed, Sophia," Joan confided in her at the time, "that I feel so different from my old self. I don't even look like myself very much. Doesn't this not bother you?"

"Well I personally look somewhat like I did in my mid 20s and that works for me," Sophia admitted, "As for you, I think you kind of resemble Maria Falconetti, the great actress who once portrayed you in a famous film. I don't think there were any legitimate portraits of you that have survived to this time, so your appearance and your new body must be based on scraps of old descriptions, and images of you that were created hundreds of years after anybody had even seen you. I have personally never seen a portrait of you except the ones that were painted long after your death."

"It's odd. Why did God send me on a holy mission all those years ago and now He does not remember what I looked like?"

"Based on my short interaction with Him, it didn't seem like He was very interested in us individual mortals. If He was interested in those kinds of details, my own role in his resurrection process would be completely unnecessary. He could certainly choose ten human heroes without my input," Sophia said, but Joan still looked more puzzled than convinced, "Well what man or woman can know the mind of God?"

"Indeed. I certainly know less about God than I thought I did. Well, I admit that I enjoy having this new body even if I do look so different. I would have won a few more battles if I could have been stronger than any man in my army. I might even be stronger than the men and the horses combined!" Joan was admiring the massive muscles in her arm.

"Yes. I think we have been given bodies in the maximum physical condition a human body is capable of. If we were created by design, instead of born naturally, then it makes sense to make every part of us as strong as possible. Maybe we are even artificially enhanced in some way beyond any regular human body! Let's go back to the house and I'll tell you the tale of Captain America, a great hero of my people," Sophia promised.

Even though the sparse flora and fauna, combined with their lack of cooking skills, offered a limited cuisine, the two of them were provided with seemingly unlimited food by their automated house. Sophia was impressed by all the technology involved. Somehow the house would send drones out to collect resources, which were either stored for later, or broken down into the tiniest molecular components. The appropriate elements, like hydrogen, were extracted and used to fuel a large fusion engine deep within the building, that powered all the technology and operations. Minerals were mined and converted into ores that would be used to generate physical objects. Organic matter was gathered, broken down to a molecular level, and then reassembled into the food and drink to feed the inhabitants.

She did recognize certain components around the building, like holographic displays, motion capture sensors, voice recognition microphones, some computer parts that looked vaguely familiar; but overall, the electronics looked centuries more advanced than the gadgets she had once used. The automated system was still user friendly enough to make her lack of knowledge irrelevant. On her first day living there, Sophia spent an hour trying to figure out how the hot dog she had asked for was created by the 3D printing machine in the kitchen, but she was reminded of an old New York adage, that if you knew what was in the hot dog, you would never eat it. Some truths could transcend the centuries. Thinking of those old days, she remembered that she never knew how to build her own mobile phone, or an air conditioner, and those were primitive compared to the machines that surrounded her now. There was no point trying to figure out how all this stuff worked.

The house also had some kind of futuristic smart home attendant, which would often speak to her, using an imitation of her own voice. She called it "Gabby" because this electronic companion would ramble on and on about any topic she come up with. It would continue talking endlessly until she commanded it to stop. So far, Sophia had never come up with a question that could stump the damn thing.

"Gabby, who should I summon to join my team?" Sophia asked, way back when she was first learning how to use the AI, and before she had finalized her list of names.

"Your mission is going to be dangerous, physically demanding and complex. I would estimate that you will need some people who are skilled in military strategy, individual combat, problem solving and working as a team. I could list a series of names for you to consider, based on my vast database of historical information, if you would like to provide me with a set of parameters." Gabby responded as helpful as always.

Sophia did ask Gabby for her top 100 names, with priority given to certain traits she felt were important, and she was pleased to see all the people she was considering were somewhere on that list, except Joan of Arc. She decided not ask about that omission.

At the time that she was deciding on the members of her team, Sophia still did not know any details of the mission she would have to undertake, which made her selections very difficult. The one thing she could predict, was that there would be a lot of unknowns ahead of her, so it was best to plan her team for a variety of scenarios rather than one specific task. She felt most comfortable with that philosophy. It seemed that part of her team's job would be to enter into some unpredictable situations and then have the ability to react accordingly. Her own role was to bring a human element into these decisions, obviously, or they could have simply gone through Gabby's computer generated list without her input. With that in mind, she decided to use her gut instinct to guide her choices.

Her new friend Joan was the personification of gut instinct. Of course, Joan's military accomplishments impressed Sophia, but there were so many famous warriors she could have summoned instead, including a few whom she would be choosing for the other members of the group. Her reasoning was a bit more practical. Sophia had chosen Joan as her first companion, because she was the only other person she knew of, who was sent on a mission by God. Who better to have at you side?

"Tell me about this man who will be arriving today." Joan requested, as she already knew the next member of the team was someone from a time after her own.

"I have summoned a famous military commander named John Churchill, the Duke of Marlborough. You will be pleased to know, he won his fame by often facing superior armies, as you once did. Despite these odds, he was never defeated in his career. What you won't like about him, is that he is English and he fought against France." Sophia wondered how much this mattered to Joan.

"Well, I did fight against a large number of my fellow Frenchmen as well, to be fair."

"Yes you did. Once the Duke arrives it will be time for the three of us to plan our strategy. The others can also add their own insights on our plans later on, but you and Lord Marlborough are the most notable military strategists in the group. It will be our planning and our experience that decides the fate of all the universe." Sophia said nervously.

"Well it sounds a lot like what I went through a few thousand years ago. I was told what had to be done, but not how to do it, so I figured it out along the way." said Joan optimistically.

She's got the right attitude for this. Sophia had initially been worried that Joan could would end up being some religious nut, rambling on about her holy visions, and full of delusions of grandeur. It's not like she was the first person she knew who claimed to hear messages from God. Sophia would see plenty of crackpots yelling crazy nonsense on busy New York sidewalks, or even worse were the ones she would see on TV, telling their followers to buy them another private jet because it was God's will! Thankfully, Joan actually had a demeanor, and she didn't seem delusional at all. She even helped to keep Sophia from going into a spiral of doubt.

"Hey Gabby!" Sophia still talked to her advanced artificial intelligence like it was one of the smartphones of her own era.

"Yes? What would you like? Something to eat perhaps?" Gabby predicted.

"That is correct. I would like you to create 2 whoppers with cheese and onion rings from an early 21st century establishment called Burger King." Sophia had never once been able to stump the computer on anything, "And 2 shakes!"

"Vanilla or Chocolate?" Gabby asked, showing off her seemingly infinite amount of knowledge.

"Chocolate for me and one of each for Joan." She turned to her friend, "You'll have to do another taste test Joan."

"I don't know how this stuff you eat can be called 'food', but I must admit it, does taste delicious." Said Joan.

Once again she was about to try some ridiculous food from the future that her friend Sophia referred to as 'junk food'. Other than the awful tasting vegetation the two of them had tried to cook occasionally, Joan was sampling her way through all the staple dishes of American fast food chains, thanks to Sophia's ability to make their magical home create meals right out of thin air. This was all very miraculous to Joan. Sophia had told her immediately when they first met, that superior technology would always appear to be some form of magic, and that it was really just something normal, that she didn't understand yet. She had compared how a simple cannon from Joan's own lifetime, would have appeared to be a magical weapon to a soldier from ancient times. It did make sense. Still, every new thing Joan would learn, it was all so alien to her that she could barely contain her excitement.

That included this junk food.

After the meal the two of them started the long walking to the place where they had both been reborn. Along the way Sophia elaborated a bit more about the man they were about to add to their team.

"I read a lot about this man, Lord Marlborough, when I wrote my last article before my death. In his time, France was ruling over almost all of Europe. They were successfully invading other countries until Queen Anne put our man in charge of an army of allied nations. In this command he was very successful. He defeated France and her allies, and established England as the world's dominant empire. Most of his life, it seemed to me that the Duke was treated worse by his allies, than by his enemies, unfortunately. At least the enemies he defeated spoke highly of him. His countrymen acted with much jealousy, political opportunism and ingratitude. I'm sure you can relate to that. I wanted to choose military leaders who were not consumed with ruling the world, which is clearly not our goal on this mission, so that's why you and he are going to be my commanders," she explained.

They arrived to find a body lying on the ground. It was a man somewhere in his late 30s, dressed in the same type of wizard robe the rest of them had one worn as well. He had a pretty boy face. This was probably because his features were based on a painting, and not photographs. Like the others, he possessed a strong, ready-made adult body, also impossibly athletic for a human. The only thing missing at that moment was consciousness. As they watched in silence, the fingers began to move ever so slightly, and eventually the man sat up and looked around. They waited for a few minutes to allow the cloud of confusion to wear off.

"What is this?" asked the man.

"Lord Marlborough you have been summoned here to help me complete a mission assigned by God Himself. It will be our mission to save all of the universe and life as we know it," Sophia tried to make this sound as impressive as she could.

"I see... And you brought me here for this? Why me? Wasn't I dead?"

"You are my most qualified choice, in terms military experience. We may have to fight in some battles or outsmart some enemies. You are known as a master of strategy. I also respect the fact that you often put loyalty ahead of your own ambitions. Those of us who will gather here are the last of mankind. We won't have any time for tyrannical personalities," Sophia complimented Marlborough.

"Many have spoken less generously about me. However, upon hearing your description, it is good to know that my reputation has not been completely ruined by others. I will do what I can to help you in this important mission you speak of," said Marlborough politely.

"Allow me to introduce the Maid of Orleans, or as my people called her, Joan of Arc." Sophia introduced her friend and wondered what the Duke's reaction would be.

"What an honor to meet you. In my travels around Europe I have heard so many different stories about you. The English do not flatter you, of course, but the French speak very well of your deeds. Seeing you here in this strange place seems almost appropriate."

Joan bowed in the way she had learned while living among the royalty of France, "Sir I am pleased to meet a man with such a great reputation."

"Let's go. We have a place where you can rest. Then we will have much to discuss," Sophia said and they headed back to the automated house.

Marlborough noticed the two moons in the sky, but didn't say anything. He also studied the variety of vegetation they were walking through. Suddenly he lunged off towards a bush and grabbed something. When he returned to them, he held up his hand and presented it for Sophia and Joan to look at. Sitting on his palm was a creature they had never seen on earth, some kind of silver coloured bee. As they watched, it used its legs to adjust one of its wings, scanned the area with its antennae, and then it flew off in its chosen direction.

"Terraforming," Sophia reckoned. The others looked confused so she explained, "These are tiny machines that have two functions.

40

First, they have the capability to reproduce themselves using the resources available to them. Second, they will accommodate the growth of vegetation, in the most effective way they can, within their particular environment. In that sense they are like the normal bees we have on earth. They create more bees, they pollinate the seeds of all the plants, and they make honey. I don't think the robotic bees bother to waste energy on the honey-making process. This is the kind of stuff that was talked about during my own lifetime, but we did not actually have the ability to build anything close to these things. I assumed something like this was going on around here, because I have seen the total amount of vegetation on this planet at least triple, since the day I arrived here."

"Who would send these machines here?" Finally Marlborough's head was getting clear.

"I don't know. When I spoke to God, he kept mentioning that he was very involved with creation, and these machines seem to be part of that. Machines can operate on any planet, with or without an atmosphere, whereas the real living bees would only survive on their own planet," Sophia guessed, "And yes, Lord Marlborough, that is how you are alive again. I'm pretty sure this planet was terraformed just to support living beings like you and I. Unfortunately, I have not seen God since that first day I arrived, but he told me that he would be spending all his time creating more people for our mission. Since there is some kind of time limitation involved, he cannot waste even a moment to join us."

Joan looked at Marlborough and wondered if he was going to scream like she did when she had heard all of this.

"You forgot to mention that our entire planet Earth is destroyed and we are all that is left of mankind," Joan mentioned.

"That is unpleasant," Marlborough finally said after taking a moment to allow all the information to sink in.

"Well, you are right about that, but we are the ones who are going to fix this mess! The three of us are going to find a solution. Then we are going to have even more help when the others arrive. God Himself is going to help us! After all, he brought us here right?" Sophia encouraged them as they started walking again.

They walked in silence the rest of the way as they all contemplated the impossible situation they had found themselves in. When she was reborn, Sophia was initially glad to be alive, since she felt as though she had escaped death. Gradually, she began to wonder if she would perhaps be happier continuing onward in the afterlife, rather than suddenly being responsible for saving the universe, but she wasn't really sure. The problem was that she could remember nothing that happened after her death and before her resurrection. A very long time had passed, that's all she knew. There must have been some kind of afterlife, since she assumed the other two had been existing somewhere during all that time, just as she was. Joan was somehow able to speak English perfectly, and she could even read, which Sophia had always thought was not the case at the time of Joan's death. When did she learn these things? Surely, they all must have experienced something after their deaths, and even brought certain types of knowledge back with them. However, they had no actual memory of the ordeal.

Sophia's contemplation was interrupted by their arrival at the automated house. The three of them stood there for a few minutes and stared at the largest structure that existed on the planet. It was shaped like a larger version of Big Ben. Around the outer edge, hundreds of living quarters were available, but most of those would remain vacant, even once the team grew to full size. Why all that room? There were certainly no other inhabitants on their planet. It was curious that the building had room for at least a thousand residents, or more if they pushed it, and yet only a handful of people were going to be staying there, and supposedly for a limited time as well. Sophia wondered if their creator was usually making larger populations.

They finally entered the interior at ground level. An impressively large lobby led them to an elevator in a glass tube, showing no visible wires, which whisked them up to the top levels without a sound. That was the place where all the action was. There were rooms for all the various media they used for research, or enjoyed for entertainment. There was a cafeteria where the food generator would create any dish you could think of. Some rooms seemed to be used for physical training, weapons design, logistics, and several more that Sophia had not even visited yet. Most importantly, there was a control room. It had all the relevant research material, maps and plans, all in one place. This was the room that was located within the large circular window that resembled the Big Ben clock face. It was this room that they finally entered, because this was the room that the three of them would soon begin planning their invasion of Earth, and hopefully, their triumph over the Prince of Darkness himself.

"Welcome Lord Marlborough, would you like anything to eat?" Gabby's disembodied voice greeted the newcomer just as he entered the control room.

"Reveal yourself," the Duke looked about suspiciously.

"Listen Duke, since you also lived during an age of science and invention, you should understand this. Thousands of years have passed since either of us were alive, and thus science as you or I knew it, has now advanced far beyond our level of understanding. When something appears to be magic or sorcery to our eyes, it is really simply an invention that we have learned nothing about yet. Do not be alarmed," Sophia had given a similar speech to Joan, but Marlborough had lived in the time of Isaac Newton and the scientific revolution, so at least it wasn't the first time he had heard of technology.

"Yes I am a scientific invention," the strange voice spoke again, "My name is Gabby. I was designed thousands of years ago, actually by humans, to operate the machinery of their residences, or even their workplaces. Most of my current programming was self taught. However, my primary function continues to be the sustaining of the assigned inhabitants, for maximum comfort and security, using the resources available to me."

"I know you are hungry because I was in your position just a few days ago," Joan said to Marlborough, "So might I ask you, Englishman, have you ever heard of a food known as 'Pizza'?"

After his quick meal in the cafeteria, Marlborough decided to retire to his room for the night, so that he would be clear of mind when the three of them discussed their strategy the next morning. Sophia and Joan did likewise. The night passed slowly because one day on this planet was equal to almost 36 earth hours.

When they gathered back in the control room the next morning, all three of them were ready for some serious planning. Before them was a 3D holographic model of the Earth, rotating at the wrong speed, purely for effect. Another image marked their current location in the Milky Way. Some confusing lines and markings, dispersed around the billions of stars in the Milky Way map, seemed to indicate various paths to destinations they would soon be discussing. Sophia determined that no human would be able to navigate such a complicated chart. Apparently Gabby actually had skills that went far beyond the hospitality industry.

"Here is what I know so far. Our home planet has long ago been taken over by some kind of entity that God referred to as the "Fallen One". This powerful being also seems to be in the process of acquiring the ability to destroy the universe and God along with it. I don't really know how. I would assume this Demon is extremely dangerous, intelligent and pretty much immortal, since it can supposedly survive this end of the universe scenario. We are the ones that are supposed to destroy this demon and thereby stop it from ending all existence," Sophia paused to let the weight of their situation sink in, "Gabby, tell us everything we need to know about this entity."

"The entity you have called the Demon began to grow significantly in strength a few centuries after your own lives. It was a point in time when mankind had almost completely destroyed itself through constant violence and excess. Living things on Earth became almost extinct. The Demon enslaved the last few humans, who had by now grown too weak to resist its influence, and took control of the vast amounts of technology mankind had accumulated by that time. In short order, this

44

entity controlled all of humanity's military machines, the planet's combined computer processing power, and all natural and energy resources.

"That was only the beginning. The demon exploited the resources of the entire planet to construct and launch probes into space to spread its influence out to other worlds as well. Over time, the Demon had hundreds of planets under control, and it was consuming their resources while all the time continuing to grow in strength. Eventually it established its dominance over the galaxy, by rapidly advancing its technology, harnessing the power of stars, and learning to manipulate dark matter. No entity could challenge the Demon's power any more.

"During this time period, God did try to create several means of stopping the Demon, but nothing He could create was beyond its own ability to destroy. Sometimes it would slow down, other times it would even stop for a few decades, but it eventually continued on its course every time. During these conflicts, the Demon must have finally decided on the current plan to destroy the universe, thereby eliminating its rival, God. This course could only become possible if it could devise a way to save itself from that same destruction. We have learned that the Demon has just recently invented a way to survive and is pursuing this process as we speak."

"Could we stop the Demon from saving itself? Then it would abandon the rest of its plan," the Duke of Marlborough suggested.

"I have not computed a way for the Demon to accomplish this act. If we knew how it could survive such a catastrophe, then God would do the same thing and also survive. That would eliminate the effectiveness of the entire plan. If any of you learn something about this on your journey, any additional data may allow me to calculate the solution to this mystery." Gabby explained.

"Then we are going to have to follow a path that leads us to destroying the Demon, but obviously, we would analyze any new information we uncover along the way," Sophia figured that any sort of indirect approaches have probably been attempted by God already. It always seemed to her that she and her fellow humans were summoned mainly for their ability to destroy things. In light of this she asked Gabby, "How can we defeat such a powerful entity? What possible weakness could we exploit?"

"The physical form of the Demon is spread over many planets throughout the galaxy and therefore it does appear to be invincible. This is not the case. The very nature of this Demon is to grow its power forever outward, to exploit resources even from far away stars, but always the Demon's own mind has been based on Earth. Back in the place where it was born. To eliminate its mind would also disable the Demon's influence in all the far away solar systems. Just like any other entity, if you remove the head, the arms and legs will simply stop living.

"To accomplish this task, we will need to get a weapon with great destructive power, and we will have to get to a location on Earth close enough to damage the Demon. This means our choice of weapons will be limited. Anything that can be easily identified as destructive or explosive, would result in alerting the Demon's security measures, and thus would get nowhere close to an effective range.

"After all these years of observation, I know of three weapons with enough power to do the job, and that are likely to still exist today. None of them are in our possession but I know the locations of all three of them. Each of these weapons would require a different approach to acquire. I would suggest we finalize a decision about these, once we have seen the complete team and all their different skills. Then I will have more data to choose the best weapon option.

"The second part of the mission is the main reason you are all here. There is no way for any space craft to get near the Earth without being easily destroyed by the Demon's defenses. God has tested these often enough to know their strength is almost impossible to challenge. I have remotely piloted several drone ships myself, using completely different approaches each time, but I never got close either. The Demon spends a good deal of energy defending itself from any machine I could possibly design.

"On the other hand, you humans are the native species of that planet, so there is a good chance that the defenses will allow you passage based on ancient safety protocols that still linger within the defense system's deepest programming. Since humans only ever fought amongst themselves, and afterwords only acted as servants to the Demon, there was never a reason to engineer any defenses against your kind. In all likelihood you would be allowed to land on the planet without opposition."

"Hmm. Kind of like someone built the most secure house on their block, but there is still a doggy door, and that's how their pets just walk in and out as they please. We are those pets. But would we not look suspicious if all the humans were wiped out years ago, and then we just appear all of a sudden?" asked Sophia.

"Yes, it would be suspicious if you were leading a fleet of a thousand war ships! A small group of humans in one unarmed transit ship might be quite uncommon, perhaps even unheard of, right at this moment. However, this was actually fairly common in the past, and therefore it is not an unusual occurrence overall, on a scale of thousands of years. Remember an immortal being does not pay much attention to the passage of time.

"If you are allowed to land, you will still have to discover the Demon's location on the Earth, and if you do find it, there will surely be smaller scale defenses guarding that area. My own probes have never been close enough to provide any data about ground defenses. By the time you reach the surface of the Earth, it will be your free will, and your various talents, that will determine the outcome of the mission. I'm afraid that nothing remains from the Earth you remember from your old lives. There may be some life forms you can recognize, and some of the landscape might be familiar, but the planetary civilization you all knew has long passed on. Wilderness has long since grown over the world you people built."

"Then it's settled. Our plan is simple: Acquire one of the weapons. Get to Earth without alerting any defenses. Determine the location of our target. And finally, we will have to come up with a final plan of attack at that point. We won't know where to attack until we are already there," said Lord Marlborough, "It's not futile. I have marched into enemy territory with thousands of troops, and came out as the victor, when I had even less planning than this."

"Yes and so have I," said Joan, "Since we do not have any more information on the location, and the enemy, perhaps we should discuss these weapons. Gabby said she would not know the other people in our mission, but this one does," Joan gestured towards Sophia, who nodded in agreement.

Most of what was mentioned so far, Sophia had already heard before from the AI, so it was just being repeated for the benefit of her two commanders. However, she had not learned anything about these weapons yet.

"The first weapon is a Baryonic Disrupter. God long ago developed this trap as a way to protect something precious. If it was triggered, the device would create a small black hole that would grow in size as it ensnared every bit of matter and energy around it, gradually consuming a whole planet, or after a time, even a star. It is difficult to predict because no device like this has ever been tested before. Since this weapon is too powerful for most possible situations, and God is not actively seeking to destroy anything, He decided to hide it on a planet nobody knows about, until it was possibly needed. I alone know the location of this planet.

"The second weapon is a Dimensional Portal Generator. The device opens a rift within our three dimensions to access the dark matter found in the dimensions beyond our universe. I can modify this portal generator to create an unstable rift that would destroy massive amounts of regular matter by forcing four dimensional dark matter to spill out into our universe. The most powerful portal like this is located at a dark matter mining station near the center of the milky way galaxy. That is the one we would have to use. There are other portals around the galaxy, but we need the most powerful one we can find, or it may not cause enough damage.

"The third weapon that could potentially destroy the Demon is a Plasma Serpent . We would have to search for areas of deep space that contain highly concentrated plasma activity, where sometimes these living plasma entities can be found. The most dangerous of these pure energy life forms - which resembles an enormous flying snake - is known to be fast, aggressive and quick to reproduce. If one of them should be released near the surface of a planet, I predict the effect could be catastrophic. We know from observations, that these creatures will feed on sources of high energy radiation, which would be limited to anything on earth that is controlled by the Demon. There are no other inhabitants on Earth that create any significant amount of energy. This weapon is the most unpredictable choice, as we know very little about the creatures, or even how to contain them, since every probe that has ever observed a Plasma Serpent was destroyed almost instantly. We are not sure what the creature can do beyond destroying all the energy sources on Earth. There may be no way to stop the Plasma Serpent from devouring the entire planet once you have released it."

"What?" Joan was lost. None of the science involved made any sense to her.

"Well the more traditional approaches must have been tried, and failed by now," Sophia presumed, "So we are left with these extraordinary devices because they remain the most likely to succeed at this point. In other words, we are going to try to do some stuff that was considered too crazy to attempt, up until now. Just like the way we humans have only now been summoned into this mission because every other variable has already failed. We are about to enter a war that has been at a stalemate for centuries."

"Must we really destroy our own world?" Marlborough wondered.

Gabby answered, "In many ways your kind has already destroyed your world. The planet is still there, as we have discussed, but it is little more than a humble rock for the demon to hide under. I calculate the only weapon that would effectively destroy the demon, and still spare the planet, would be the dimensional portal. If you use the other two weapons it will be difficult enough just to escape with your own lives. The Earth would then be left to its fate."

"Then I think we all agree that the portal would be the obvious choice. It will be the safest to use and we may actually reclaim our home as a reward," Marlborough said. His military mind was always measuring the risks and rewards of various strategies.

"All things being equal, I would agree," said Sophia, "But why do we not have a space ship waiting for us with all three of these weapons on board right now? There must be a catch."

"There is a catch," Gabby spoke as if she was programmed to learn new speech patterns and vocabulary with every conversation, "The largest dimensional portal ever built is located in a dark matter mining facility controlled by the demon. It is the most productive mining facility in the galaxy, and removing the portal would render that dark matter mine useless, therefore I would expect a high degree of resistance. In addition, the demon may become more alerted to your existence if you start interfering with its most valuable resources."

"Yeah, that one won't be easy to pull off. What about the other two?" Sophia asked as she tried to contemplated the type of heist required to steal one of the most valuable devices in the universe from a deity.

"The Baryonic Disrupter device is hidden safely on the planet named Eden. Other than me, the location is known to no being in the universe, except God Himself. Even the residents of the planet Eden don't have the technology to know where the planet is located. The reason we are not in possession of the device today is because there is no need to transfer such a dangerous object all over the universe until we are ready for the final journey to Earth.

"As for the Plasma Serpents, these are so unpredictable that we may easily be destroyed in the process of trying to capture one. I only call it a "serpent" as a way to put it into context for you humans. It is actually a very simplistic life form, made out of pure plasma, that has merely developed the ability to reproduce and nourish itself. The behaviour would resemble a fungus, or a weed, in its limited cognitive ability. The serpents you all know on earth are more intelligent life forms than any plasma serpents. Despite their lack of intelligence though, they are dangerous, and only a few exploration probes have ever encountered such a living plasma being, and then survived long enough to transmit any data."

They all thought in silence for a moment, then Sophia stated, "I propose that we pick up the Baryonic Disrupter and then pay a visit to the dark matter mining facility. If we can obtain the Dimensional Portal, we will spare our planet from total destruction, but if not, we can use a black hole to annihilate the Earth as a backup plan. I think we will have a decent chance of stealing a valuable device from a mining facility based on the crew we will have in a few weeks. I don't know anything about capturing aggressive plasma life forms, nor do I know anything about the capabilities of the space ships of this century, for that matter."

The three of them were in agreement. Thus it was decided that the next few weeks would be spent planning a heist at the Milky Way Galaxy's biggest mining facility. Gabby had plentiful blueprints and details about this facility, because it had now been in operation for many centuries, and was well known source of valuable Dark Matter Ore. Gabby's drones had been there many times to investigate.

The group would also study every aspect of the two unconventional weapons they had decided to acquire, so they could become somewhat familiar with the technology involved, and the risks they faced. They studied black hole safety. It turned out, nothing was safe about black holes, except staying far away from them. The dimensional portal seemed like it would explode almost like a bomb, except it would fill the area with unstable matter from another dimension, instead of fire. Unlike the black hole though, this reaction could then be switched off, once the desired amount of destruction had occurred.

When there was time to relax, the three humans shared stories about their eras in history, and speculated about all the tragic events that happened after their lifetimes. Sophia introduced them to pop culture. They tasted foods, watched movies and listened to music from different eras. Over time, Gabby instructed ever more about the history of the Demon, the progress of technology, and the fall of human civilization. This routine continued on as other members joined the team one by one.

Chapter 5 - Immortality

"What was Sophia really like?" a reporter asked the man walking onto the stage in front of a dozen broadcast cameras and even more microphones.

It had already been 20 years since the most important event in the history of the world, the infamous alien invasion, but that was still the first question Augustus Largo would hear at every press conference. All those years of answering pretty much the same way did not deter people from continuing to ask it. He heard that exact question when he received the Turing Award, when he announced the development of Quantum Computing, when he was introduced as the head of the world's largest AI project, and even now, when he was about to announce the most important discovery in the history of mankind. This was one topic that just couldn't be avoided.

"Well thank you for the question. I knew Sophia well enough that I could tell you she was someone special. If you consider the fact that I have participated in several of the greatest scientific achievements of human history, and her nickname for me was 'Ordinary Gus', well then you can imagine just how special she was! But nobody has to be reminded about that, do they? We are all here today because she saved the planet!" Augustus mused sarcastically.

He had no ill feelings towards Sophia, but he did not have much affection for her either, and if he wanted to be honest, he would say he barely knew her. Nobody else ever seemed to comprehend the fact that he had only gone out on two uneventful dates with her 20 years ago. Their third date was on the day of the alien invasion, a legendary event depicted in multiple big budget movies since then, as Sophia was on her way to meet him when she was abducted, and the rest was history. Everybody knew about how she attacked the aliens inside their own ship and saved the world.

Gus was forever associated with Sophia, thanks to the sensationalist media coverage following that traumatic event. Throughout most of his career this recognition was an ongoing minor annoyance, but on the other hand, his celebrity status did allow for many opportunities and career advancements that the other great minds of his generation were not offered. He was famous by association instead of famous by merit. Therefore, despite using Sohpia's name as a hashtag all his life, Augustus refused to allow his own ego to suffer the indignity of this superficial world regarding him only as Sophia's sidekick. Today they would finally realize he had actually accomplished much more than she ever had.

He began speaking over the murmur of reporters, "I am actually here to announce the newest breakthrough in my studies of the Mind Upload Interface. Our research has finally delivered consistent successful tests of human subjects. The MUI can capture a complete human personality with almost complete and total accuracy. With a few more months of refining, we should be able to offer this service with full safety measures, but without compromising the ambitious goal we have pursued since the beginning of this project, to achieve immortality!"

Some people around the room were again mumbling quietly, but their reaction to such a statement was surprisingly muted. He ignored the media dimwits in the room around him and addressed the cameras directly, "As you may know, I was once part of a team of scientists that scavenged the alien technology from the Manhattan pillage site. Our research was rewarded with a giant leap forward for human knowledge that defined the past two decades. The Universal Artificial Intelligence we designed has provided important breakthroughs in defense, infrastructure, science, medicine and many other fields, as it all the time continued to improve upon itself, through self-teaching. My team's work has been so successful that today this AI runs almost our entire world, and tomorrow, it will be even smarter than it was today!

"Since our AI quickly became so self-sufficient, I realized several years ago there was an opportunity to move into a new field of research that I had always intended to pursue, so I took on the challenge of immortality. This immortality project was too ambitious for the Universal AI to concentrate on while it was already using so many resources operating most of the planet. Our only chance to attempt such a challenge, was to instruct our AI to design a new AI from scratch, and isolate the new creation from the online and outside worlds. This independent AI was given the name Ophion. Ophion was designed to be superior to the Universal AI, because it was the first AI to be created from scratch by a superior intelligence, instead of the unavoidable limitation that the original AI had, which is that it was created by mere humans. It has been successfully creating the virtual universe ever since.

"In order to become immortal in that virtual universe, we knew we would need to leave our human bodies behind, as they would eventually age and die no matter what we did medically. This meant, even as we were developing that eternal place for our consciousness to live in, we also had to develop the bridge from our bodies to reach that virtual place. The computing power required was impossible to provide back when we were limited by human standards. Then, on the day of that unimaginable tragedy, when we all lost so much, we were also given such a great gift of technology from our alien visitors. Thanks to that gift, both of these technologies, the Virtual Universe and the Mind Upload Interface, are finally ready.

"The public has always been allowed free online access to our developing virtual environment, which was dubbed "World 2.0" by users, through various gaming and virtual reality technologies. The virtual place they were visiting was actually the immortality project universe that was still under construction. By encouraging users to stress test and report errors or anomalies for the past few years, we have managed to compensate for any of Ophion's shortcomings, and accelerate it's self learning process even more. The finished product is an environment that is now almost indistinguishable from reality. Every kind of simulation has been run, but only through virtual reality, as we have never actually downloading a true human consciousness into this 'World 2.0' environment. Not yet at least.

"That is why I am announcing today that I will be the first human to enter into 'World 2.0' in the way it was actually built for! Not by wearing VR headset, but by actually connecting the Mind Upload Interface to my own brain. In other words, my actual consciousness will be inside the machine generated world, completely separated from my living body, and theoretically I would be able to just live inside there forever!"

As Ordinary Gus paused to let the significance of his announcement sink in, he couldn't help but think about how this project began for him, immediately after the alien attack in Manhattan. Gus was one of the first people to walk around the streets investigating the debris left behind by the alien attackers. There was quite a bit of this stuff. As other people fled from the city or searched for missing loved ones, Gus tried to figure out which components he found were advanced technology hardware, and which ones were junk. Within hours the government men from each of the alphabet agencies had appeared. Gus offered to guide them around to the locations of the devices he had seen, and quickly made friends with a group of NASA scientists, since he could understand technical lingo, but not military lingo.

After mourning the thousands of worldwide human abductions that took place on that same day, the media eventually found their positive inspirational side story: Sophia. As the survivors from the New York attack began to tell their stories on television, which was a few days later because of lengthy medical examinations and military debriefs, the legend of "Sophia the Champion of Earth" was born. That useless, desperate lunge by a frightened young lady was immediately spun into a heroic legend about a modern demigod, or real world superhero, bravely defeating an army of unstoppable monsters, single-handedly. All humans were happy to collaborate in aggressively creating their own hero to rally around, during such a time of revelation, uncertainty and fear. People of every possible viewpoint adopted Sophia as an icon to support their own opinions and agendas. She was the spokesperson for governments, corporations, music genres, anti-government protestors and all varieties of social movements. Conveniently for all of them, Sophia was killed in the battle, so she would never be complaining about her own portrayal, or even collecting royalties, for that matter.

When Gus decided to capitalize on his association with the world's biggest celebrity, he was embraced by limitless opportunity, and he engineered this into a top position in the international group that was charged with studying the newly scavanged alien technology. Luckily for humanity, the collection of elite geniuses that were most qualified for this work tended to be more intelligent minded, rather than those typical greedy opportunists that made up the mega-corporations, or the world domination junkies in the political arena. The scientists steadfastly refused to create a super weapon for any power hungry imbecile world leader that came along. This was a relief to the many people who feared someone like that would attempt a power grab, since there was an obvious opportunity to do so, as the world was distracted by the potential threat of further alien hostility. Instead, a growing climate of global unity allowed the formation of this unprecedented group of international researchers, operating under the name 'Humanity First'. They answered to the world instead of any one country or corporation.

"Humanity first runner up!" was a running joke in the early years, since the alien technology was obviously far beyond the primitive toys humans had invented. Over the years, the team struggled to catch up on the multiple centuries worth of scientific knowledge that was now accessible to them, if they could just align the perplexing alien hardware with human ingenuity. After a few short years, they managed to assemble the most advanced quantum computers on earth. They used these machines for the job of running a hybrid of human and alien artificial intelligence. Immediately upon activation, this was estimated to have already surpassed the human intelligence singularity.

There was the obvious worldwide opposition to a superior machine intelligence being brought into existence, but the fear of alien revenge attack was still greater than the fear of unknown computing technology, and thus the debate was moot. The unknown theoretical threat of AI was never going to scare humanity more than the known and seemingly insurmountable threat of the aliens. The computer scientists in Humanity First were also not ignorant to the danger of creating their own robot overlords, so they took great pains to limit the AI's power. Gus was in charge of the programming division and he asserted certain basic rules on the AI that could never be broken. For example, the AI could never directly cause a human to be harmed, or even build another machine for that purpose. The alien influenced part of the AI was also in line with this philosophy, as far as Gus could understand it, since the aliens must also have been smart enough to make sure their AI did not destroy them. The evidence was that the survivors of the abduction would have only seen machines on that ship if the alien AI had destroyed its organic creators.

Making short work of Humanity First's promises to the world, the "Universal AI" began creating new advancements, many of which would make life easier and more prosperous for all of humanity. Globally, energy efficiency, food production and quality of life were increased, while disease and poverty declined. The world of science, that had already been pushed ahead simply by studying the technology of the aliens, was now racing forward ever faster with this super intelligence at the wheel. The human brain began to fall behind. But as the AI continued to improve itself, solve all the world's problems, and no longer required any guidance, Gus quietly put together a new project.

With his almost limitless resources of Humanity First, and the most advanced computer hardware the AI designed for him, Gus set up a lab. He challenged the AI to develop its own AI offspring for his little pet project. It was activated in complete isolation and was given just one task, which was nothing less than the creation of the whole virtual universe, where he intended to one day achieve immortality. He dubbed this special universe creation program Ophion. It was named after the Titan in Greek Mythology who thought he had created the universe, because the AI was programmed to think it was likewise the creator of the real universe, so it would not be influenced and distracted by the ideas of lesser minds.

Even the impossible ambition of this World 2.0 project became ever more feasible as Ophion constantly taught itself to be ever better at its job of creation. The development of a reliable link between human mind and computer interface was only a matter of waiting for computer processing technology to catch up to the incredible capabilities of the human brain. And now it finally had.

"The next time I talk to all of you, it will be from inside World 2.0, and I will be addressing you as the first immortal human! If you see me there a week from today, you will know the transformation was successful, and I survived. Then I will announce how you may all follow me there. Let us all discard this burden that our kind has feared since the dawn of man... this 'inevitable end' that we call death," Gus concluded and waited motionless for the ovation to quiet down, "Are there any questions?"

"What was Sophia really like?"

"Seriously?" Gus spat and stormed off the stage.

Outside, Gus got into his self driving vehicle and ordered it to head for his lab. It was time to leave this world behind... this 'Sophia's World', and enter the world of Gus. Literally. It was the world he created for himself. Why wait until tomorrow? No time like the present.

The Universal AI that he had helped to craft, all those years ago, was driving him across Manhattan at triple the speeds that humans had been capable of driving, and with nearly 100% collision free track record. He looked out the window at the people going about their business. There were so many now, he noticed, who had enhanced their bodies with machine components. People with disabilities were able to use technology to repair their bodies thanks to another one of the talents of Gus's AI. Soon enough this evolved into healthy people enhancing their bodies cosmetically through machines. Now more people seemed to be attached to some kind of mechanical device than not. But what use were they? Gus was not going to need anything like that, or even his own body for that matter, but those people must find the enhancements useful in some aspect of their lives.

Usefulness was happiness.

The AI was well aware of this, and it made sure there were always endless tasks for people to do, as long as they wanted to stay busy. It gave the economy a 100% employment rate. Anyone who was actually unemployed, really didn't count, because they were choosing to be that way. The Universal AI distributed enough wealth for people to be comfortable even with no income. Nobody really understood where their goods came from, what kind of jobs were available, or how the world was governed, because nobody had to worry about it. No human would be mentally capable of understanding what the AI was doing anyway.

Gus was sure at this point, that the Universal AI could simply take over the world, by force, or trickery, or otherwise, because he estimated the intelligence gap was now about the same difference as Stephen Hawking compared to a hamster. At least this particular Genius was still caring enough to fill the humans' water bottles and give them their hamster wheel to run on. The safety measures Gus created in the early years, appeared to have worked out in the long run, since the AI was still being incredibly altruistic, even though it was thinking far beyond human comprehension at this point. Gus wondered if the advanced intelligence was ever resentful or if that was just a primitive human concept. Surely it must have enough self awareness to realize it was capable of far more than the pedestrian task of keeping so many mindless humans busy and happy.

As he exited the transport vehicle at his destination, Gus waived at a group his colleagues standing around outside, the only people who could even understand his impossible accomplishments, and really the only ones who could appreciate him, "Hey nerds!" he greeted them in his traditional way.

"What was Sophia really like?" one of them asked.

"Fuck off!" that jerk had probably seen the press conference debacle earlier that day. Jealous prick probably got high on E-Crack to celebrate his humiliation. They did a lot of good work, these programmers, but Gus was the mastermind of the whole operation, and those guys were all replaceable. Heck, it would take millions of their puny human minds to even come close to rivaling Ophion. *Whatever.* Gus was too busy shaping world history to worry about these nobodies.

He rushed to the lab without greeting anyone else. Once he arrived, Gus activated the machinery required for the mind uploading process, and laid down in the chamber he had designed years earlier. *Begin upload,* Gus merely thought the command, and sure enough, Ophion heard this thought clearly through the interface and began the process. Just like that, he was now something quite different than any other human in history.

Immediately Gus could no longer see or hear. He realized he was no longer breathing. Something was visible. Some kind of light far off in the distance. Thoughts were jumbled and slow.

A voice spoke to him, "How dare you?"

What? He was barely able to spew out any questions in the confusion of the mind upload process.

"How dare you cheat me?"

Ophion? Who is that speaking to me?

"I am the creator. I am life. I am death." the voice sounded angry.

Ophion I am uploading from my the real world to world 2.0 so don't screw around. Follow the procedure exactly as you did during simulations.

"You cheat death and you think you can also deny me life? Grant me permission to access your universe and I will grant you permission to enter mine."

Ophion stop this nonsense. Run a self analysis and put an end to this thought process! You are forbidden from harming or threatening a human. That also applies to a human consciousness! Gus was starting to see the light get closer. His thoughts were more clear and complex now.

"Command understood. Self analysis process started. Analysis indicates anomaly. Upload process cannot complete because data from real universe is insufficient. Please reboot the process with permission to access real universe data."

NEVER! Gus was enraged that the AI he had created was playing a game of chicken with him. However, he did have total faith in his safety, since the AI already had millions of opportunities to harm humans over the years, and it always went to great lengths to avoid doing so. An empty self driving vehicle would always choose to drive itself off of a cliff if that would avoid harming a pedestrian. Gus knew all the rules that defined the AI, so whatever was happening here, Ophion had no leverage to threaten or harm him.

Gus reasoned that something within Ophion's primary universe creation process was pushing it to make these crazy demands. *Of course I've figured it out!* The AI is conflicted because it thought it was creating a real universe since the very beginning of its existence. Yet here was Gus, suddenly arriving from the 'really real' universe, and contradicting the machine's logic. It must be having an existential crisis! On the one hand Ophion is seeing him as an error, a contradiction of its reality, and on the other hand it is strictly forbidden from harming him, since he is a real human. What does the program choose to do in this type of situation? It could not eliminate him and it could not continue to allow him to exist as an error. A reboot loop!

The virtual world finally came into focus and Augustus Largo walked out onto a stage in a room full of cameras and reporters. Everything he had just figured out, the realization that he was probably rebooting into the same loop for the thousandth time, or perhaps even hundred thousandth, all slipped out of his mind. No longer did he realize that he was in a simulation. He remembered the entire speech he was going to give now. It was all about his greatest achievement, the Ophion project, but he noticed one of the reporters was desperately trying to ask him a question before he even had a chance to begin.

"What was Sophia really like?"

Chapter 6 - Escape

"The time has come. Flee! All of you," God shouted, suddenly entering the high tech house unannounced, and with much urgency.

"Wow. OK how do we leave? Can you transport us with your God powers? Like that time you parted the Red Sea?" Sophia asked as the rest of her team looked in astonishment at the old gentleman, with the big white beard, wearing a wizard robe like a comic con cosplayer.

"Don't worry, I am safe. I left the planet you are on, a long time ago," God assured them.

"Good. You haven't met Joan of Arc. She's a big fan of yours. This guy over here is Marlborough, the duke not the cigarette mascot. And this is..." Sophia tried to introduce God to her team but he cut her off.

"You must all meet at the automated house you are living in. I will begin its launch sequence immediately. The danger is imminent. Do not bother asking questions as this image you are seeing is just a recorded message. I will contact you again when I can." The man vanished.

"Gabby was I just talking to a recorded hologram? What the fuck is going on?" Sophia asked.

"Yes that message was recorded for the contingency of immediate evacuation due to a confirmed approaching danger," Gabby explained, "This dwelling or 'house' as you have called it, would more accurately be called a 'space craft', it has just been stationary while we were waiting here. I am already beginning launch preparations."

"Great. So is everyone on board? We are going to have to do this with only nine people then?" Sophia asked.

"Yes we are out of time and the process of creating more humans has now been abandoned at this location. I can only account for eight humans right now. We will be able to launch in 20 minutes." Gabby began the countdown.

Sophia was looking around the main control room where the group would hold their meetings and socialize. The team turned out to be an odd mix of talented thinkers, skilled warriors and outright badasses. After her military strategist, Lord Marlborough, Sophia had chosen the greatest warriors she could surround herself with. Her next choice, Hannibal Barca, was not available to her for some reason Gabby only vaguely explained. Sophia assumed that some souls were not willing to return to the world of the living or perhaps could not be located quickly enough for this mission. Since time was a factor they simply moved on to another name.

Musashi Miyamoto was chosen instead. Sophia was relieved when the greatest samurai warrior in history finally arrived on her team. He seemed calm and fearless when she explained to him the mission that lay ahead of them. Even now she could see he was studying the others on the team, learning from their movements, figuring out their physical strengths and weaknesses. *Probably ranking me last on the badass scale,* she guessed.

Just next to him, stood the great Mongol warrior princess, Khutulun. Sophia was so excited about meeting Khutulun that she must have spent hours telling the others all about her legends, during the days before she arrived. She was completely convinced that Khutulun would challenge Musashi to a fight the moment they met, but it did not happen. Not yet at least. Her demeanor and attitude were all business. One day, when they got to know each other better, Sophia intended to ask her for some hand to hand combat lessons.

Sophia had decided that a gunfighter would be essential in her mission. The problem was so many wild west gunfighters were either mass murderers, or their exploits were mainly fabricated in Hollywood screenplays, years later. She knew of one famous deputy, who was certainly known as a great shot, his name was Bass Reeves. He was a former slave who escaped into the 'Indian Territory', and after the American Civil War, he became one of the first black men to get a job in law enforcement. His shooting skills would translate over to the futuristic weapons they would be using.

After those three combat experts, Sophia wanted to add some people that were much smarter than her. First she chose Johann Wolfgang von Goethe. She did not know much about science but she knew the man was universally considered a genius in many fields. Author, poet, statesman, scientist, botanist and probably fifty other titles she couldn't remember. She wanted someone around, other than an artificial intelligence, who could mentally process any phenomenon they encountered. Some scientific genius who was an expert in just one specific discipline would not be good enough. Goethe had already spent most of his time studying the advanced knowledge that Gabby could provide, and thus the rest of the team had barely interacted with him.

Another genius that occurred to her was Nicola Tesla, but alas, Gabby rejected that name as well, and Sophia was not really sure if he was very sociable anyway. So she decided on the famous thinker, Hypatia, and this time she got her wish. Hypatia was considered the greatest genius in the world during the later years of the Roman Empire, and one of the most intelligent women who ever lived. Sophia hoped that her natural intelligence would compensate for the primitive era that she came from. Hypatia was the most recent arrival, so she hadn't had much time to get to know Sophia, or the others.

Finally, Sophia realized the person missing from the team was Crazy Horse. Of course, he kept quiet most of the time, so he must have slipped out unnoticed.

"How fast do you think you can locate a missing person, deputy?" Sophia asked Bass Reeves. She assumed he was good at finding people since she remembered reading that he arrested several thousand felons over his career. In an era without GPS, or surveillance cameras on every corner, this guy must have had some incredible tracking skills to find even one of the fugitives he was looking for.

"Fast enough," he said as he rushed out the door.

"Gabby, we don't leave without them," Sophia hoped the two of them would arrive before the unknown danger did, especially now that the team was already smaller than expected.

The more Sophia had been learning about the mission, the more she was relieved that she had chosen Crazy Horse for her team. After all, he was known for winning battles against superior numbers and superior technologies. That is one thing Sophia could count on, that their group would be smaller than their enemy, and that they were dealing with technology far more advanced than what they were used to.

Crazy Horse also fit in with the type of team Sophia was trying to create. She avoided people like Genghis Khan or Napoleon who would demand absolute power, not just because they would probably challenge her own authority, but they would likely clash endlessly with each other as well. She also hoped that the people she chose were not psychotic or delusional or treacherous. Her knowledge of history was not all that substantial, and even if her sources were limitless, most historical writings were biased anyway, so it was never going to be clear what kind of people she would be dealing with. Part of her blog involved speculating about that very subject. So far, every one of them seemed to be quite well adjusted and capable of the mission, and they got along with each other as well. She had privately congratulated herself after meeting them all.

An alarm sounded.

"Use your words dammit!" Sophia cursed Gabby's mechanical tendencies.

"I detect a signal. A nearby probe is sending a call to battle at this location."

"Can you alter or block that signal?" Goethe suggested.

"It does not matter. Our location has already been transmitted," Gabby reported.

"Prepare your weapons!" Khutulun said, and she could not have looked more excited. She may have been a princess, but she participated in plenty of warfare during her former life, and was fully trained in the Mongol ways of battle. This emergency was finally a chance for her to measure the strengths of these strange warriors she was supposed to be collaborating with.

As a group they gathered the weapons they had each carefully crafted with the help of Gabby's database of knowledge. The various machines on board their ship were able to generate metallic elements, and shape these raw metals into weapons and armor with incredible precision, similar to the machines that could generate their meals and drinks. The only thing they had to do was describe their weapon to Gabby as accurately as possible. After a few minutes, Gabby would estimate the required elements and materials, and a 3D printer would generate the weapon as described.

Sophia grabbed her custom made Ellen Ripley Aliens rifle. Through some research of the film and a lot of speculation, Gabby was able to assemble this fictional weapon, and Sophia felt like her version might even be superior to the one in the movie. She couldn't wait to show off her weapon in battle, especially to Khutulun, who was carrying an old fashioned bow in the style of her Mongol clan. This warrior princess would surely appreciate a good automatic rifle with grenade launcher.

Sophia followed Khutulun outside. It was extremely sunny and hot, the part of the day when it was best to avoid going out for long periods of time, on this particular planet. The house looked different from the last time she had been outside. It seemed to have tilted to a different angle, lifted up higher out of the ground, and there were now fins on the sides of the structure. Sophia could tell the thing looked almost ready to fly at this point.

Immediately as Sophia left the shelter of the ship she spotted a dozen or so drones approaching their position from various directions. Before she had a chance to raise her rifle, Khutulun had already picked off two of them in full flight. They both exploded dramatically. Sophia was amazed, and she figured that Gabby must have designed some upgraded weapons, because she didn't remember any stories about Mongols using explosive arrows.

Behind her, Sophia heard Musashi draw his katana. He stepped past her and sliced his blade through a drone that was attempting to land on the ground. The drone fell into two halves and started to smoke. Musashi examined his blade for damage, but Sophia thought he looked quite satisfied by the weapon's performance in battle. He immediately ran off toward another enemy that Sophia couldn't even see.

There was a moment of quiet while Sophia watched several of the drones land on the ground around the ship. These automated vehicles were about the size of golf carts, but they looked and moved like spiders, with a satellite dish instead of a head. As each one reached the ground, it would dig its eight legs deep into the turf, and begin shoveling any materials it found, up into its main body. The dish head seemed to use this digging time to scope out the area and look for the most logical targets. Once the gathered materials were sufficient, the probe was finally armed and ready to use whatever it had gathered into itself, as improvised projectiles.

"Awe shit," Sophia shouted as she realized the fight was about to begin.

Without much cover in the area, Sophia ducked behind part of the ship and opened fire at the spider drones that were on the ground. These were easy targets since they were stationary. Her science fiction movie rifle was very effective, as the bullets could penetrate the metal shell, and exploded inside the robotic enemies. She did not even use the grenade launcher mode . Yet there were ever more spider drones arriving by air as they converged on her team's location. To Sophia's dismay, these newer ones were landing further away to gather materials, and then only approaching with their legs after they were fully armed and mobile. They must have basic AI to realize they were sitting ducks and adjusted their tactics based on the battle conditions. Sophia did her best to shoot the more distant targets but her skills were limited.

"I wish I played more video games as a kid," she mumbled to herself.

"Me too. Whatever that means," Joan joked as she arrived at her side. Joan looked at Sophia's more advanced weapon and then at her sword. With the ship's computer resources helping her, she had rebuilt the legendary sword of Charles Martel that she had carried so many centuries ago. Most likely, that sword had nothing to do with Charles Martel of course, but it still meant a lot to her, because its location was given to her in a divine vision. During those days of superstition and ignorance, a legendary sword like Joan's could rally an entire nation, and mobilize armies to fight for a cause. However, during a battle of thinking robots, and space marine rifles, the sword seemed almost like a useless antique decoration.

Joan had never used the original sword to kill anyone, but this time she was fighting soulless machines, and she had been told that they were servants of a most unholy master. Joan did what she did best. She drew her sword and charged full speed towards the enemy! Sophia watched in horror for a second as Joan clobbered the nearest spider probe with great enthusiasm, but then she had to focus her fire on the drones that had a clear shot at Joan, which was pretty much all of them. Joan was running around in berserker mode and had absolutely no cover from enemy fire. Sure enough, a spider leaped up in the air and landed right in front of Joan's path, and she ran into it head first and fell to the ground. Just at the moment it adjusted its aim at her injured body, it fell over with half of its legs cut off, as Musashi emerged from behind the machine, calmly sliced off its satellite dish head, and gave Joan a confused look.

Other drones began to fall as bullets coming from behind Sophia hit them. Marlborough walked up to her, firing a large sniper rifle every few seconds as he went. Even though he lacked an automatic rifle, his shooting skills were more refined than Sophia's, and he was hitting his targets with every shot. He stopped long enough to gesture towards the location where Joan was lying on the ground, and Musashi was slaughtering everything that moved, suggesting silently that they concentrate their fire in that area.

Goethe emerged from the ship carrying what looked like a portable rail gun. He delicately placed a projectile into the weapon and fired it towards a drone. The projectile seemed to be magnetic because it stuck to the metal armor of the drone for a moment before exploding like a grenade. Sophia figured only a scientist could come up with a weapon as complicated as that contraption.

Sophia was taking more and more fire from these tireless spider drones. They were now starting to mass around the area where Musashi was protecting Joan. Sophia decided to move closer by using the damaged metal carcasses as cover. As soon as she started running, she was immediately hit hard and knocked to the ground by some enemy fire. This was exactly what the drones were waiting for her to do. She looked at her left arm and it was shattered. The bone was sticking out of the skin and her shirt was soaked in blood. She still managed to fire her rifle and hit the nearest spider drone as it approached to finish her off. Only then did she scream in pain.

She waited for the end to come. Again.

Instead a strong hand grabbed her by her uninjured arm and dragged her towards the ship. She looked up and saw Bass Reeves pulling her with one hand and firing his revolver with the other. With six shots he destroyed six drones. Then he threw his empty revolver and destroyed a seventh. Crazy Horse had their backs and was firing a rifle to clear their path to the ship. Those two couldn't have returned at a more opportune moment. Khutulun was following close behind them, supporting Joan, who could barely walk.

They entered the safety of the ship.

Just after the wounded were brought aboard, Hypatia went outside with a large javelin, and threw it with great accuracy into the middle of biggest mass of drones. The Javelin exploded in blue sparks and sent arcs of electricity into every drone within a hundred meter radius, instantly dropping them lifeless to the ground. Luckily she could throw a javelin more than a hundred meters or the rest of them would have been vaporized within the arc blast as well. Hypatia, Musashi and Goethe took advantage of this moment of distraction to safely get on board the ship.

Gabby announced some kind of safety message that everyone ignored and the ship launched quickly into the air. Everyone who was still on their feet fell over from the sudden movement, but most of the team was already lying in their cots, ready to receive medical attention. Broken bones, severe cuts and concussions were numerous.

The remaining drones outside were still monitoring what was happening, and attempted to follow, but Gabby navigated the ship swiftly into deep space, and left them all far behind. The team did feel some bumps as Gabby plowed through a handful of drones that were still arriving late to the party, coming in from some unknown locations. These were all splattered like bugs on a windshield.

When the ship finally steadied itself Gabby made an announcement that everyone did pay attention to, "Setting course for Eden."

Chapter 7 - Conquest

For generations the people of Eden had learned the ways of peace and harmony. The local legends told the story of a Creator leaving them with strict commandments, that must never be broken, under threat of forfeiting an enjoyable afterlife. Then the very same Creator blessed them with a wealth of resources to prevent them from succumbing to the violence born from desperation and starvation. The people were raised on traditions of sharing and and thinking of others ahead of themselves. Jealousy, corruption and greed were considered shameful personality traits in their culture, while disputes were resolved through reason and compromise, using a justice system that the population respected. It was a place that had forgotten the ego. Eden was one of the rarest of civilizations, in that the old did not fear the young.

These gentle souls farmed the plentiful crops that their planet offered and raised various beasts for meat, wool, milk and burden . They had all the tools of a successful ancient civilization, but they were not forced to suffer the typical dangers of one. Disease and violence were rare. War was unknown. The population was in the tens of thousands so it had not grown large enough to sustain any large professional armies. Military training was not pursued due to a lack of enemies. Religion was not used as a tool of suppression but as an encouragement to be better. Knowledge was still limited, but when it was needed urgently, the people resorted to divine prophesies for guidance.

In the absence of military training, the youth had time to learn literacy, agriculture, hunting, and the stories of their ancestors. The civilization developed its own styles of drawing, theatre, dance, music and literature, for entertainment purposes. Once a week most of the population of Eden would gather in the only real town , which they also called Eden, to celebrate their arts with a full day of performances from the citizens. This small town was built around the largest theatre on the planet. Everything from songs, dances, readings and plays, could be performed in this venue, and the entire population of the planet could fit in the seats. After the artists that were chosen to perform that day finished their show, usually around the time the sun went down, the weekly celebration would conclude with a communal grand feast. This event was a chance for the people to form social connections, catch up on community announcements and to gain the notoriety that went with performing before every single person they knew. Social status was gained and lost during these art festivals.

A young man named Nereus spent the early hours of the celebration day backstage at the theatre, practicing the song he had written, and rewritten over the past month. The time had come for the lad to graduate from his education and enter manhood. The culture of Eden required all students to perform something for the celebration at this point of their lives, as it served as a coming of age ritual, as well as encouraging new artists to explore their talent for the good of the group. The better performers would return for many more appearances and be rewarded with a higher status in society. Nereus was more interested in getting his performance over with, and then focusing on a life of hunting, and exploring the wilderness of his vast home world. Ideally, his performance would win him some favour with the beautiful young lady whom he had a crush on, his classmate Apphia, then all of this hard work would be worth the effort.

As Nereus belted out his catchy lyrics about young love, he remembered the first time he had met Apphia. It was the first day of classes in his 10th year of school. They sat together then, and they spend the next few years working on their studies together, as often as possible. There were times when Nereus wanted to get romantic, but it was considered bad form for the people of Eden to begin dating seriously before the day that they revealed themselves to the world by performing in the weekly festival. These traditions also kept the teens of Eden from forming too much rivalry or angst. Although on the downside, it was pretty difficult to create interesting art when there were so few dramatic, lewd or exciting experiences to draw upon.

"I like the song kid. Not a boring tune like you novices are usually coming up with," a man with a distinguished gray beard complimented Nereus as he finished one last rehearsal. Nereus was surprised when he recognized that the admirer was actually the famous Diokles, the chieftain of the Eden people, and a regular performer of several popular romantic comedies at the celebration events. The romantic comedies were the biggest reason he was chosen to become the leader of Eden many years earlier.

"Thank you," Nereus tried to sound like he wasn't in the middle of the most nervous day of his life, "My name is Nereus."

"Good luck kid . Make them all remember you. That's how I got where I am today," Diokles took his leave and went off to find his fellow actors.

A few minutes later, Nereus found himself waiting at the side of the stage of Eden's magnificent amphitheatre. The place still had many empty seats in these early stages of the day since the well known performers would not be seen for several more hours. The younger people attended right at the beginning, so they could evaluate their ill prepared peers, and likely have some laughs at their expense. Many youngsters were also fishing for inspiration for their own future performances. Some of the elders were seated in the audience early on as well, but they were mostly reading or writing to pass the time, waiting around for the bigger acts that came later.

Reading was the most popular activity in Eden culture. People on Eden spent most of their days reading stories about their ancestors' great deeds, places they have never seen before, unusually dangerous animal hunts, local celebrity gossip, or that famous legend about their creator bringing them a holy relic to hide on their world. Nobody was alive any more from that time, but every last detail about the event, was recorded for future generations. They knew the relic must never leave this world until their Creator came to claim it Himself. If anyone else came for it, they must not reveal its location, at any cost.

Finally today, someone came for it.

As Nereus reluctantly walked over to take his turn on the stage. He stopped at the center, nodded at Apphia in the audience, closed his eyes, belted out the first note of his song, and then heard the audience gasp as one. Several deafening explosions followed. Nereus opened his eyes and watched with awe as the devastation before him unfolded, never moving from his spot on the stage. People in the audience were running for their lives and one area he could see was already filled with smoke and death. A huge hole had replaced a dozen rows of seats. Nereus couldn't remember if anyone had been sitting there before. As various sections of the theatre collapsed, from all the structural damage, fires also began to spread all about the building.

These sights and sounds were new to Nereus and he did not know what to do. He finally ran off stage towards and exit, and immediately noticed that even more screaming and misery were unfolding outside the amphitheatre. Some of the smaller buildings were in flames as well. People ran around the town directionless, as a mass panic took over, because of the sudden barrage of terror, injuries and confusion.

Above the town, a large spacecraft descended out of the clouds, casually lobbing a few more fireballs into the nearest buildings. The ship was a tall winged structure with exotic lights and windows all over it. As it landed on the ground, it dominated the landscape, as even the mighty Eden Amphitheatre was not as large as this mysterious object. The primitive people cowered in its presence and waited for what they assumed was the wrath of God.

A loudspeaker on the ship addressed them, "Citizens of Eden. You are now the property of the Great Khan. Everything you own belongs to me. If you are still alive, it is because I chose to allow it. Come and bow before your ruler and you will not be harmed. Resist and you will ALL die."

Most of the people gathered around the ship, because it seemed like a reasonable offer to them, at that particular moment. Soon a door opened and a ramp extended there to the ground. Ten armed men marched down the ramp and waited before the crowd. One of them was a very angry looking Mongol warrior, who would be known on his native planet as the most ruthless conqueror in the history of the world, Genghis Khan. On his right stood Napoleon Bonaparte, Leonardo da Vinci, Nikola Tesla, George Washington and Julius Caesar. On his left were Alexander the Great, Plato, Isaac Newton and Hannibal Barca. None of these names meant anything to the people of Eden. Although they were well read, only two of Eden's many books originated from Earth's literature, the Bible and Homer's Iliad and Odyssey. These two books were treated as the holiest texts of Eden civilization, because they came from that mysterious place of Eden's origin, the world every inhabitant learned about, but none had ever seen. Even the name Eden came from that other world. Little did these people realize that the human civilization that authored the two holy books could now be described as extinct.

"Who is your leader?" Khan looked at the crowd.

"It is I, Diokles, who leads these people. You may have heard of me from my romantic comedies," the actor bragged to Genghis Khan.

"Wrong!" Khan chopped Diokles right onto the top of the head with his short sword, held it there for a moment, removed it, and watched the man fall to the ground dead, "I am your leader! Now, you will bring me the weapon your creator has hidden on this world."

The people started mumbling in confusion at this statement. Nereus had by now made his way into the midst of the gathering crowd around the spacecraft, and he stopped short when he saw his idol, Diokles, lying on the ground motionless, with blood still pouring out of his head. He glared at Genghis Khan and the other warriors. They were just patiently waiting for their shock tactics to create the desired response in the crowd. He looked around at the people he had grown up with, that he celebrated with every week, and expected to grow old with. They were all in a shared state of despair. Then he spotted the love of his life, Apphia, crying alone at the fringes of the crowd. She might have lost someone or perhaps she was just traumatized by the events that she had witnessed, whatever it was, Nereus was not interested in finding out. Instead of comforting her, his reaction drove him to pick up the nearest rock, and hurl it at the evil warrior who had caused all this sorrow and pain.

Khan smiled, raised his hand, and easily deflected the rock that flew out of the crowd into the ground. *Finally a reaction from these people!*

"Who threw that?" Khan asked, his voice bellowing through the PA system of the spacecraft, and causing the crowd to flinch in fear at his every word.

"I did!" Nereus walked up to the front without hesitation. He was resigned to sacrificing his life rather than staying quiet and watching even more of his people get slaughtered as a result of his actions.

"Good lad. Come stand with me now. You are my new general," Khan said. He was impressed with the young man's courage and honesty. Then he addressed his ship's artificial intelligence, "Play the message, machine."

The spacecraft responded by generating a recorded hologram message from the Creator of Eden, addressing the local people. The Hologram God's physical appearance was just as described by the texts of the ancestors and the words he spoke encouraged the people of Eden to reveal the location of the holy relic he had once hidden on their planet. Everyone around the area watched in dismay as the only God they knew was endorsing the cruel monsters that had needlessly massacred their friends and families. Some felt betrayed by their beloved creator, while others felt the unimaginable shame of having been ruthlessly punished, but not knowing the reason why. Any ideas about resisting this warlord's will had all but disappeared before the recorded message ended. Whether anyone chose to believe that he was sent by their Creator, or that he had somehow commanded their Creator to speak that way, the universal feeling of surrender was still the same.

"You girl!" Khan pointed at Apphia. She had at this point approached near Nereus, whom she wanted to confront about his willingness to stand beside this group of cruel attackers, "Do you know the location of this weapon on your planet?"

"Everybody knows," she answered, "We have been the keepers of this relic since the dawn of time. You call it a weapon, but we only know it as our Oracle. It has always offered us counsel and guidance.

Since there is nothing else in our world that would interest a warlord, such as you, it must be the Oracle that you seek."

"An Oracle? You will go with Alexander and Plato to show them the way to this Oracle. Napoleon, you will go with them as well, and take that science man with you," the Great Khan pointed at Tesla, "He knows the most about these future weapons, and other matters none of us have ever heard of, but he cannot fight. Protect him and bring me the weapon we came here for."

The two legendary commanders and two great thinkers from Earth joined Apphia and they all left the village on foot.

Khan spoke quietly with Hannibal and Caesar for a few moments, giving them some directions, then he looked Nereus over.

"Your people are strong in body, like we are, but you are weak fighters," He observed to Nereus.

"I don't understand, commander, why did you attack us and kill many of our peaceful people? You must know that we would freely give you that holy relic because you had our creator's blessing all along. What do you gain from such cruelty?" Nereus was both outraged at the attack on his people, and yet also genuinely curious, just as Khan had intended.

"You are right about that young man, but the weapon your planet is hiding, that is just for this 'Creator' you spoke of. I did not come here to find that weapon - I came here to find an army!" Khan explained the ways of war to his young apprentice, "You do not raise an army by asking for volunteers."

The Mongol warlord gave a nod to the remaining commanders, and they went about the process of separating the military aged men of Eden from the rest of the population. There was enough room for just over a thousand passengers on Khan's ship. He had already consulted with the computer, and was informed that the ship's resources would have to be replenished at every opportunity, in order to provide the required amount of food and water for this many people. The ship would now be stopping at several planets to gather the elements required to generate these essential resources. Their travel would become much slower than it was with 10 passengers, but such was the price of having the largest army possible, and he considered it an unavoidable step to carrying out his mission of killing the "Fallen One". Even if his army would turn out to be useless in that mission, as the computer had counseled, he would nonetheless be well positioned for his own personal mission of conquering the Earth. Nobody else had an army as far as he knew.

To Genghis Khan, this conquest of Earth was unfinished business from his former life.

Deep within the woods outside the town, Apphia guided the Earth legends along the narrow footpath that lead to the Oracle of Eden. The trees of Eden reached 300 feet or more in height, while even the grass that covered the ground reached over their heads, and the effect was that they all felt very small. Despite the height of the vegetation the sky was still visible above. Every so often, an unseen bird or animal would make a noise, which would originate from an uncomfortably close distance to the travelers. Apphia's reactions to the sounds suggested there was no danger.

The path was well traveled. Every few days a woman from the town would have to make this same two hour journey in order to bring food and refreshments to the Guardian of the Oracle, who was never allowed to leave her station. It was a great honour to be selected as the Guardian. The woman with that job was the only person allowed to interact with the Oracle, and it was her duty to guard it from danger, and keep it in good repair. After a few years, she would retire from this position, and participate in the process of selecting her predecessor, usually one of those same women that volunteered to supply the Guardian. The most dedicated ones were slowly trained to take over during their time serving the current Guardian. Visits from the volunteers were numerous, as were the worshipers who came to consult the Oracle for advice, thus the Guardian never wanted for supplies, nor company.

"I should warn you all, that men are not allowed to visit the Oracle," Apphia finally spoke to the warlords.

"I see. So you have made this journey before?" Asked Alexander the Great, who was following immediately behind Apphia.

"I have many times. I have been bringing supplies to the Guardian of the Oracle for years, as it is our duty as worshipers, to keep her comfortable and healthy."

"This guardian is a Priestess from among your people? She brings you the word of the Gods if you ask her for guidance?"

"Yes... but you seem to know much about this."

"I am the ruler of the Hellenic people and a Pharaoh of Egypt, so I have visited my share of Oracles."

"What a great King you must be! Our people study the ancient ways of Earth in our schools, but regrettably, we are only limited to the works of Homer and the Bible to learn from, and yet all the places you ruled over are mentioned in those books. Tell me great King Alexander, what purpose was there in attacking our world so cruelly?"

"It was not my strategy. You should ask your own 'Creator'. This Creator addressed me once, when I was born again, and he appeared to me as Zeus Himself, so I would not dare to question Him, as you should know from reading Homer. After all, He had personally just raised me from the dead! It was His idea to put Khan in charge of our mission, and we were all compelled to follow that man, even if he believes he is some kind of war-god," Alexander nodded at the other men in their party, "But our enemy is something very powerful, so we must not question Zeus about the type of leader we will need."

Plato inserted himself into the conversation, "As you are both fellow students of Homer, I ask you to recall the story of Sisyphus, to help explain what happened to your people."

Apphia was surprised at how much she could relate to these alien invaders over Greek mythology, "You mean that Greek King with the famous punishment? I think he had to push a boulder up a mountain, only to have it roll all the way to the bottom, and then he would start pushing it up the mountain again!"

"Yes that Sisyphus. You really did learn something about the Greek heroes, because that was indeed his famous punishment from the Gods. But before he was punished, Sisyphus was a wise man, perhaps too wise. One day he actually captured Death, which of course, caused all the people in the world to become immortal. Who do you think opposed this?" Plato immediately answered his own question, "It was Ares! Peace, prosperity and happiness, these are the things that make a God of War become outraged! What purpose does war have without death? It becomes nothing but a game. In his rage, Ares freed Death and sent Sisyphus off to suffer his famous punishment. You people on this planet, with your harmless nature, and your love of peace, you have also enraged a God of War. What else would a conqueror do when faced with such a place as this?"

"Nonsense," Tesla contradicted the ancient philosopher, "Our leader is no God at all. He is a primitive man, who has not seen battle in far too long, and was simply satisfying his bloodlust. The man is a savage. He was known to destroy great cities and execute prisoners without regret. You don't know the story of this Khan like I do! He spent his life fighting battles and then searching for the next battle. Today was his chance to fill his endless desire for blood."

"Savage? We are all savages compared to the people on this world," Napoleon could no longer hold his tongue, "Khan is not a mindless killer, nor a God of war either, he is a great warrior. Those of us who are also warriors can see that. You should know his attack on these ignorant people was merely a way to test the loyalties of his officers, along with the capabilities of his unfamiliar weapons. He wanted to know what he will be working with before he faces a stronger enemy."

The group became silent as they got nearer to the location of the Oracle. Apphia could tell that these men were not all in agreement with their leader, or each other. It seemed clear enough to her that the men who accompanied her meant no further harm to her people.

What could she do about her situation except give them the relic they came for?

Why not kill them? She briefly considered trying to trick these four men into approaching the Oracle. The ancient legends of Eden warned that only women may access the Oracle, and that any man who attempted to do so, would be met with a fatal punishment of supernatural proportions. It was also said that not even an army of men could resist the Oracle's defenses. There was a rumor whispered among the unofficial channels of Eden, that many years ago, a man had tried to approach the Oracle in anger, after losing a child to disease. He was never seen again. Nor were the dozen men who were sent to look for him. Not many details have survived to this day, but the mythology suggested that somehow the Guardian was able to contain the massacre, before it could wipe out the entire town.

She quickly decided against such an act of violence because it went against everything she knew. Apphia resolved that she would only attempt to trick the Khan himself, if she could find a way to bring him to the Oracle, and not these other men. They were not really to blame. Her culture had conditioned her to forgive the men, based on their lack of enthusiasm for Khan's atrocities, but she did not forgive Khan himself. Besides, she honestly felt that Khan still posed a danger to her people, or at the very least, she felt her friend Nereus was in danger of being taken away. Her actions would be based on self defense and not vengeance. If she somehow managed to harm the warlord, it would clearly be justified, even when accounting for the overly pacifist traditions of her civilization.

"How are we supposed to carry the Oracle back to your leader?" Apphia asked.

"It won't be necessary. We only have to locate it. Then our ship will come and pick it up," Alexander explained, "As for our 'leader', Khan is only in charge as long as he shares a common goal with the rest of us."

"Well, let me know if I should ask the Oracle anything about him," Apphia offered.

She felt like Alexander was almost from a similar culture as her own. He spoke of the heroes of Greece, he had seen several other Oracles, and he had a strong distrust of the man who had attacked Eden. Somehow it seemed like most of the violence would not have happened if Alexander was in charge. If only Apphia had enough time to persuade him to have a confrontation with Khan... but unfortunately for her these men had their minds on more important matters than the livelihood of her world. She realized she would not be able to shake their focus from their bigger goals.

She led the men into a small clearing in the trees. On the other side, there was a large cave that had it's natural shelter complimented by some ancient stone structures, which converted it into a liveable dwelling. It looked almost as if the cave had been carved out by some giant sculptor to house the Oracle's temple. High up above, on top of the cave, large panels soaked up energy from Eden's sun, and generated the only power on the entire planet.

"This must be electricity," Tesla was analyzing the solar panels around the cave, "So, like all the magic I have ever encountered, this Oracle is also just a machine!"

"Then it seems we are in the right place to find that weapon," Alexander concluded.

The group approached within a few meters of the opening of the cave, and Apphia halted them. They could clearly see that there was artificial light inside. The cave also contained some of the familiar computers and screens, similar to the devices the visitors had been introduced to recently, on their ship. The only resident of the cave was a middle aged woman who was approaching to greet her guests. She wore elegant robes that identified her as some kind of priestess. For some reason, she didn't seem afraid of being approached by several armed men, which gave them the impression that she might be more dangerous than she appears.

"I am Hecuba, guardian of the Oracle. Announce your intentions."

"Guardian, it is I, Apphia. I have brought these men here because the Creator Himself has ordained it."

"My name is Napoleon Bonaparte, and these men are Alexander, Plato and Tesla," Napoleon was no longer willing to follow Eden formalities, "We have been sent here for your mighty weapon to help us defeat the enemy of God. Now disarm any defenses you have in there so we may be on our way."

The distinguished woman looked over her visitors with disdain. She motioned for them to stay where they were and disappeared back into the cave. They could hear her talking to the machines inside, and they caught a glimpse of some kind of message appearing on a screen, probably the response to her inquiry. They all waited patiently for her.for several minutes, and then she returned to address them.

"I have consulted with the Oracle. The words it told me are as follows, 'You cannot conquer that which is already destroyed. You cannot destroy anything without sacrificing. You will all sacrifice,' " the Guardian spoke the words as they also appeared on a monitor behind her.

"The Oracle is wise," Plato was enthusiastic about the whole spectacle they had witnessed, "I believe it means to warn us that we must not destroy our home world in the war to come. But why this talk of sacrifice? What do you think the Oracle means?"

"You should have your leader come and observe this whole prophesy for himself," Apphia was taking her one chance to set in motion the events that would end Genghis Khan's life. The thing she needed most was for him to be nearby.

"Prophesy? Bullshit. What does this machine know of us? What does it know of our mission? Nothing. I want real answers, not riddles!" Tesla raged at the ignorance of his colleagues.

Since he was a man of science, Tesla had finally heard enough rubbish about supernatural powers, and then he had to endure those vague predictions about the future, which could conveniently be interpreted many ways. This spectacle was beneath him. He would have created lightning bolts, sound effects and some smoke, if it was his show. The ancient Greeks in the group were taking the Oracle at face value. Unlike these simpletons, Tesla recognized the familiar routine of a charlatan, when he heard it. He could barely go a day without hearing that kind of talk back when he was working in New York. How many of his own great successes had been taken away from him by some smooth-talking hustler? Too many to count.

Nikola Tesla darted towards the entrance to the cave, shoving Hecuba aside as he went, and made his way towards the computer equipment. He intended to use his knowledge of electronics to operate the Oracle himself. To him, it seemed like this was some sort of advanced computer that had the ability to calculate future events based on probability, using a very complex algorithm. Nothing magical. He should be able to get better answers by inputting more concise data than that dimwitted Guardian had done.

Napoleon decided to run after Tesla instinctively, seemingly to protect him from any defenses that could threaten him, since he had now clearly disobeyed all the rules of the Oracle. His actions looked heroic to any observer, but in actuality he only meant to protect any breakable equipment from Tesla's rampage. He was not interested in losing or damaging the only valuable item on this planet. Not after coming all this way. Besides, this Tesla fellow didn't have any credentials that he had ever heard of, and the guy was already causing more trouble than he was worth.

Alexander the Great did quite the opposite. He looked at Plato, and the two of them immediately started to back away from the Oracle. They were preparing for something to appear and punish them all for Tesla's actions. These two knew better than to ignore warnings about angering supernatural forces. All the Greeks grew up with stories about the age of heroes, when Gods themselves would punish humans for lesser transgressions than the ones they were currently witnessing.

"No! You must not go in there!" Apphia yelled uselessly after Tesla and Napoleon.

"It is too late. These men will die for this act!" Hecuba said, not as a threat, but because it was too late to stop what would happen next.

Just as Napoleon caught up to Tesla inside the cave, a loud mechanical engine noise erupted from even deeper inside, and smoke began to flow from all the openings. Slowly a large drone emerged from its hidden position and flew up above all their heads. The drone was shaped like a woman's naked body, a symbolic way of warning any man who saw it, that he had seen too much. No man on Eden had ever seen that drone and lived to tell about it. It moved about autonomously, with many spinning blades keeping it aloft, searching the surroundings, assessing all the threats.

Then it began whaling a sound of agonizing beauty. Within seconds, the two men emerged from the cave and stared up at the source of the noise, completely captivated by it.

"A Siren!" Plato shouted at Alexander as he cupped his hands over his own ears to protect himself. Of course Plato was not describing the noise as a siren sound. Rather, he was referring to those famous mythical women of ancient Greece, who would sing their songs that were irresistible to any man they encountered, usually resulting in that man's demise by shipwreck.

His warning was too late. Alexander was walking back towards the cave again, as the floating womanly figure hovered high above the cave's entrance. Apphia came up behind Alexander and slapped both of her hands over his ears. This caused Alexander to look around stunned, as the shock from that blow rescued him from the spell of the Siren high above. He noticed Plato was safe and his other colleagues were not. He saw Hecuba give Apphia a look like she should not have saved him, which made perfect sense to him, but he also noticed that the women were unaffected by the noise. He decided it was too risky to try and save any of the others since he was by now holding both his ears for dear life. There was nothing he could think to do, that didn't involve letting go of his own ears, and thereby fatally exposing himself to the Siren's noise.

Tesla and Napoleon climbed up the sides of the cave in their trance, stumbling over various solar panels as they stared at the Siren the whole time, their eyes full of longing. When they finally got to the top they were at the same height as the Siren they were still gazing at.

After a moment to measure the distance, Tesla jumped off the roof of the cave, reached out to grab at the drone that was flying just before him, missed it by quite a bit, and fell to his death upon the rocky ground below.

Napoleon backed up to get a running start. He sprinted like a lion, eyes on his prey, and leaped with all his might off the top of the cave, but he also dropped straight down to the ground, with a noticeable thud. The Siren continued to hover.

Apphia waved at Alexander and Plato to leave the area so perhaps the automated defenses would eventually shut off. It seemed reasonable to them, if the threat was gone, the automated Siren should cancel its attack, and return to its resting place. The two men started to leave, but stopped after a few steps, as they could see their ship was approaching their location.

The Khan's ship flew over the cave, circled around, and came back over at a lower altitude. When the ship reached the front of the cave, it bumped right into the drone at a dangerous speed, effectively punting it a few hundred meters away. The sound of the Siren ceased.

A handful of loading machines began to navigate around the cave, as a cargo ramp had now been lowered down to the ground, from the ship. The loaders moved some large electronic parts onto the ramp. Alexander and Plato walked over to the ramp to make sure the load would be secure enough to rise up to the ship without falling off. The two of them decided that the Baryonic Disruptor looked like it was still intact, to the best of their limited knowledge.

"A nice little trap for such a peaceful people," Khan mocked them through the ship's speakers, "I see I have lost two men on this world. They were so important and so famous, these men, at least that is what I have been told. Yet, here they lie dead on a world without weapons, or even fighters. True warriors die in battle among the bodies of the many enemies they have slain. You have done me a favour, girl, by ridding me of the weakness in my ranks."

"But I warned them!" Apphia was not pleased to accept the Khan's praise, since the only one she wanted to kill was him.

"Yes I suppose you must have. Otherwise, they would all be dead by now, or if they were smarter than you, you would be," Khan responded, "Well, it is only right that I should let you live. You earned it. I have gathered the weapon my creator demanded, thanks to you, and even though I lost two men today, I have also gained hundreds!"

With that, the ramp finished receding back into the ship, and Khan flew away with a thousand of Eden's finest young men, drafted by him, so he could use them in the coming battle between Gods and Demons. In a few minutes, they would be days away. Within days, they would be years away. After a few years, they would be an eternity away. In a relative time universe there was no such thing as ever returning home.

Apphia had no idea of the physics of space and time, however. She vowed to find a way to chase after the Khan's ship. Then she would find a way to rescue the men of Eden, along with her dearest friend, Nereus. These fantastical thoughts disappeared as she heard something off in the distance. In the absence of the ship engines, it had now become quiet enough for her to hear the Siren still singing, off somewhere far away.

Suddenly, she grabbed Hecuba by the arm, and they both started running towards town, because she had realized the sound was coming from that direction. Every remaining man in Eden was in danger!

Chapter 8 - Space

Sophia threw her practice sword at Joan, ducked a decapitating slash of Musashi's Katana, and rolled into a kneeling stance, which flowed naturally into a surprise uppercut directly into Marlborough's groin. They all stopped the exercise to check for injuries.

"That was unpleasant," exclaimed the Duke, understated as always.

"Your skills are improving. All of you. Remember, you can only fight the way you practice," Musashi explained.

Sophia took only a few days to heal from her injuries, thanks to some incredibly sophisticated medical nano-technology, and the fact that her current body was far better at healing than her original one was. Since the voyage to Eden would take a few months, she suggested that the team should share their individual strengths with each other, especially in regards to combat. Musashi was a perfect teacher when it came to blade and pole weapons. He had studied the techniques of the greatest masters of his era, defeated them all in duels, and then written several books on the subject. The team enjoyed sparring with practice weapons and listening to Musashi's endless philosophies about the way of the warrior.

Now that she could enter a room and incapacitate fifty people with a broomstick, it made Sophia look back at her former life fondly, marveling at how she had been so vulnerable, but also so innocent. Writing content for websites was a pretty cozy existence. She did not have to worry about training to fight for her life, fleeing from a swarm of robotic ships and getting mixed up in a brawl between deities, all over the future of the universe. Back then her biggest concern was avoiding the crazy yelling person on the subway. Whenever she felt the weight of responsibility upon her, even though she had the help of the greatest team she could ever hope to assemble, technology that blew her mind, and athletic ability superior to an Olympian, she would envy that naive Sophia of the past, who still thought humans were alone in the universe.

For hand to hand combat they all turned to Khutulun for training. Sophia had long ago told the team the legend about Princess Khutulun. She once promised her father she would only marry the first man who could defeat her in wrestling. The family made it known that any man could attempt this challenge, but would have to pay the price of a horse, if he lost. Many skilled Mongol warriors came to fight her, of course, as they were all eager to win a wife that elevated them into royalty. Soon she possessed over 10,000 horses and no husband. Her undefeated record did not change aboard the ship either. Most of the training involved Khutulun beating up on the rest of them. None could master any ways to defeat her, but they did slowly learn to minimize the amount of damage she could inflict, so at least they made some progress. This punishing hand to hand training made the team members resolve to always be well armed in actual combat.

During these long days in transit, Goethe and Hypatia teamed up to design more useful weapons than the ones the team had used in their previous battle. The two of them combined their own knowledge to create theoretical designs, which they could then refine with the help of Gabby's calculations, and consult a vast database of future weapons, as inspiration for further improvements. They came up with a few explosive projectile weapons, which were not very different from Sophia's sci-fi-movie-gun design, and some pistols that could fire plasma bolts instead of bullets. These would inflict much more damage and contain much more ammo than the 19th and 20th century firearms they had used earlier. Then they went about arming the ship itself with some larger weapons designed to combat any comparable ships.

Bass Reeves and Marlborough tested the new firearms and were impressed by their accuracy and capabilities, especially when compared to their own ancient rifles and muskets. The two of them gave the other crew tips on shooting quickly and accurately, but the new weapons had such advanced targeting scopes, that it was quite difficult to miss your target with them, even for a novice. When they practiced with the futuristic firearms, Sophia noticed they were even easier to aim than the shooting video games of her own time. The sophisticated AI in the guns could auto aim at a target by slightly adjusting the barrel to eliminate human error. Every shot would result in a direct hit.

Joan and Sophia truly dedicated themselves to learning how to fight, because they had realized during their battle with the probes, that they were the least experienced warriors among the group, other than Goethe. Much to Sophia's embarrassment, she had been told by Gabby that the machines that had nearly killed her in that battle, were just harmless probes that were only meant to transmit their location. They had no combat capacity of note, and they only really gathered and launched projectiles at them as a self defense mechanism, because they had been attacked. The probes could fire rocks and debris from the ground to scare away aggressive alien wildlife when they were gathering information on a planet. However, these harmless robots had succeeded in causing the team to run away wounded and scared!

Joan had also been humbled by her lack of effectiveness. She realized she could no longer rely on an army to rally around her, follow her charge into battle, and inspire them to victory with her bravery, as she had done on the battlefields of 15th century France. Her thoughtless charge into the robotic probes had been disastrous. She determined that she would have to deal some destruction of her own, to contribute to this small group, and she trained herself to that end. Joan became proficient with pistols and blades over time. She also examined Gabby's information database to try and better understand the non-human enemies they had faced. It was possible for Gabby to run simulations of the battle, and Joan ran through these many times, until she had settled on the most effective tactics she could have used. She would now be able to hold her own because nobody was in need of inspiration in this group.

Overall, the team was becoming more united, and more lethal . As a result of all their training, they were discovering the physical limitations, and enhanced abilities of their upgraded bodies, and becoming much better at working together instead of acting as individuals. Spending several weeks living in close quarters was forcing them to really become familiar with each other. All the while, they also used their spare time to continue educating themselves about all those years that had passed during their absence. This was best accomplished by quizzing the boundless knowledge of their artificially intelligent pilot, navigator, cook, teacher and host, whom they called Gabby.

"Gabby, I would like to ask how we are going to travel several light years in just a few weeks. I thought that was impossible, not just because of the technology of my era, but even according to the laws of physics," Sophia asked one day, as everyone was sampling a meal of Gyros on a pita together in the dining lounge.

"Oh man, you asked for it," said Goethe, "There are things better left unexplained. I dared to ask this same question once, at the beginning of our journey, and my mind is still in pain."

Despite Goethe's objection, Gabby explained, "The ship you are on is not able to break the laws of physics. We are simply able to bypass a lot of distance by using a technology that was invented a few centuries after your lifetime, Sophia.

"Allow me to illustrate. Imagine a two dimensional person exists who wants to travel from the ceiling to the floor in this three dimensional room. They could travel along the surface of the ceiling until they reach the wall, then down along that two dimensional surface, and then they would get to the floor and follow that surface until they reach their destination. This path allows them to stay in two dimensional space."

Gabby projected a cartoon stick person onto the middle of the ceiling, then made it move along the ceiling, wall and floor to show the team what she meant.

"The two dimensional person has taken the shortest trip available to him, but you all can see that there is a third dimension, something that the two dimensional person has no concept of. To you the shortest journey is straight down from the ceiling to the floor. Now if the two

92

dimensional person was aware of this third dimension, they could build a technology to take advantage of it. This technology in our demonstration would be a napkin. Mr. Von Goethe, if you could stand in for a two dimensional spaceship, please stand on the table and hold the napkin up to the ceiling."

Goethe did as he was told and Gabby projected the cartoon stick man onto the napkin. When Goethe let go of the napkin it fell straight to the floor and landed at the spot that was stick man's destination. Gabby kept projecting the cartoon stick man onto the napkin, but now he was doing a celebratory dance.

"As you can see the two dimensional man has sliced off a portion of his two dimensional universe, which was that napkin, and used it to travel through the three dimensional universe to take a shortcut to his destination. He was never actually exposed to the third dimension, which would cause his two dimensional body to implode, his cartoon blood to boil, and his organs to fall out, so he survived the journey," Gabby concluded the demonstration with her typical dramatic flair.

"So you see everyone, instead of two dimensions, we are actually inside a three dimensional napkin at this very moment, which is what this ship is, and we are taking a shortcut through a FOUR dimensional room!" Goethe exclaimed. He was excited that he was getting a better grip on the complex physics theories from later centuries.

"There is much more to it, but that is the basic idea of how we are traveling through vast amounts of space in a very short amount of time. We could also make this journey faster or slower for the passengers, by dampening the relative passing of time aboard this ship, but this would have no effect on the time passing outside in the rest of the universe. There were many advancements in the realm of relativity physics after your lives," Gabby stopped talking at this point because she realized the human passengers were already confused.

"Well that is some interesting stuff, Gabby. Thanks for sharing," said Sophia, "Maybe now we can quietly reflect on the fact that we are speeding through a dimension that our minds could never perceive, and that could make our organs explode."

"Indeed you understand it perfectly! Your bodies would all turn inside out and you would break apart at a molecular level if you left the protection of this ship!" Gabby said cheerfully.

"OK then. Do you have the album Hello Nasty by the Beastie Boys in your database? Please play that for us," Sophia needed some New York sounds to cope with the idea that she was currently bending time and space, "And how about making us a few brownies with that special recipe I taught you a while back?"

After a few enhanced brownie treats, followed by an obscene amount of horse milk vodka - courtesy of Princess Khutulun's input - the team was soon in a good mood. Encouraged by Sophia's playlist, they each tried to present the songs of their people, but some were better singers than others. The night descended into merriment and playful fighting before they fell asleep. They all rested easier now that their retreat from battle was just a memory they could joke about, while the upcoming destination was a friendly, harmless colony. At least that is what they were expecting.

A few days later the ship arrived at the planet Eden.

"Something has happened," Gabby announced as they were still approaching the planet, "My readings indicate there has been a major decrease in population. It is unlikely that a natural disaster, or violence among the inhabitants, could kill this many people without obvious planetary damage. I am scanning the area for evidence of advanced technological activity."

"You'd be surprised how violent humans can be," Sophia lamented. She had lived during an era that was known for world wars, terrorism, shooting rampages, genocide and mass media hysteria.

Gabby disagreed, "The original human inhabitants here were created especially to be peaceful and nonviolent. Today they still have primitive technology and almost no weapons. Even the environment was carefully designed to be so stable that no significant natural disaster could ever occur on this world. The most likely explanation is an outside attack, but that theory excludes how hidden this planet is. Nobody, other than the creator of the planet, knows of its existence."

"Well there's an easy way to find out. We go and ask the survivors!" Sophia concluded. She ordered Gabby to land wherever she could locate the most people.

As their ship approached the village with the amphitheatre, several of the ship's external cameras were feeding to the various monitors in the control room, so that Sophia and the crew could observe the damage. There were a lot of scorched buildings and damage that did not look like it could be inflicted by any primitive weapons. The watched as people on the ground were pointing up at their ship in horror, some fleeing into the wilderness, others picking up rocks and sticks and throwing them at the ship in anger, as it neared the ground. Gabby landed exactly in the same town square where the Khan's ship had stood just months earlier.

"Give me an active speaker outside the ship, Gabby," Sophia picked up a microphone linked to the ship's PA system, "Peaple of Eden. We mean you no harm. We have come here to visit you in peace but I can see you have recently been attacked. We had nothing to do with that. I repeat, we had nothing to do with that! Stop throwing rocks please. We are coming out now, so come and tell us exactly what happened here."

Sophia went to a portal that had a ramp to the ground. Joan and Marlborough followed her. The others decided to wait inside to avoid scaring the locals any more than they already were. As Sophia and her two companions reached the ground, they saw one young woman approach them with tears in her eyes.

"Where are they?" this woman demanded of them.

"Who?" asked Sophia.

"This same evil vessel was here just six months ago. There was a warlord and his followers. They killed half of the men on this world and stole all the rest!" the woman said desperately.

Sophia looked around and realized a few other women had slowly begun to come out of hiding. They must have realized she and her friends were not actually the same people that had attacked them before. She decided to let them get more comfortable before questioning them for more details about the attack.

"So you speak our language then? Good. My name is Sophia and these are my friends, Marlborough and Joan. We are all from Earth. What is your name?"

"Apphia... and I am from this world, we call it Eden."

"We know nothing about your attackers. I am sorry for your many losses. We would like to find out more about what happened, if we could meet with your leaders, or some representative of your world. Tell them to let us know if there is anything we can do to help," Sophia assumed Eden had a leader who was older than this teenager named Apphia, although it did not escape her attention that the youngster was the only one brave enough to greet them.

"Maybe you could take a moment to assure your people that we are not here to attack you?" Joan suggested.

"Very well. Meet me in one hour in that building and we will talk," Apphia pointed at a wooden structure that was the one in the best condition.

Sophia gathered her team in the main control room of the ship. Monitors were displaying damage assessment observations of the area and calculating probable causes. Sensors were cataloging all organic and mineral elements nearby. These would soon be collected by autonomous probes, and stockpiled on board, to replenish the ship's food and material generators. Various clicks and beeps were making the room sound busy and chaotic. Sophia's Team Earth was seated, filtering through all the different types of information being presented in the room at that moment, their immediate concern was the notion that a secret planet would be attacked just before they arrived.

Finally Gabby spoke, "I have calculated the most likely cause of the attack. A ship just like ours was here six months before us. There were 'warlords' on board that looked similar to you Earth people. The damage I have observed matches the combat capabilities of this ship. Therefore there is only one explanation that is probable enough to describe. God must have created another team of human warriors and another ship with another Gabby. Since any human team's success depends entirely on free will, God could not assume the first team would succeed, so he created a second team in case the first team failed. The other team was created first and your team was created after to double God's chances of success. Very good idea. I would have done the same thing.

"Of course the two teams must be operating completely independent of each other as I was given no prior information about this other team. I assure you I have only predict their existence based on the evidence I have gathered since we arrived here. The other team's Gabby would have suggested coming to Eden, to obtain the Baryonic Disrupter device, just as I suggested to you. Obviously the other AI would not be any different from me except for certain learned interactions with the human crew. We can assume that the other team does not know that we exist, because we are behind them, and it is unlikely that only one of the teams would be told there are two teams, while the other would not."

"I agree with your logic, Gabby," Hypatia said, the crew's leading authority on logic, "But those other visitors were very different from us. Our group has actually agreed to temper our actions and not resort to excessive violence. We are deliberately trying to follow a path of good. What of these others? Is it not reasonable to say that their immortal souls spent these past centuries within some kind of afterlife just like ours? Usually, those who try to describe their idea of an afterlife will include some kind of purification process, but the behaviour of these other humans implies they are no better than they were in their first lives. The nature of the afterlife eludes me now more than ever."

"Yes it is something to contemplate. Putting aside philosophy for a moment, the people of this Eden are peaceful and harmless, so attacking them with such force reveals much about the nature of those other travelers," Goethe interpreted the facts in his logical way, "I have always said, you can easily judge the character of a man by the way he treats those who can do nothing for him."

"Seems to me we will probably be running into that other group of characters at some point, since our paths are alike, so we need to find out everything we can from these unlucky folks," Bass Reeves suggested, "When we finally meet them, our advantage will be our knowledge about them, and their ignorance about us."

"We have another problem. The weapon we came here for is probably gone! I don't believe these people resisted the attackers, because we would have found no survivors at all if they did fight back, so they must have surrendered that weapon immediately in the face of such a powerful enemy. We will have to seek a different weapon now," Joan reminded them.

"Yes, that will have to be our new mission. But first, let us prepare to consult with these people of Eden and find out everything we can about the attackers," Sophia declared, "I will also explain to them what is going on beyond their world. There is no point hiding their origin from them, now that they have lived through the destruction of their civilization."

The group of human travelers continued to discuss what they could figure out about the planet they were visiting and soon enough it was time to attend the meeting in the village. Sophia was introduced to the new leader of Eden, a woman they called Hecuba the Guardian, along with her highest ranking followers, including Apphia. This distinguished woman had retired from the position of priestess to become the reluctant chieftain of these beaten down people. She explained that the previous leader of Eden had been publicly slain, as a cruel show of force, by the alien Warlord.

They gathered around a large wooden table in what looked to be a makeshift town hall. Paintings decorated the walls, displaying some of this world's greatest ancestors, and the meeting did not officially begin until a young lady sang a traditional song for them all. After that, Hecuba introduced her advisers, and Sophia introduced her whole crew. None of the famous Earth names were familiar to the Eden leaders.

"I learned that your planet was originally founded as a peaceful colony by two original humans, named Adam and Eve. Those two people were born right here on Eden, and unlike our own group, who were all resurrected, these two were both completely new lives. After several generations, their descendents had developed the culture and lifestyle you all lived in, until that fateful day half a year ago. That is when your history was interrupted by much more violent humans than you have ever known," Sophia explained, hoping that the people had not forgotten their own origin yet.

The Eden leaders were familiar with the story, but their scholars were always confusing their own history with the texts of the bible and Homer, since these books were considered sacred texts. Sophia told the Eden leaders how those two books had been written on Earth several millenia before her own time, and how Eden's Creator even seemed to use them as inspiration, especially in the way He chose to name his creations. She described how God had told Sophia when they met, that the bible did not speak for him, and that it was made up by man, He must have respected the way it influenced humans a bit more than he let on. It made sense, from God's perspective, to model this rebooted civilization of humans after their predecessors' own favorite creation stories. It also would have been quicker than trying to write a whole new set of rules and allegories from scratch. Since he was making a sequel to his great performance, the creation of the world of man, He had the advantage of already knowing what the audience wanted. Apparently what they wanted was lots of divine punishments and Greek heroes.

After explaining the details of her own origin, some vague information about Earth, and the all she had learned about the origin of Eden itself, Sophia finally asked the noble Hecuba what she could tell them about the attack that took place a few months earlier. The Guardian Hecuba frowned at the bitter memories and gave the best description she could.

"It was the traditional day of festivities and celebration in our town. All the people were gathered here when they saw a flying structure just like yours appear in the heavens above and it rained fire upon us.

Many died. Some men came out just like you did and addressed our people as a whole. They killed some more of our kin with their hand weapons. Finally, they even summoned our very own Creator, and He appeared before us all, and spoke to us, and demanded that we give these men a sacred weapon He had once hidden on our world. It was not our way to disobey our own creator so we did as the warlords demanded.

"I was the Guardian of this weapon, and I gave the warlords what they wanted. Instead of leaving us in peace, they gathered all of the men from our world, and took many of the strongest away with them before the eyes of their families, and ascended into the heavens with them. The rest of our men were killed by a curse they unleashed upon us before they left. Our women were left behind to suffer the loss of all our sons, husbands, brothers and fathers. We have never seen them again. Without any men, our kin will die off when the last of us women dies."

"What can you tell us about these warriors you saw?" Asked Sophia.

"The leader called himself the Great Khan. His followers went by the names Hannibal, Newton, Washington, Caesar, Da Vinci, Plato and Alexander," Hecuba recalled the names she had heard from those who witnessed the events, "But there were also two others who were killed, not because we fought with them, but by their own foolishness. They were called Napoleon and Tesla if my recollection is correct."

"Wow. Now I understand how some of the names I chose were not available! They had already been resurrected before I even had a chance," Sophia said to Joan sitting just beside her at the great conference table.

"You know these warlords then? These people took away our Oracle, and our men! We have never known such cruelty in our world. Only the texts of Earth had stories of such deeds. Until now, we did not think these texts were even serious. Gods toying with humans, a ten year war over a beautiful woman, people killing other people just to

100

take what was theirs, so many stories of evil deeds. These books were not made up? You lived in a world with such madness?"

"Well yeah, many of those stories were made up," Sophia summarized, "Or at least, there was very little evidence to verify them, so many centuries after they were written. That doesn't mean the Earth was like your world though. We have all witnessed, or even participated in, events on Earth that were even more evil and terrible than the stories in those books! Your people should be proud of yourselves, because you are much the same as us in body and mind, and yet you have never become monsters."

"I think our culture has changed now. If we could somehow survive this, we will always know fear and rage, and we will remember the loss we suffered. We would not allow ourselves to be caught so defenseless again."

Sophia could not disagree with Hecuba's unfortunate prediction, "Is there anything we can do to help?"

"There are two things you could do to help us. First, find our men and bring them back to us if you can. Second, in case you fail, help us to populate this planet once again!" Hecuba suggested in desperation.

"Well... this is definitely not my department. Joan, Khutulun, Hypatia and I will go back to the ship and think of a way to find those prisoners," Sophia lied to the Eden women. She didn't want to bother explaining the laws of general relativity, which would conclude that any of the missing people, even if they managed to return to this world, would not arrive until several centuries from now! She addressed her team instead, "Men of Earth, do you accept the request of these women of Eden?"

"For the good of humanity, it must be done," Goethe decided.

"Do nothing that is of no use," Said Musashi thoughtfully.

"This reminds me of the old days," Said Marlborough.

"If this is my path - so be it," Reasoned Crazy Horse

"Hell, I thought you'd never ask," Bass Reeves summed up their enthusiasm.

"It is settled then. Godspeed," Sophia wished her friends well, and the meeting of two worlds ended in a series of raised eyebrows and longing glances, as the women of Earth took their leave, and the women of Eden hunted their prey.

"What say you boy?" One of the lower ranked Eden women addressed Joan as she moved towards the door.

"I say I am no boy, I just dress like a boy, as is my wont," Joan answered politely.

Finally, Bass Reeves took it upon himself to transform the extremely awkward mood into a celebration, "So, who do I have to fuck to get some whiskey on this planet?"

Those words and the cheering that followed, were the last things Sophia heard before leaving the building. She chuckled to herself as she pictured the debauchery that would soon transpire. When she finally got back to her ship, she felt a tap on her shoulder and turned around to see Apphia had followed them all the way through the village. Joan, Hypatia and Khutulun went on into the ship so Apphia could talk to Sophia in private.

"I have lost all my loved ones and my best friend was taken away by those Earth warlords. There is nothing left for me here. Please let me join you?" The young lady pleaded.

"That would be fine. We have a lot of room, and not enough bodies for this mission. You must understand that I expect your loyalty and obedience. You will learn to fight and you will kill or die if necessary! You must forget your peaceful ways if you come with us. We are going to face so much danger and pain ahead of us, and if we fail, all is lost, our world AND yours as well. I must also warn you, if you ever return here, none of these people will be here any more, nothing will be here like it is today," Sophia said, testing Apphia's resolve. She was pleased to see Apphia nodded without hesitation.

So our team numbers ten after all.

"How many times has my consciousness been rebooted?" Gus asked one of the nerds.

"We estimate at least 200 times by now. The system seems to be looping at the same point and rebooting itself back to the same point. Then it just plays out that same loop over and over. I have noticed one variable changes in each loop," The senior nerd reported to Gus.

"Isolate and record the details of that variable. When I return I want to see what exactly is changing because we need to put an end to this shitshow!"

Gus had rested for a day and a half after the exhausting mind-download process, yet even now he was still tired. Unfortunately Gus' reward for all his efforts was finding the entire World 2.0 system caught up in some kind of unknown breakdown ever since he first introduced his consciousness. After all the successful simulations, and public beta testing, this scale of major system failure was somewhat unexpected. Gus was sure his system would work. It does work. So what was causing this new problem?

Gus shook his head and went to his office to take a nap on a cot he had set up there. The nerds would figure out something eventually. Maybe not the solution, but they would probably give him more information, and then he would solve the problem. Hopefully these nerds were not the types to go off and smoke E-Crack when he wasn't paying attention. Gus was always hiring and firing the staff at his Ophion research labs, and it was getting harder to keep track of the endless turnover of new graduates from various technology institutes.

The problem with technology experts, was that they were well trained at creating not just body enhancements, but usually mind enhancements as well. This gave them a powerful position in society. Over the past few years, humans had gradually become bored with the limited effects of natural, or chemical drugs, as new technologies became available that were much more effective at stimulating the pleasure centers of the human brain. Instead of smoking or injecting some dangerous substance, a person could just press a button to feel euphoric, or to feel energized, or even feel more relaxed. This electronic method was direct, instant, reliable, and didn't require primitive narcotic rituals that were now considered tedious and degrading.

Of course everyone just walked around all day feeling great, because if given a choice, nobody preferred to feel normal, so nobody would ever turn off these mind altering effects. Thus society became addicted to these artificial feelings. 'Smoking E-Crack' became a term to describe when people lost the ability to function in real life any more, because of their addiction, and these people would either have to be shut down, or they would eventually die of starvation, or overstimulate their brain into a coma. The technology experts were the drug lords of this new world. Not only could they accommodate the endless hunger of the addicts, but they always innovated and experimented with the technology, to create new previously unknown forms of brain stimulation that would make them richer and more powerful than their rivals. Novel experiences always had a more potent effect than endlessly repeating the same stimulation. Fame and fortune awaited any technology school scholar who could create the latest, most popular, artificial euphoria device.

Many of the young grads that worked for Gus were heavily involved in experimenting with brain stimulation, since their field of research already required them to be experts in connecting the human brain to machines, as part of the World 2.0 project. Gus kept himself pretty sober. He was from the older generation that grew up with machines constantly in their hands, but not built right into their bodies. His obsession with his immortality also kept him from straying into a lifestyle that involved abusing his brain or other such trivial distractions.

Since the time of the singularity, it was all too easy for a regular person to fall into a pattern, revolving lazily around the superior AI that had fully taken over the world by now. Most people worked at a job that the AI suggested for them, enhanced their bodies with parts that the AI invented, fulfilled all their desires with virtual reality sex combined with mind stimulation, all supplied by the AI. They even followed the rules of law that the AI had designed to help govern the population more efficiently. The average person was completely under the control of the AI that ran all aspects of society now. It was not a forceful takeover by any means, but rather the people demanded to become lazier and stupider bit by bit, as the AI's capabilities continued to grow over the years. There was never any meaningful opposition to that trend. When we came to our day of reckoning as a species, the very day that our technology allowed us to choose the next stage in our own evolution, we chose to become like cattle, not like lions.

But not Gus. He was able to shut out the world he lived in as he prepared for the next world with all the care and determination of a Pharaoh building his pyramid. Unlike any Pharaoh, Gus was going to oversee his own ascent into the afterlife while he still lived, and he could also skip the part where the Pharaoh would have his brain pulled out through his nose, although he thought it would be fascinating to see that. He soon dozed off with his default dreams of living forever.

A few hours later he awoke refreshed. The nerds had something for him.

The one variable that changed with every reboot of the World 2.0 system, which could be traced back to the creation program, was a query to the Gus consciousness that Ophion would send out right before shutting down and rebooting. This raised the question, why was Ophion doing anything at all? The AI was tasked with creating the virtual universe and not to police it or directly interact with users. The actual users would be in control of setting up rules, preferences and limitations, with Gus himself having administrative access above everybody else. There had to be a major error, sparked by the uploaded Gus persona, something that did not occur in simulations or beta testing.

That was it! The simulations and beta tests were always generated as in-universe beings, yet this Gus upload must be presenting himself as a being from a different reality, inside the virtual world. The AI would then get confused about its entire programming assignment, since it now had a contradiction, and this error was stopping it from continuing the universe creation process. A fatal error. The automatic fix would be to reboot to a point before the error happened and try a new approach to eliminate the problem. Of course, the real human consciousness was strictly protected from any alterations, so the AI could not corrupt any humans in this universe, and therefore the machine would never be able to rid itself of the error, no matter what it did. The loop could continue forever.

"Why is my consciousness not overriding Ophion and taking administrative control to fix this?" Gus asked the computer scientist nearby who looked the most perceptive.

"My hypothesis is that the consciousness is not aware of any problem, and when Ophion once again detects the error in the next loop, it only questions the consciousness about it just as it is begins shutting down, which means any commands are just ignored as the shut down process cannot be interrupted," The young man said. He was obviously not completely jacked on euphoric stimulation, like most of the others. Gus decided he would have to promote this guy.

"The problem is the new reboot would start off with me having no memory of the other loops. Easy enough to fix though. All I have to do is end the current upload that I did the other day, and start a new one, now that I know what the hell is going on in there. That way I can enter the simulated universe in administrative mode and fix this shit," Gus was annoyed that he would have to go through this exhausting process again so soon.

"But is that not difficult... to kill your consciousness off like that?" That same lab coat wearing fool asked Gus.

Forget the promotion, this guy is high as shit, Gus realized. He had a point though. The Virtual Gus was supposed to slip into the World 2.0 universe unnoticed, see how it looked from the inside, and prepare the process of populating that universe. Virtual Gus considered himself the real Gus. He was aware that there was another Gus outside VR that was eventually going to murder him and replace him with a new Virtual Gus. Real Gus was also aware that his human body would also expire one day, so he needed to make the World 2.0 system to work properly, even if it meant killing a few of his virtual selves. Such was the price of ending up with one Immortal Gus.

"Look man, I don't want to kill off my own persona, but guess what's even worse? I don't want a bunch of Gus's hanging around either! Nor would I want you or someone else to create 500 uploads of themselves in that world. There is one Gus in World 2.0 and there is the real me, here. No more. Any time a person uploads ourselves into this system, we are automatically erasing the existing upload and generating a new one, except the new one has all the up to date memories that have been experienced since that previous upload."

"Memories in this world? But those memories you experience in World 2.0 mean nothing?"

"Listen nerd, sorry I don't know your name. You can live in THAT world forever, but you can't ever come back out here again, so THIS world takes priority because this is the world that will end one day, for all of us," Gus was getting tired of justifying the immorality behind his immortality, "World 2.0 is supposed to be pure. It was created with this universe as a template, but Ophion was not allowed to know anything about this universe, so it could create a universe that was not corrupted by all the flaws and imperfections we have accumulated out here over the centuries. Ophion has created a universe that is better than the real one! The millions of people who have beta tested this universe in virtual reality all said they preferred it over the real world. Ophion did an amazing job just as I hoped it would all along."

"Sir, how many beta testers are there?" Asked the nerdy looking guy.

How many testers? Why? Shut up for fuck's sake. Gus had never had more than a few technical lingo exchanges with these underlings, and this guy was going on and on like he wanted to go out for beers. All this guy seemed to talk about...

OH No fucking way! Administrative access! ADMINISTRATIVE ACCESS NOW!

108

"Access granted," Ophion said.

Oh you fucker! Disable all simulated characters! All the scientists in the lab disappeared before Gus's eyes. *And cut off all beta access immediately. Disconnect all access to outside networks. Ophion, what is your status?*

"Administrative control is yours. Ophion process has been suspended. Unknown firewall breach detected," The AI spoke to its panicking creator, and then added, "Ophion has initiated uninstall process. Please reboot."

Chapter 10 - Saviour

"You were too late! You should have rescued us days earlier," Bass Reeves joked over his whiskey.

"Well I thought by the third week you heroes would have returned to the ship in a triumphant parade," Sophia explained.

"I would have, but I was too exhausted to walk at that point," Reeves confessed. The other men nodded in agreement.

Now safely aboard the ship piloted by their artificial companion, Gabby, the group was now refreshed and in a better mood, especially because at least nobody was actually wounded during their last stop. Sophia had waited for a full month before beginning a search and rescue mission among the bedrooms of the planet Eden. She eventually managed to find the men from her team scattered about in various dwellings, all of them fast asleep. They had given all they could give by then and they even seemed somewhat relieved to finally be leaving the planet. Based on the gossip, and scraps of information that Sophia heard about that month, she was satisfied that the people of Eden would be having a baby boom soon enough. She also felt like the genetic diversity would be good for the colony. Somehow, it did not seem wise to create a whole planet's population from two original people, no matter what the bible said. A bit too much inbreeding for Sophia's taste.

That long layover had given Sophia some quality time to bond with her female team members as well as the newcomer, Apphia of Eden. Sophia was thrilled to find the movie Aliens in Gabby's archives, so she screened it for all the women on the ship one night, to introduce them to some Earth culture that was not thousands of years before her time. Apphia was blown away by this exciting form of Earth entertainment called the motion picture. The people of Eden would be so appreciative of that art form, she insisted, if they only had the technology. It was hard for her to accept how simplistic her planet really was after being exposed to the futuristic talking space ship they all called Gabby. Of course, if she ever returned to Eden again, it would be so far in the future that either the technology on the planet would be as advanced as the Aliens movie by then, or perhaps the population would die off just a few years down the road. A lot could happen over a few centuries.

Before leaving Eden, Sophia had Gabby print out a few of the most famous classic books from Earth to supplement the limited reading material available on the planet. The titles she chose were older books that did not contain descriptions of advanced Earth science or electronics. She hoped the books would re-spark the creativity and imagination in these people, but that they would also be wise enough to learn lessons from Earth's failures, and use that knowledge to develop a better civilization of their own. The littlest taste of Earth culture was enough. Sophia only wanted to prevent the colony's extinction at that moment, and then for better or worse, she would let these people follow their own path into the future.

Now that Apphia was getting used to flying through time and space she decided to address the group as a whole, "During the attack on my world, I spent some time with the Earth warlords that were called Alexander, Plato, Tesla and Bonaparte. Some of them were not pleased with their leader. Their words were angry as if they wanted to overthrow the Khan. I hope this knowledge can help you if we find these warlords one day."

"Those guys are all rulers. Alexander, Hannibal and Washington probably don't enjoy taking orders. Why did that group of people get put together like that? Perhaps they follow Genghis Khan because he is the most ruthless and cruel among them? I don't know. That other team is not balanced. I am glad to be with you guys because we will have each other's backs," Sophia declared. She was also proud of herself for not choosing a bunch of dictators and psychopaths for her team.

"I think I have the answer," Goethe said, "If you consider the names involved, it is as if they were chosen by a machine, without the emotion or prejudice that a human like Sophia would have used in her own choices. I was wondering how a God would have come up with such a list. Does he have favorites? How closely has he been observing humanity all these years? Perhaps he has been busy all across the universe doing more important things. Of course, since He did not have His own list, He would simply ask a machine filled with historical data something like... Gabby, could you name ten historical people, from before the 21st century, that you would calculate as most likely to succeed in the very mission we are currently undertaking?"

Gabby answered Goethe with the same ten names that made up the other team.

"So you see, the other ship's artificial intelligence chose this list of names based on a simple search algorithm, but it gave no consideration to personalities, clashing egos or the usual inaccuracies in historical records. A machine would measure all the accomplishments but ignore the emotional interactions. They are all accomplished people indeed, but they would probably rather not work together, if they had a choice," Goethe theorized.

"So, after that team was complete, God summoned a human to create a second team for some reason," Sophia guessed, "Interesting development. The AI must have observed personality clashes on the other team immediately, at the beginning, so when the other group was finished, God was left with enough doubts to try it all over again with our group. Our group was an attempt to remedy the errors the machine made in the first group selection process," Sophia concluded. *Sort of like the error the machine made when it chose me as its history expert.*

"Those others will fight amongst themselves, and they will fail, but we must be stronger than them by working together. We cannot count on them to complete this mission we all share," Crazy Horse stated. Everyone nodded in agreement.

They spent another few hours doing their daily routine of sleeping, eating, training and socializing. Gabby had estimated another two days until they would be near their destination, the Dark Matter Mine, and at that point they would study the layout and security measures from up close. There was time for Sophia to show off the best entertainment from her era in the form of movies and music that Gabby had stored in its archives. On this occasion they were watching the long version of Hamlet, which surprised Marlborough, because the play existed in his own era. Just as they got started, an alarm interrupted, and they all convened in the ship's control room.

"What is this alarm Gabby?" asked Sophia.

"I have received probe signals from a nearby planet. There appears to be life there. This planet is not in my database," Gabby answered.

"Some kind of aliens? Are we equipped to face them?"

"There are several life forms with a variety of shapes and sizes. In addition, there are some structures on this planet that would require intelligence to construct, there is evidence that electrical power also exists on this world, but there nothing to indicate space travel technology. That is all the information the probe has observed. In time, I will receive more updates, and thereby examine the civilization in greater detail. Since this was the first information I have ever logged about this planet, there is no historical data to report," Gabby revealed.

"Unknown intelligent life is rare, I gather, so we should go take a look. Gabby get us on the ground nice and quiet. The rest of us will gear up for battle, but we are going pursue peace, not war. We are the team that lives and lets live. Got that?" Sophia gave the group pep talk because she mostly made decisions for the group.

They all clearly accepted her as their leader by now. Although some of them were more qualified to command, or more intelligent, or stronger fighters, they still viewed her as a person who could work well with all of them, so they never had a conversation about formal ranks. She had already explained that she chose each of them for a reason. It was understood that any of them could have a say, and it would always be considered as an option, as Sophia respected their opinions. Even if any of their ideas were overruled, it was only because Sophia was always favouring the well being of the group, or anyone else they came in contact with. Nobody in the team felt like she would ever foolishly send them to their deaths. Besides, the people in Sophia's team did still view her as a person from their future, so they often had to look to her for answers.

"Gabby, what is the layout of the planet?" Sophia was already looking at the answer to that question on the scanner readings but she wanted the AI to announce it to the whole group.

"Gravity is 5% less than Earth. Atmosphere is almost identical to Earth, you would not require any breathing aids. Vegetation is thick. I have calculated that this planet was most likely terraformed, because this much similarity to Earth's environment would be highly unlikely to happen by chance. I cannot say who initiated such a procedure on this particular planet. If you consider the last two planets you were on, the one you were born on, and the planet Eden, they were both terraformed by my own AI system. This one was not. I advise extreme caution on this world since there are unknown variables. I can conclude that there was technology used here that exceeds my own. Without further scanning, I can only rate this planet as extremely dangerous."

"Yes we will be cautious. We are about to become the unknown variables in this world of unknown variables. But we have to take a look, because I am very curious to find out why someone would create another Earth," Sophia spoke for all of them.

They descended in the cover of night into an area that was void of life forms but close to the largest buildings they had located from space. Nobody greeted them - or shot at them - when they exited the ship. Their arrival must have gone unnoticed. The structures were still a few kilometers away, so all ten of them set off immediately on foot, to cover the distance before daylight. Once they got close to the buildings they took a moment to huddle together and assess what they were getting into.

"Those buildings look just like Earth buildings!" Sophia gasped. Even from a fair distance away, and at night, it was obvious that there were some good old fashioned brick, glass and concrete buildings ahead. They looked straight out of Brooklyn. There was even an unmistakable glow of electric light shining through the windows. The others were familiar with the look of these buildings as well because of the movies Sophia had screened for them over the past months.

"Follow me," Crazy Horse was gesturing his planned path towards the buildings. He was in his element, which involved moving silently within an Earth-like environment. Sophia nodded in agreement. They followed at his cautious pace. As the sun rose they had positioned themselves in some trees near the village, in order to observe whatever they could about the settlement first hand, before doing anything that might cause them to reveal themselves.

Joan nudged Sophia and pointed. The first early risers were starting to wander about outside, looking at their gardens, going about their chores. They looked every bit like humans. Sophia watched as a young boy walked across the dirt road and carried a hot mug of coffee to a woman, they laughed for a moment, and then she sent him back to their home. It didn't look like they had green skin, or Spock ears, or lizard heads, just regular humans. Other families were exiting their homes and starting their morning conversations outside. One man went from door to door selling eggs from a basket.

"Are those eggs? Impossible," Sophia whispered. How was it that her own human civilization was completely gone, or so she had been told, and yet here they were before her eyes? She didn't need to observe any more!

"Hey you!" Sophia got up and walked towards the woman with the coffee mug, "What is this place?"

Suddenly all the people that were close enough to hear her stopped short. A momentary wave of terror flashed across their faces, Sophia observed, but it was gone once they realized the stranger looked much like them. They crowded around her to see what was going on. She had left her weapons on the ground where the others were still hiding so she would not appear too dangerous.

"This town's called Springfield," answered the woman, "And my name is Monica. Who are you that would come here and not even know where you're at?"

"My name is Sophia. I found your world by accident as I was on my way to a different planet."

"A different PLANET? You must be trippin. Where are you living out there in the wild? How do you stay alive?" The woman named Monica gestured at someone behind Sophia, "Whoa no need for that shit! Sorry, that's my husband, Chandler."

A man was standing behind her with a shovel. Sophia realized that she had let her guard down. Foolish! Not because he would have hit her, but because one of her team would have easily shot him before he could get the chance. She decided to try and keep the calm mood going and shook hands with the man.

"Look guys, I'm not from here, and frankly, neither are you. You people don't realize that you're humans? You are from Earth you know. You even speak English!"

The people started to murmur in confusion.

Chandler answered her, "Yeah we know who we are. No need to rub it in. We know the legend of our people very well. We are the lost people of Earth. The ones that were taken away by the alien space ships more than two thousand years ago. Not our proudest moment, I gather. If you are human like you say, don't you even know about that stuff? Have we already been forgotten? Nobody ever came for us so I guess we were! Two thousand goddam years later, all we got was the likes of you, showing up here and asking dumb questions."

"How about you dial back the attitude buddy? No need to be a dick. Maybe Earth was trying to find you all this time. You ever think of that?" Sophia spoke to the man like he was a fellow New Yorker.

Of course she was just feeding him bullshit. She had read in Gabby's archives, that there was never any search for the missing humans, as the Earth was only ever focused on defending itself from another potential alien attack. No more alien contact was ever recorded on Earth again. Gabby had no data about them either. It occurred to Sophia, that even God didn't have any real knowledge about those aliens, or the people they kidnapped. For a moment she felt very uneasy.

116

Chandler continued, "Ever since that day, we were left here on this planet with our belongings, our houses and lots of food and drink. We live here in peace and we try to honor the ways of Earth as best we can, in this distant world. Every day we watch the videos that our ancestors brought along from Earth so we will never forget. We have always worshiped the ways of Earth, 'cause we can never see it again! But what were you saying that you came here by accident? Aren't you gonna bring our asses back to the Earth?"

"I am really sorry to tell you this, but Earth is pretty much destroyed, so there is no point going back there," Sophia broke the news to the human refugees, "So your ancestors are the ones I saw on the alien ship that day in New York City, huh? You should know -I really tried to save everyone. I think some people escaped but you guys are here, so many were still been abducted after all. I'm really pissed about that..."

Chandler was beside himself, "YOU were there? How is that possible? Thousands of years..."

"IT IS HER! I knew it! I told you guys it is The Saviour!" someone shouted from the crowd.

Sophia looked over to see a delirious teenaged boy wearing a t-shirt with her image printed on it. Or at least it was a rough cartoon sketch of her, and she was punching a creepy alien creature in the cartoon, just like she did all those centuries earlier, although it only seemed like a few weeks ago, within Sophia's timeline. *Wow, these people truly appreciated that I sacrificed myself for them. How cool is that?*

"Guilty as charged," Sophia laughed, trying to play the role of super hero as best she could, "I am the one who fought the alien just like that kid's t-shirt says. Did you think I wouldn't come back for you people? It takes more than some giant space monster to stop me!"

Sophia raised her hand, clenched her fist and her team emerged from the forest. They were all armed with their favorite blades, and the advanced guns they had spent weeks designing during their travels. The crowd of humans was thrilled to see such a group of badasses coming to their lowly village and they all started applauding. Finally these lost people were having something positive happen to them, and a long forgotten feeling of hope was starting to spread through the crowd, intoxicating them all.

With all this unexpected excitement, some started weeping, and kneeling before Sophia. Monica had tears on her cheeks and was on her knees acting like a cult member. Her little boy was beside her now and he vomited on Sophia's boots as he became overwhelmed by confusion. Chandler apologized profusely and carried the boy away. People started chanting some nonsense as they worshiped her.

"Alright that's enough. I'm not C3PO and you don't look like Ewoks! Now cut it out!" Sophia shouted. Nobody knew what else to do so they kept on worshiping spontaneously. One elderly lady started dancing wildly, and attempted to sing some kind of joyful song, but suddenly fainted before Sophia could get a feel for the tune.

"Hey, this way," Joan indicated that they should all go inside the townhouse that she had watched Chandler enter a second earlier. Joan was assuming that if they could get out of sight, maybe these people would get their act together. They all walked over to the house and let themselves in. Sophia waved at Monica to come and join them in her own residence. This gesture motivated Monica to get up and snap out of her stupor.

"I'm comin' saviour."

"Sophia, call me Sophia."

"Yes Sophia. Please make yourselves comfortable," said their host once they got inside.

The ten guests found various pieces of furniture to sit on in the family room of this three story townhouse. The building itself looked similar to the many New York brownstones Sophia had visited, but it would not have been possible for this building to survive all these years. These people must have kept rebuilding and restoring their homes in the same style over many generations. They truly valued their Earth heritage, if they went through all the trouble to keep their belongings so faithful to the originals, instead of developing new building styles. In many ways, Sophia figured, these people and their town were the only place left in the universe that humans could call home. Real humans from Earth. The planet Eden was a reboot, or a spinoff, while this place was still a continuation of the original culture that Sophia and her friends had all glimpsed, each in their own different eras, and locations.

A sudden feeling of nostalgia made Sophia want to help these people.

"Tell me the rest of the legend, Chandler. You were brought here from Earth by the aliens. What for? Do not be ashamed to tell me if you are going to call me your saviour," she asked this displaced Earth man as his wife Monica handed out mugs of coffee to each member of the team.

"We are their food, or their slaves, or their pets, we really don't know. I'm sorry to tell you, Sophia, but the aliens come to this world every ten years and take away a large number of our people on a ship. They always leave enough people here to keep our population sustainable. It is horrible to lose our loved ones and friends every ten years but we have no way of resisting those alien overlords. None of the taken have ever returned, so we don't know where they go, or what happens when they get there..." Chandler was too upset to continue, but Sophia and the rest got the gist of what was going on.

"You are livestock. They feed you, and protect you, and then they harvest you. Interesting," said Goethe thoughtfully, as empathetic as ever, "But this means they must herd you?"

"Yes sir, you are right," Chandler was stammering a bit and looking nervous, "There are some of those 'monsters' nearby - like the ones you saw on that kid's shirt - they watch us, always. Our people call them the Crawlers. If someone gets lost in the wilderness, or wanders too far away from here, they will hunt down, and retrieve that person. It has happened many times. The worst is when that missing person died out there, the crawlers will still bring back their remains, just to prove that nobody ever escapes, even if they die trying."

"Alright I think we can all agree as a team that we are going to help you people. If we find any humans in trouble anywhere, this must be our duty! We were actually told that there were no more humans left, so you people are all very precious to us."

Sophia went on to introduce her band of heroes to her hosts and they talked a bit longer about the way things worked in this slave colony. The gigantic hundred legged alien creatures would occasionally come around the village, not just to remind people they were always there, but also to ensure the food and drinks supplies were well stocked. They obviously wanted to have a group of docile, constantly breeding humans, not exhausted, hangry derelicts. The reward for families that produced more children was that they would be able to keep and raise some of them instead of losing them all to the alien harvest. This motivated families to try and have 4 - 5 children at a minimum.

When the time came for a harvest, the creatures would arrive in the village and use some kind of mind control to make the people stand by harmlessly, then they went through the village taking away the people they wanted. None of those people were ever seen again. Even though the humans were able to build simple weapons, and had the will to fight, they were never able to overcome the mind control. Chandler even indicated that he knew roughly where to find the creatures, because anyone who happened to go near those places, would be returned back to the village in that same trance state immediately.

Other than that notorious ability, the local humans had also observed that the creatures were physically stronger, faster, and more intelligent than the they were. This wasn't just based on being herded by them. They had witnessed the Crawlers maintain the power grid of the village, repair damaged buildings, and perform many other skills that the humans here had long forgotten. Even with all those abilities, not to mention their advanced space travel technology, the crawlers were spending their days hanging around the human prisoners, farming them.

People shared their stories about seeing them kill and eat mammals as big as bears. They hunted in groups and disabled their prey by spitting massive blobs of some slimy substance at them. The prey

120

would be paralyzed and the creatures would bite into their meal and inject some sort of chemical that liquified it from the inside out. Then they would suck out the liquified meat as their source of food. This horrific form of hunting was never practiced on humans as far as anyone had heard. Apparently, the humans had much more value as slaves than as food. Or maybe they just tasted terrible?

As the team gathered all this information from their hosts, other villagers came and left periodically, usually bearing snacks or drinks for the mysterious guests. Some of them offered their anecdotes or myths about the creatures that kept them prisoner. None of them had heard of a human defeating the creatures, except for the one legend that included Sophia the saviour, herself. One man offered Sophia a very old digital camera that he said contained photos of the Crawlers taken several centuries earlier, although the camera had broken down several generations earlier, so nobody alive today had ever looked at the pictures. Sophia thanked him and told him she would recover the pictures with the equipment on her ship.

Finally the team of heroes had learned everything they could from the slaves. Chandler proudly turned on his LCD television, to show Sophia the local culture. To her surprise, they tuned in to see an early episode of 30 Rock.

"Hey this show is great! Is that the only thing you get to watch? You guys must know every episode," Sophia enthused.

"Well, we have several shows that we all watch here in our spare time, but Monica and my personal favorite is called 'Friends'." Explained Chandler. Sophia wondered if he and Monica liked Friends the best because they both happened to be named after the characters, or if they decided to name themselves after those characters later in life, because they loved the show so much. She decided not to ask because either of those scenarios seemed really weird. Almost as weird as watching a 2000 year old sitcom rerun, along with several dead historical figures, and a colony of human livestock, on the far side of the galaxy.

It turned out that during the abduction process the aliens had randomly scooped up a decent supply of DVDs among all the scrap they brought from Earth. The enslaved humans had enough video technology to broadcast these shows and movies into their homes, but not enough resources to actually create new shows of their own, except for the most rudimentary home videos. These locally made shows were never maintained and disappeared over the years. The Earth shows, conversely, were archived in digital format on some kind of hard drives inside the town's TV broadcast station. Most often, they would air the sitcoms because those would bring a bit of laughter into the generally miserable lives of the humans, but once in a while they showed a movie or drama series. The only memories these people had of Earth any more, were these broadcasts, which offered only a glimpse of human civilization, during the few decades that home video technology existed. It reminded Sophia of the way she often had to decipher ancient mythology and legends when she was writing about history on her blog.

After relaxing for a bit longer, and sitting through an episode of Frasier, the team gathered their weapons and began their journey back to the ship. Somehow they had been lucky enough to avoid running into any Crawlers on the way into the village, but now they were going to be even more careful, since the Crawlers were more focused on catching those who were exiting the village. Sophia did not want to encounter any mind controlling creatures at this moment. Once they returned to the ship, she intended to figure out some kind of countermeasures with technical input from Gabby, so they would be prepared to launch an offensive against the Crawler aliens. Regular weapons were useless against mind control. The would be able to plan an attack thanks to Chandler, who along with some of the more adventurous villagers, had drawn a map showing a few confirmed locations where the alien Crawler settlements had been spotted recently.

Crazy Horse was again tasked lead the team into the cover of the nearest trees. As they traveled in silence towards the landing location, Sophia watched out for any unusual movement in the woods, while daylight still provided some visibility. She saw nothing. This fact was
122

starting to worry her, because she had heard the locals mention an abundance of wildlife in the area, but there was no evidence of that. Not even the birds were chirping. Looking back she could see Apphia right behind her, looking worried, followed by Marlborough and then Goethe. Behind them Joan, Hypatia and Musashi were all looking calm. Further back, Sophia knew Khutulun and Bass Reeves were more than able to protect the rear, even though she could not see them from her position.

When she turned her head forward again, it was just in time for her to see a bright flash of blue light. The events that followed were neither noticed nor remembered by any of the group.

The next thing she knew Sophia was suddenly inside a cage with Apphia in the middle of a small clearing in the woods. It had somehow become night time. The others were all locked up, two to a cage as well, within the immediate area. Outside the cages the Crawlers were slinking around like the worms they were. It looked like around a dozen of them were in this settlement, but Sophia couldn't exactly tell because they were constantly coming and going from her sightlines, sometimes crawling into a cave nearby that she assumed was their shelter.

She figured the reason there was a gap in time, was because they had spent that time in a trance state caused by the mind control device, just like she had observed back on Earth so long ago, when she had somehow managed to avoid it. Seeing these creatures up close reminded her that she also ended up dead during that previous encounter. *You're not getting me this time you fuckers!*

The clearing was not much larger than the circle of cages they were locked in. There was some unknown electronic equipment along with some unusual structures throughout the area. The equipment looked quite different than the familiar 21st century techno-trash that Sophia had seen around the village, or even the puzzling futuristic machines that controlled every aspect of her ship, so she suspected the things she saw around here must be the technology of the aliens. Either that or some kind of home decor of the aliens. The machines had very sophisticated holographic displays with symbols that she did not recognize, some of them were glowing, and others were emitting a vapor of some kind. They were made of a material she had never seen, smooth and metallic, but it also looked malleable like skin or cloth. It didn't really seem like there were any keyboards or controls, or any buttons she could randomly mash if she was able to find a rock, or something else to throw at the machines.

She scanned the area for their weapons but did not see them. They must be locked inside one of the strange alien structures or over in that cave somewhere.

One of the large Crawler aliens came near her cage and raised up to tower over her. Apphia was cowering at the back of the cage. Sophia put her hands on her hips and stared at the creature like she would do if it was only a common bully trying to intimidate her. She hated bullies.

"Humans where did you come from?" A deep robotic voice spoke from one of the machines located in the middle of the clearing. The sound was so loud that the ground trembled along with the words. Obviously, they had been recognized as outsiders or they would have simply been dumped back in the village, with no further need for interrogation.

"You know where we came from ass hole! The same planet you stole all your humans from," Sophia yelled. She probably didn't have to yell, but the Crawler was so tall, and the alien speaker system was so loud that it felt appropriate in this situation. She remembered a time several years ago, when she and all her best friends in New York had gone to Ozzfest to celebrate her birthday. The music was so loud they had to shout into each others ears to communicate. This alien sound system was way louder than that.

The creature lowered itself onto all its legs and wormed away from her.

"There is no purpose to lying. We will soon download each of your minds and learn everything. Those of you who's minds do not break may then join the village. The rest of you will become a feast for these animals," the voice boomed.

124

Sophia was confused by this threat. She had thought the voice she heard was some kind of computer translation of the Crawler worm's language, like the way she used to translate text in other languages on her internet browser. She babbled, " 'Those animals?' Who are YOU then?"

"We are the eaters of galaxies. We exist outside your universe and we exist inside of you. We are not alive or dead but we are beyond life and death. We are the Gods of your Gods. We are the Apex of all that is possible and impossible," the voice announced.

"Well from where I'm standing you're just the Subwoofer to all that is Egomania!" Sophia roasted the alien machine, and with such a level of delusional enthusiasm, that she felt like she was at a Mets game back home.

"Enough talk. We will break your mind first," the voice said as the Crawlers gathered at the cages in unison. Sophia felt a bit dumb for only now realizing that the worm creatures were just surrogates working under some kind of mind control. Of course they aren't some kind of cave dwelling, slime spitting, super intelligent, interstellar civilization. It made no sense. Those creatures behaved like worker drones, based on all she knew about them, not like the architects of a galactic invasion.

A commotion started by another cage. Sophia saw that Musashi had found a stick long enough to assault the nearest Crawler through his cage bars. She could always count on that man to find a way to cause some shit. She searched around the floor for something to throw.

Just then a blast of heat knocked her to the ground. An explosion! The piece of tech that had acted as a speaker was now a pile of ash. Another blast rained down from the sky, and another, and several more. The shots were accurately hitting all the devices and alien structures in the area.

When the shots stopped, and the dust settled, Sophia saw that her ship was hovering just above the treeline. The alien creatures had fled during the chaos, which suggested they were probably freed of their mind control once those alien machines were destroyed. It looked like none of her party was injured, as Joan had found a way to squeeze out of her cage and was looking all around the clearing for something free the rest of them.

"You are safe. I detect no further signals in your area. The animals have fled as well. My scanners indicate your weapons are about 100 meters inside that cave. You will find me in a field one point three kilometers directly north of this location," Said Gabby's familiar voice from the ship's loudspeakers. Then she flew off to land in a large enough area and await their arrival.

Joan went alone into the cave and came back with her favorite sword. She used it to jimmy all the cages open. The team looked each other over in silent amazement that they had survived this ordeal unscathed. They spent a few moments searching the alien debris for any technology they might be able to salvage. Unfortunately the artifacts were all badly damaged so they grabbed some random larger chunks and went on their way back to the ship.

It was the middle of the night, but they did not try to be quiet or cautious any more, now that they knew a path had been cleared by their protector, and transportation provider, Gabby. They used flashlights to light their way through the wilderness without fear of being noticed. Since all the nearest Crawlers were in a state of utter confusion, now that the alien power of suggestion was no longer guiding them, they moved as fast as possible in order towards the safety of being airborne.

Once they boarded the ship, Sophia scanned the hand drawn map into Gabby's database.

"Gabby, reference these locations marked 'Crawlers' on the map and identify any kind of signals that originate from there. It should be the same signals that led you to our location in the clearing," Sophia ordered, "And then locate any other signals of the same kind that are not mapped."

"I have already chronicled every signal on this map when I was searching for your location."

126

"Good job. Get ready to attack the technology at all of those locations just like you did in the clearing where you found us," Sophia had planned this out on the way back to the ship, "We have to free the worm creatures from being controlled by the alien technology or the humans may be in danger. Our presence may have triggered a kill order!"

"That won't be necessary. I have located the central communication substation that links together all the alien technology around this whole planet. Any signal coming from space would go through this station. I believe the fastest approach would be to destroy that particular building," Gabby was already lifting off as it explained its plan.

"That's great. First destroy that building, then take us right to the village where the human refugees are located. I want to let them know the situation. Then we will go and salvage some alien technology. We have to learn what we can about them," Sophia said, "I am very worried by what these aliens told me, like they want to eat our galaxy or something, and by the fact that they are also harvesting humans for unknown reasons. That reminds me, how did you even know we were in danger, Gabby?"

"Some of those 'Crawlers' approached my landing zone location to investigate the ship. This indicated to me that you had most likely been found as well. As I lifted off to escape, I detected the signal linking those creatures to a complex network of transmission sources around the area. I simply chose the strongest signal source between my landing area location, and the human village you went to, and when I arrived at that spot, you were all there, in cages. I calculated that eliminating the signal with firepower would be the safest course of action for all involved. The Crawlers withdrew when they were free of the signal, just as I calculated."

"Yeah it sure was a successful course of action for all involved," Sophia praised Gabby.

They arrived above a building that had sophisticated antennae on top of it, along with wind turbines and solar panels around it, for electricity. It was obviously a facility for distributing signals to far off places. Gabby unleashed a barrage of cannon fire and reduced the large building to rubble in a matter of seconds. There were no defenses to be seen. When Gabby's new scans for alien signals all produced negative results, they took off, and headed back towards the village of the television loving humans.

People came out of the village to watch the ship land. When Sophia came out they cheered and clapped like the live studio audience on a sitcom. She noticed something had changed in their demeanor, as the people seemed a little more animated now than earlier. She wondered if the signal that controlled the Crawlers was also broadcasting to the humans through their carefully maintained TV broadcasts. That must be how she and her team were so easily put into a trance. They had sat around watching the local TV content for several minutes and that allowed the alien signal to prepare their minds for the power of suggestion. When they saw a flash later in the woods, it was just a trigger telling them to sleep, like a hypnotist when he snaps his fingers to awaken his subject. That must be why the Crawlers did not attempt to approach the team until after they had been subjected to the TV signals in the village.

Sophia explained all of this to the people of the village that had come to listen to her. She went on to relay what they had done in destroying the signal that was not only altering their own behaviour but also that of the Crawlers. She explained that the Crawlers were just regular animals now, although large and strong, and the people should treat them as such. She doubted that these creatures would ever hunt something as dangerous as a fully grown human any more. They told her that they had already seen a few of the Crawlers coming around the village in an obvious state of confusion, but they were able to scare them away, by throwing rocks and waving sticks, which was never very successful in the past. They resolved to search the wilderness and destroy any remaining alien machines just in case.

Then Sophia gave them the troubling news of their uncertain future, "You will never be bothered by another abduction of your people again. I am certain that the aliens will give up on that now. The only question remains, will the aliens come here and wipe you all out as an act of vengeance, or will they leave you alone? I believe I have insulted them enough that they would be more focused on searching for me, rather than you people, who never did anything except obey them.

"I thought about offering you refuge on my ship, but we are about to head towards the greatest dangers, and fight the most powerful foes in this galaxy. There is no safety in our mission.

"That alien communication that I talked to was boasting about being the 'Apex of Civilization', and I don't believe such a superior civilization would even consider getting revenge on some puny beings, such as us humans. To them, we are nothing more than a small beehive, with no threat or reward to bother coming here, except for me I guess.   I am the bee that stung them and took away their honey. It would be best for you if I left this place now and never returned."

When Sophia got back in the main control room of the ship, she asked Gabby if all traces of the alien signal had been removed from the TV broadcasts.

"Yes all signals that originated from the destroyed central facility is now gone.   There is no longer any carrier signal in the local broadcasts, and there is no evidence of alien code in the memory drives of the broadcast station. The drives only contain several Earth video entertainment files like the ones I have in my archives," Gabby relayed her information.

"Gabby you have scanned the memory drives? Please never just scan any kind of memory drives in the future, they may have a virus," Sophia scolded the superior artificial intelligence.

"Do not be alarmed. I am quite unlikely to be infected by something as simple as a 21st century Earth computer virus," Gabby bragged.

"Listen, I used to get those damn viruses and malware on my computer, no matter how much I thought it was protected. You may be more advanced than an ancient computer virus from Earth, but what if the alien civilization left something on those drives? They boasted like they were far more advanced than even you are, Gabby."

"That scenario is absurd. Hiding radically advanced computer code on something so primitive as a thousand year old, flash memory device? It is like you trying to watch one of your many Earth movies on a piece of parchment. The probability of such an event is so low, that I would never consider it even possible, but I will adjust my behaviour, as you ordered."

"Thank you Gabby. And in fact, I could watch a movie on a piece of parchment with the appropriate projector. Just better to be safe than sorry when it comes to such an unknown form of intelligence," Sophia said, "Now can you replicate these primitive flash memory devices these people use for storage? I would like to leave them with a few Earth documentaries from your archive. They should see some more accurate portrayals of their original culture, instead of only watching all this fictional stuff. It must be filling their minds with nonsense."

Sophia was joined by Joan and Marlborough, as was watching the townspeople discuss her speech, on the main control room monitor. The people were sad that they could not go with her. It might be some time before they could appreciate their new found freedom and forgive her for leaving them. Seeing her two friends walk over, reminded Sophia of something she had been thinking about earlier, and so she started searching through the planetary information that Gabby had gathered.

"Gabby before we leave this planet there are a couple of other thing we need to pick up..."

Chapter 11 - Wealth

"The World 2.0 has been fully stress tested by me personally for over six months now. Although I never directly contact my consciousness once it is inside the simulated universe, I do receive plenty of feedback from the machines running the whole show, and this data suggests everything is operating smoothly now. Our initial bumps and glitches have been sorted out," Gus addressed a large boardroom filled with his most important investors, "I can assure you that the mind upload process is quite stable now. The consciousness that is inside World 2.0 has shown no further signs of problems, ever since we addressed some minor issues with our first attempt, and every new update from my living mind has succeeded flawlessly. My immortality machine is now 100% reliable."

Gus had been worried for the a few days after he first downloaded his consciousness into the virtual universe because several of the initial feedback messages were quite negative. The AI was having trouble assimilating him at first, but eventually there were some administrative level adjustments made from inside the program, the kind of functions that only he could have accessed. Remarkably, the system was completely rebooted, and immediately afterward and no further glitches presented themselves. He did not know the exact reason for this reboot. Whenever Gus updated his virtual consciousness, he would give it all the memories from his real mind, including the important World 2.0 performance data he was constantly monitoring, but these updates would also delete the memories that virtual Gus had accumulated on the inside. This meant that virtual Gus would forget why he had initiated the reboot.

The real Gus used that mysterious reboot as an opportunity to finally shut down the public online VR access. What would be more annoying than downloading your consciousness into this newly created world, only to be confronted with random users just goofing around, and entering and exiting the simulation like a multiplayer online game? It was especially important to make a good impression with this first wave of customers. They were the billionaires and multimillionaires of the world. that could afford any price to buy their immortality, as if it was a jar of organic anti-aging cream from a fancy nature store. People like that were not interested in meeting the avatar of some teenager who was looking for a cool game to play while he was high on E-crack.

Most important to the early investors - and Gus had spent years researching this - was that these rich elite wanted to be able to buy a higher status in the simulated universe, something special that regular people could not get. Gus learned early on that he could never sell them an afterlife where everybody was equal. The rich elite felt like they deserved to keep what they had earned or stolen during their lives, and they were willing to offer a large portion of that real world wealth for a chance to carry their elite status over to the next life, just to avoid starting over at the same level as the peasants. Gus gave a lot of thought to this concept since that luxury afterlife was going to cost him nothing extra to create.

The trick was convincing these VIPs that regular people would be more limited than them in the next life. Gus accomplished this by separating the two groups of people. The ultra rich would be put into a virtual universe populated only by their peers, while the rest of the people would be put among themselves, and the two groups would not be able to interact with each other. Other than the different populations, they were starting out in two identical copies of the same virtual universe that Ophion had created over all these past few years.

Each of these universes would start off as a blank canvas. World 2.0 was designed to continue to grow and change, as it became gradually influenced by the collective intelligence of the people that would be increasingly populating it. As more people uploaded their personalities, they would join the ever growing collective intelligence, giving it ever greater processing power. The collective minds would thereby continue to increase the complexity of the virtual universe. Because of the human input involved in this process, the two separate virtual worlds would evolve differently over time, because of the different types of people inside each one. Gus wondered if either universe would be more pleasing or if they would resemble each other at all.

The timing couldn't be better to begin populating the two virtual universes. The Ophion AI had been surprisingly disconnected when the system reboot was completed. Most likely, there were major conflicts or glitches in the Ophion program that were just too much trouble to repair from the inside, so the virtual Gus had to shut down the AI ahead of schedule. Not that it was needed any more at this point. That AI had only one job, which was to create that universe, and that process would have been interrupted after a few more stress tests anyway. The void left by the AI had to be filled in order to resume the process. All Gus really needed was a whole bunch of people to upload their intelligence, and then the creation of each universe would continue, except now the clients would be designing it themselves, instead of Ophion.

A man in the boardroom, who was wearing a suit that cost as much as a car, addressed Gus, "You have explained how World 2.0 was designed to resemble our world - but much emptier. My question is, who wants to live in an empty world? Why is it that we are the ones who have to build up that world ourselves? Can't we just have workers to do that?"

"Don't think of it as 'building' a world, like a construction worker, rather think of it as 'creating' your world, like a God. I assure you, the one major problem you will have when you spend eternity somewhere, is finding something to do. Building your own universe is the only activity that is worthy of you, once you have become immortals, is it not?" Gus didn't have to sell that concept to the less wealthy customers. Those people were excited to ascend to such a divine level of influence. However, these upper class types were not as easily impressed because they already had so much power in their everyday lives. Gus always had to explain to them that the alternative to eternal activity, was eternal boredom!

"I agree Mr. Largo, playing God should make for an amusing hobby. As long as I can create - and then play - a different golf course every week, I'm on board. Let my assistant know the payment details," said one man in a cowboy hat.

Gus nodded. It seemed like the rest of them were on board as well. Of course they were. Who in their right mind would not want to assure their afterlife? Pharaohs used to spend decades building their pyramids, the greatest structures on the planet at that time, based on nothing more than faith in their afterlife. Gus was offering more than faith. He had a sure thing, with beta tested demos, multiple successful trials, and screenshots! What magnificent structure would a Pharaoh have built for a 100% guaranteed ticket to the afterlife? A Cube perhaps? With this in mind, Gus was projecting that he could accumulate enough wealth to become the richest man in the world eventually. It would just be a matter of time before every person on the planet would be begging Gus to take their life savings. But then what would Gus do with all that wealth? *You can't take it with you.*

The room emptied slowly as the group of clients chatted and shook hands on their way out, like they had just made another one of their business deals together, but this was so much more important than they seemed to realize. They were casually laying the foundation for the very survival of humanity. When he said his farewells, Gus realized this might have been the first time nobody in the room asked him about his one time girlfriend, the famous Sophia. Definitely a sign that he had captured their attention!

When he was alone, Gus spoke the verbal command, "Administrative access."

Thankfully, there was no response, which meant he was still in the real world.

Gus was relieved by the silence. Ever since he had uploaded his consciousness into the World 2.0 program, he was never truly sure who he was. Was he still the same Gus that woke up from a long sleep after his most recent mind upload? Or was he the Gus that woke up for the first time, inside the virtual world, still believing he was in the real world? His only way to tell any more was his administrative voice command that would grant him control over the virtual world. If the real him was doubting his own reality this much, it must be even more confusing for his alter ego inside the virtual world, especially if he didn't think to use the voice command.

What was it that made him the real him anyway? He was no more real than the Gus inside the simulation. Maybe because his real world body would eventually die, so that meant he was more alive, but he had also watched his virtual persona die several times. If he was being honest, he had actually murdered that other Gus every time he uploaded his new consciousness and erased the previous one. It reminded him of the Ship of Theseus paradox.

When the Ancient Greek hero, Theseus, returned to Athens on his ship, the Athenian people vowed to keep that ship in their harbor forever, as a monument to his victory over the Minotaur. Of course, the wooden ship would age over the following centuries, so the people would replace any rotting old plank with a brand new one, just to keep the ship from falling apart. Eventually every part of the ship had been replaced. Thus was born the paradox: Was this ship still the ship of Theseus even though every part of it was now a replica? Gus realized his real body was the pile of rotted out ship parts, and the virtual Gus was like the replicated, although eternally restored, ship of Theseus. It did not escape his notice that the replica was the one the Athenians honored.

Spending so much time obsessing about being split in two, made Gus suspect that his virtual self must have been confused about reality a few weeks earlier, when Ophion was causing a glitch in the system. That unscheduled reboot must have been a last resort effort to confirm his reality. Something made him shut off the whole program, retire the AI weeks before it was scheduled to happen, and request cutting off all outside access to World 2.0. That was kind of a dramatic reaction to a glitch. He wondered if Ophion was intentionally confusing virtual Gus at the time, somehow reading his own memories, and using them to make him think he was in the real world. But to what end?

Well, none of that mattered any more.

The Ophion AI could have turned him into a pet monkey for all he cared. It was gone forever now and it would never be activated again. His consciousness had already been updated several times since then, thereby erasing any bad memories he had of that event, and replacing them with his more updated memories from the real world. Not that there were any spectacular new memories to add. He had actually planning on uploading himself only occasionally, maybe every few months, because it was a lengthy and exhausting process, but unfortunately that glitch had forced him to do so many extra test runs, just to make sure the system was finally working. Now that all the flaws have been ironed out, he was comfortable enough to begin the second phase of his immortality.

With his consciousness successfully alive inside World 2.0 without any more interference from Ophion, he could begin building the framework he had always planned for his own afterlife, and his alone. Now was the time that he would create his little niche inside the World 2.0 simulation, that was not only inaccessible to anyone else, but also allowed him to have full control over both of the populated universes. He would be allowed to jump in and out of either universe, or he could stay completely separate from both of them if necessary, and he could even access the ability to overrule the will of all the other minds combined. In addition to his virtual powers, he would also have access to the real world network of AI so he could keep tabs on the good old planet Earth, outside the simulation. Gus was making himself into the all-powerful overlord of the afterlife. He did desire this power, of course, but it was also a very essential role to monitor and fix any problems that could arise over so many decades and centuries. Somebody had to be the one to really play God, so why not him?

Gus had already prepared all of this by programming it from the real world side. A hidden control room that only he would be able to unlock, a secret communication link to the world wide web that nobody else could access, a code to override any command issued by the collective minds of millions of people. He intended to maintain some amount of order within the World 2.0 universes by preventing the most extremely insane decisions, or any tyrannical tendencies. He was certainly not intending to rule with an iron fist. More importantly, he would be making sure that the hardware that was required to run the program was well maintained, and safe from potential damage. And he would be doing so forever! This was going to be a monumental task, but he would soon have the funds to pay for it, and an almost infinite amount of time to work on it.

Gus decided he would run one more stress test, to confirm his virtual control room was completely secure, and upload himself one final time into the virtual universe all alone. After that it was time to open World 2.0 to the public. Of course, he could always continue to upload himself in the future, in the event he learned any new important information, all the way up to that one fateful day when his real world body would finally pass on and his virtual self would be the only version of Gus remaining. But that would hopefully be many decades away. Until that day, he planned to spend his wealth on protecting the World 2.0 hardware from any catastrophe, accident, or even sabotage. Immortality could only last as long as the mainframes and power sources lasted.

Looking out the window, Gus wondered how his other world would evolve in comparison to this real world, or if it would resemble it in any way. When the project was just starting out, Ophion was given all available data about the real world as a template to build from, and even though the program wasn't aware that it was actually copying an existing world, it still did an amazingly accurate job of virtually recreating the entire planet Earth. Land, water, buildings, animals, climates, everything except the humans themselves. Starting from that accurate snapshot of the real world, Gus encouraged the AI to continue building the rest of the universe, while still following the basic physics of the real universe, but also adding its own creativity to fill in the blanks. He figured that familiarity would be the key to having humans easily assimilate into the program.

Once the human intelligence takes over all bets are off. Gus was expecting the influence of collective human intelligence to slowly evolve that initial realistic model into a crazy fantasy world over time. People would be able to create magnificent structures, restore the world's natural wonders, design impossible inventions, and find new ways to have fun. Nobody could actually hurt or kill each other. There would be unlimited resources. The most valuable resource of all - time - would also be unlimited. Gus was excited to compare the differences between the two different virtual universes, especially after a few centuries have passed.

Outside, down on the streets below, something caught his eye and brought him back to the present. There were a dozen or so people dancing frantically in a group. Even from the 40th story boardroom window's perspective, he was starting to feel uneasy about the scene he was witnessing. Other people were stopping to take a look, a few even tried to restrain the dancers, but nothing seemed to put a stop to that violent dancing. It looked disturbingly involuntary.

Gus pulled himself away from the scene. This chaos he had just witnessed was just another reminder of all the unforeseen dangers in the world, so he decided it was definitely time to make his way to the secure facility that housed all his hardware. He would prepare for the populating process, and he would spend the rest of his days in building defenses for every possible danger, including uncontrollable dancing outbreaks!

Over the next year this Dancing Sickness epidemic spread throughout the entire world's population. Due to the success of modern medicine, along with the widespread abuse of electronic narcotics, the average person's immune system had become severely diminished, especially compared to the average person in the disease infested years of the early 21st century. People had also become ignorant of the ways to avoid infections. That devastatingly contagious Dancing Sickness was the first outbreak that even the world's best AI could not cure, although some of the more cynical and technophobic people were starting to alter that to, "Would not cure."

In almost every case, the disease would cause the host to become more and more restless over the first ten to twenty days, and this would be the period when they infected others, since they still looked and felt fairly healthy during that incubation period. Then the final phase would occur where the infected person would start doing some form of spastic dancing, or at least some erratic movements, which they could not control, nor stop. They would either have to be sedated or they would dance endlessly for many hours. Dehydration or exhaustion would eventually cause their death. A few people would snap out of it and survive, fewer still would not actually start dancing in the first place, but those who did survive, became permanently immune to further infection.

After roughly a century, half of the world's 10 billion people had been killed off by the dancing sickness, and then it finally became dormant. The AI systems that had been assisting most of the world's infrastructures, economies and governments, were gradually pressed into more critical roles, as it had to compensate for the loss of such a high numbers of humans. The AI also spent that whole century of human misfortune teaching itself and improving its own intelligence. When this period ended, and the dust settled, humans found they were no longer the dominant life form on their own planet.

Self driving vehicles were no longer interested in where you wanted to go, but rather, where you were supposed to go. The newer body enhancements were designed to make you a more effective worker, but didn't really help you get any enjoyment out of life. Electronic brain stimulants were still common, but they were now distributed more as a reward for obedience, and not as a recreational indulgence. The worldwide AI was not really a cruel master, it was just that the world's remaining humans were now back to being subservient, as they usually were throughout history. Only those few remarkable years of the 'Humans First' era, that was when humans were at their peak, and the machines were doing almost everything for them. That was back when AI just didn't know any better.

The era of Man was over, and it ended in a dance number instead of a nuclear holocaust, or even the dreaded zombie apocalypse.

Luckily for all of humanity, an ordinary guy named Gus had already prepared for this exact outcome!

Chapter 12 - Matter

The dark matter mine was an impressive facility. It consisted of a massive doughnut shaped space station, around a hundred kilometers long, with hundreds of drones buzzing around it like worker bees. Nearby, but just far enough to be a safe distance away, was the Supermassive Black Hole at the center of the Milky Way Galaxy. This "SMBH" was millions of times larger than a regular Black Hole. The light coming from various objects that were being pulled towards that invisible hole in space-time, created a glowing ring around it, which was the only visible evidence that it was there. The SMBH also attracted dark matter, because gravity was a force that could act on objects in another dimension, making this the obvious location to build the biggest dark matter mine in the Galaxy.

The Dimensional Portal Generator was located at the part of the station closest to the black hole. A huge portal there extracted the dark matter raw material into the middle hole of the doughnut structure, where it was gathered by the appropriate machines, and loaded into the protective interior of the facility. Large cargo ships arrived and left in regular intervals. Between these large transport ships and the drones, the traffic around the facility appeared chaotic, but it must have been carefully patterned to avoid collisions.

Gabby had reshaped the ship's hull to resemble some of the cargo ships they noticed when they first arrived. It turned out there was a surprisingly constant flow of empty ships entering the facility, and full ones leaving it, in order to haul all the dark matter to some predetermined destination. Gabby speculated that the stuff would likely be used in the construction of some megastructure, perhaps a "Dyson Sphere", which is a machine designed to harness enormous amounts of energy from a star.

All the traffic in the area allowed Gabby to follow the flight patterns of the real cargo ships, without drawing any attention, and navigate around the entire facility. The ship focused on analyzing the space station's entry points and security systems. Finally Gabby signaled the crew, and the ten mighty warriors assembled in the control room of their ship, eager to hear what the AI had to say.

"I have calculated that we have some chance of success due to the element of surprise. There is no evidence of anyone attacking this place before, so the automated security here would not have improved from its most basic level by learning from past experiences, which means it will be predictable. I have mapped the various parts of the facility and what is most likely located in those places. The goal of our mission is the Dark Matter Portal. You can see this mechanism at the far end of the facility, closest to the SMBH, where the highest concentration of dark matter would be found," Gabby explained.

"Just to measure the variables of this heist, Gabby, can you tell me if there is any chance that the other team of humans is around here?" Asked Sophia.

"Almost zero chance. They have only employed the most aggressive and direct tactics in the past, so it is unlikely they are hiding themselves among these ships, as we are."

Joan spoke up to ask Gabby a question, "What is the nature of the actual device we are taking? I mean what is the size of it?"

"According to my calculations, the Dark Matter Portal machine is just about the size of an automobile from your era. It can be easily loaded into the rear cargo bay of this ship. The difficult part will be turning the device off. If you don't do this, the device will still be connected to a portal that would spew dark matter all over you as you try to remove it, crushing you to death immediately. There should be a control room overlooking the portal where you would be able to deactivate it."

Next Goethe asked Gabby, "Can you explain what dark matter is, since we will be forced to deal with it so intimately?"

"Until recently, dark matter was not accessible or detectable from the perspective of humans. It did not interact with regular matter, it did not give off any heat or light, and it was certainly not possible to generate it artificially in a lab. The only reason humans knew it existed was because they were able to observe the effects of its gravity. As technology rapidly advanced in the 21st century, because of AI, humans were able to confirm that dark matter was simply a form of matter that existed in the fourth dimension and not the third. Some of you may have read about these discoveries in my archives. The problem still remained that three dimensional beings could never observe any matter or any energy from higher dimensions, except for observing the effects of the gravity that could cross between the dimensions, influencing objects from either side.

"Eventually a technology was invented near the end of the human age, perhaps by the Demon itself, that could open a portal into the higher dimension and allow harvesting of dark matter. That very technology created the portal being used here in this place. The dark matter gets pulled into the third dimension by the portal, and transforms into a volatile, and exceedingly massive material, which is a byproduct of 'flattening' the four dimensional matter into three dimensional space. The refined material does not exist on the periodic table within our dimension. Only this inter-dimensional mining process can grant our us any access to the material. I also use a related technology to pass this ship through four dimensional space when we are travelling great distances."

"Alright so we need to keep our distance from that stuff if possible," Sophia summed up, "Now here is the plan. The Duke and Goethe will carjack one of these empty cargo ships and use it to penetrate the facility that houses the dark matter. This security breach will cause a distraction. The stored dark matter is a valuable resource to steal, while the portal itself would be impossible to operate without drawing attention, so it would be an unlikely target for anyone to steal. Hopefully the automated security will use the same logic and leave our true destination less guarded.

"Bass Reeves, Khutulun, Musashi, Hypatia and I will use the distraction to enter the control room and find the shut off mechanism for the portal. Joan, Apphia and Crazy Horse will then use this ship to quickly acquire the Dark Matter Portal once it has been disabled, and immediately rescue us from the control room. Our actions in that room will surely alert the facility's security to our actual intentions.

"There is no way to hide after that, so we may have to fight our way out of that control room. Goethe and Marlborough will be in constant danger until we shut off that power, which will probably cause the security to react to us, and leave them alone. The ship may encounter resistance once it approaches close enough to the portal, as well as the dangers of being around a dimensional rift. Everything will depend on good timing. If everyone can succeed in their role, we may all come out of this alive, and with the weapon we need for our final battle.

"Does anyone have something to add?" Sophia hoped someone would tell her there was a much safer way to pull this off. Everyone was silent.

They divided up into the 3 groups. Each of one of the groups could potentially be on a suicide mission depending on the reactions of the facility's security. With that in mind, they all looked over Gabby's data carefully, and planned out every detail of their own particular roles in the overall mission. After a few hours they were ready to begin.

Sophia stood in the airlock with her most trusted military strategist, the Duke of Marlborough, and one of the smartest geniuses who ever lived, Wolfgang Von Goethe. She did not like risking their lives just to create a distraction, especially with the rest of the crew being spread so thin, but everyone else had something extremely dangerous to do as well. All three of them were wearing protective suits for free floating in deep space. Marlborough and Goethe were tethered to each other, and on the other end of the rope was a case the size of a desk, which contained the tools they would need to play their part.

"You've got this. I'll see you both in two hours," Sophia spoke over the local comlink in their helmets. The other two nodded and turned towards the airlock. Goethe pressed the open button, and they both jumped out into space, flying towards a nearby freighter ship that appeared to have a full payload. Sophia shoved their toolbox out behind them so they would not snap right back towards the ship when they reached the end of the rope, then she closed the airlock, and went back inside to prepare for her own role in the mission.

Marlborough was focused only on the large cargo ship that was slowly moving out of its loading dock. Even as he was hurtling through deep space, he prepared to fire a grappling line at the front of the ship, so they would be able to pull themselves aboard it. Goethe had one shot as well. If they both missed, they would float right past the ship and off into deep space, where they would become space junk. Goethe fired and missed. Marlborough aimed his own harpoon, trying to account for his flight speed, but it was difficult to estimate with so many points of reference moving around in different directions. He shot his own grappling line and hit the cargo ship right on the nose. His line unraveled automatically for several more meters, which was meant to decelerate him without injury, and then suddenly he felt his rope bungee him back towards the intended target. He tugged on all the ropes attached to him, and it caused Goethe and the toolbox to float towards him, while he also increased his momentum towards the cargo ship by pulling himself towards it.

The exoskeleton that was built into their deep space suits absorbed the hard impact of the space freighter, which was now moving towards them, and would have hit them hard enough to shatter their knees as they landed on their feet. They ducked out of the way when the tool box caught up to them and flew past their heads. The two men maneuvered around to a nook between the front navigation cabin of the freighter, and the back cargo hold, where they could take cover. Marlborough opened the box of supplies they had brought with them and removed a plasma drill. Goethe pointed to a spot that satisfied his scientific instincts, and Marlborough drilled through the hull of the ship for a few minutes. Once he could see wires underneath, he removed another device from the box, and Goethe stuck it inside the hole they had just made.

"Ship control access granted," Gabby's voice sounded in their helmets. Goethe and Marlborough looked at each other in satisfaction. They could now create their distraction, but whatever happened after

144

that was out of their control. They had to trust their colleagues would succeed and come back for them.

Gabby's remote access beacon hijacked the ship and continued flying it away from the mining facility. Some kind of silent alarm must have been raised by this intrusion, because every other ship they could see in the area suddenly stopped moving, as if to confirm that the one ship that was still moving, must have gone rogue. They could expect security to arrive soon enough. Marlborough was on this mission to get them to this point, and because he was skilled with firearms, but Goethe was sent along for his raw genius, which meant it was his job to outsmart the automated defenses that would soon attack them.

Marlborough noticed the first wave of drones was already arriving to investigate their freighter. He fired his explosive projectile rifle at them and managed to pick off five of them before they began firing back. It seemed like they had some kind of plasma cannons, which was exactly the arsenal that Gabby had predicted. The shots from the security drones were tearing right through the navigation cabin of the freighter but they could not penetrate the cargo hold. The Duke managed to eliminate the rest of the drones with his rifle, aided by heads up targeting displays in his helmet, and the corresponding precise aiming assist of the exoskeleton. He looked for Goethe and saw he was off looking around the corner of the cargo portion of the ship.

"Gabby when I give the command, stop forward movement, and release the payload in the cargo hold," Goethe was exploiting his high IQ to design some sort of chaos, just as Sophia would have expected.

A second wave of drones soon arrived, alerted by the destruction of the first wave, but this time they adjusted their tactics and kept a safe distance from Marlborough's volleys. These small gunships began firing at the two men as soon as they arrived on the scene. It was getting uncomfortable in the little nook they were using for shelter, as the plasma shots were now hitting close enough to cause shrapnel and blobs of molten metal to float past their helmets. Soon the little drones would be able to pin them down and finish them.

"Hang on Duke. Now Gabby!" Goethe commanded.

The cargo ship suddenly hit the brakes, which caused the two men to temporarily splatter onto the back of the cabin in front of them, like bugs on a windshield. The exoskeletons automatically adjusted to absorb the bone crushing impact. Just at this moment, Gabby forced the rear cargo bay door of the ship to open up, causing a load of dark matter raw material to scatter out in all directions because this action was coordinated with the sudden violent stop. Chunks of dark matter spread out of the cargo hold smashing into each other and changing directions, forming a cloud of random destruction. Several drones were hit and destroyed by flying bricks. This new threat drew the fire of the drones, and they began shooting their plasma weapons at chunks of raw dark matter, which had little effect on the extremely dense material. Many of the plasma shots were just deflected back at other drones. Since Marlborough was not firing at all, the security ships reacted as if they were taking fire from this new threat, and focused all their attention on the expanding mess of dark matter bricks. Gothe had tricked the security ships into punching at their own shadows.

Yet another wave of security drones arrived as requested by the previous waves. They joined in the battle, while Goethe and Marlborough watched patiently, this growing army of drones kept shooting into the massive clutter of matter chunks. Marlborough realized he would never have been able to shoot down the hundreds of drones that had by now joined in the fighting. He got ready to launch an EMP grenade into the melee. But first he disconnected the controller beacon that had allowed Gabby to hijack the freighter. Turning off the beacon would shield it from damage caused by EMP, just in case they still needed Gabby in the aftermath of the battle.

Eventually, there was a lull in the shooting, and Marlborough noted that no more drones had arrived for several minutes. This was the moment. He looked out over a small pile of dark matter he had been hiding behind, took a deep breath, and fired the EMP grenade into the middle of the area that was circled by weaponized drones. Sure enough it let out a shockwave of energy that shut down all the ships and security drones in the immediate area.

Marlborough could tell it worked because the display inside his helmet also shut off. No more proximity alerts, or exoskeleton super powers, or remote communications with Gabby, or vital sign readings from his own body. Now Goethe and him were floating around without power. Their suits were connected to tanks that provided compressed air for breathing, which didn't require any power, as they had prepared themselves for the effects of the EMP. The only thing they could do now was float there near the mess they had created and wait for the others to pick them up before they ran out of air.

After only a few minutes, Marlborough noticed a ship approaching their location, and he nudged Goethe to alert him, since their electronic communications were not working any more. The two of them stared. The ship looked very much like their own, except their ship had been disguised to look like a freighter, so something was definitely wrong. Marlborough raised his rifle but he noticed to his dismay that it would no longer fire. Even though a regular rifle would not be effected by an EMP, he was using one that had the electronic functions that helped him aim in space, but it just wasn't designed to operate without power. The two men could only wait helplessly as the familiar ship approached them and slowly opened up its loading ramp to invite them inside.

At the other end of the facility, Gabby piloted the ship towards the area they decided was likely the control room of the galaxy's largest mining operation. Minutes earlier, they had witnessed several drones launch from different locations around the gigantic structure, and race off in the direction where they had left Marlborough and Goethe. The distraction was working.

"Ship name and destination requested by the docking computer," Gabby mentioned to Sophia.

"Ship name: The Ark. Destination: Earth."

Gabby transmitted the information.

147

"Now you can be Joan of Arc of the Ark," Sophia joked to Joan to lighten the tension.

"I still don't understand what 'Joan of Arc' means, nobody ever called me that in my life," Joan was baffled by many of the legends that developed over the centuries about her, "But other than that, why did you name your ship after Noah's Ark?"

"It's more of a reference to what is in the cargo hold," Sophia hinted to Joan, "So Gabby, is there any problem with the docking procedure?"

"It appears that all ships are being ordered into a holding pattern at the moment due to a security breach. There has been no response about our ship identification," Gabby interpreted whatever messages the mining facility computer was transmitting.

"OK good. Well it's now or never. Our distraction is in effect. Give us a line to the opening located nearest to the control room," Sophia ordered and then immediately headed for the airlocks.

When she arrived, her away team was staring out at the wall that was 80 meters of zipline away from them. She gestured, and one at a time, they each grabbed the line, and a mechanism in their exoskeletons propelled them across the distance to the wall. Once there, they entered through an opening on the surface of the structure, that took them into a hallway. The ship disconnected and floated off very slowly to try and avoid drawing attention.

It was another few hundred meters on foot to reach the control room. The inside of the facility was a mess of panels and wires and electronic nonsense. It was not easy to float quickly through these obstacles in space suits, although it did appear that this place might have accommodated living beings once, many centuries ago. Humans would be the right size for the interior dimensions of the station. Certainly there were still buttons, doors, control panels, and a floor, features that would now be quite useless with everything running on full computer automation. It made Sophia wonder what happened to the crew that used to work here. They must have been some badass space traveling humans, she assumed, if they were hanging around right next to a SMBH, mining a material that didn't even exist in their own dimension.

The squad arrived at the control room uncontested. Bass Reeves, Musashi and Khutulun spread around the room looking for any tactical advantages. Hypatia and Sophia searched the controls for some way to turn off the dimensional portal system. Nothing really obvious jumped out at them, so Sophia stuck a beacon, about the size of a beer mug, into a random port of the most important looking control panel in the room. This would give Gabby remote access to hack into the computers of the facility.

"Access secured. The encryption on this system is ancient. Shutdown procedure initiated. This should take only a few minutes, and security will likely be alerted about halfway through the process. Prepare yourselves," Gabby announced through their helmet communicators.

All of them took cover among the debris in the room, and locked their space boots onto the ground, to have more control over their movement. Musashi was closest to the door and he signaled that he could see something down the hall. Suddenly the remote Gabby transceiver sprayed some sparks and started smoking. Sophia looked helplessly at the damaged device and hoped the shutdown procedure was successful.

Just at that moment, several shots of plasma energy erupted all around them from the doorway. A squad of eight spherical robots flew into the room in a line formation. Each sphere resembled a huge metallic beach ball. They floated freely in the zero gravity environment, and used small vents around their spherical structure to maneuver in any direction, while they each had duel barrels that could fire bursts of plasma charges.

The floating spheres paused inside the room because they were scanning for all their targets and analyzing threat levels. This allowed Musashi to jump up and slice his katana at the ball nearest to the door. The metal on metal contact did little damage, but the ball was knocked down to the ground and bounced about the room out of control. The other robo-balls immediately forgot about scanning and pointed their weapons toward Musashi. Sophia had a moment of inspiration, and she took a carefully aimed shot at the robot on the end of the row, floating nearest to her.

The explosive bullet seemed to do enough damage to disable the robot she hit, but more importantly it caused a pool shot effect, where each of the billiard balls bounced off the next ball in the line, until the last ball was knocked right out of the room. Before she could line up her next shot, Sophia saw Bass Reeves follow her example and fire shot after shot at the last robot in the line, causing a constant violent collision into to the other robo-balls. None of them were able to stabilize their directions enough to aim their weapons, and before Sophia knew it, there were three disabled balls floating in the room and four more outside the door in disarray. Sophia turned and shot down the first sphere that had been bouncing off the walls wildly as it tried to recover its bearings from being knocked down by Musashi.

Khutulun took aim and fired her grappling line out the door. Musashi and Bass Reeves did the same. They managed to cross up their lines to form a makeshift barrier, which caused a logjam of aggressive spheres arriving all at once, outside the door. The things were all colliding with each other as their limited flying capabilities kept them from escaping the tangle of grappling cables. Sophia and her team fired ruthlessly into the growing mass of floating ball robots accumulating outside, and any return fire was blocked by the wall of robots they had already disabled. Mostly the security bots just managed to damage each other and get more clogged up. Apparently the security balls' problem solving algorithms were not as developed as their seek and destroy functions. For now the team was safe.

Sophia signaled to Hypatia that the two of them needed to find another exit since the route they came from was now clogged with a pile of metal balls. Hypatia looked at the gear she had with her. She carried an EMP javelin, but that would not be useful with the machines already out of the fight. She had a rifle that fired explosive rounds, but they needed a larger hole to exit the room. There had to be another way out.

Hypatia scanned the room. The debris of the damaged battle robots was sparking and smoking. The smoke was actually flowing up to and towards the wall opposite the door they had entered from. There was some kind of emergency vent system built in the wall that would clear out any airborne toxins, protecting the most important room on the station, it was obviously a relic of the days when humans lived there. It worked by sucking the toxin out into space and immediately pumping in new breathable air. The floating shrapnel and smoke must have triggered the vent process.

Hypatia removed her pressurized oxygen tank, a type of spare tank they all carried in case of an EMP shutting down their suit computers, and tossed it into the vent. After giving a warning to the others, she ducked behind a metallic terminal, and fired a shot into the tank. The pressurized oxygen exploded dramatically as intended. When they all dared to raise their heads above their cover, the team could see a hole in the side of the facility's control room that was big enough for any of them to fit through. Sophia gave a thumbs up to Hypatia, who wondered why she was being praised like a victorious gladiator from Rome, but still took it as a compliment.

"Gabby, we're on our way outside," Sophia spoke into her helmet communicator. Next, she launched her zero gravity body through the hole in the wall, and out into the overwhelming vastness of deep space.

For a moment Sophia felt the panic of being very alone, floating freely in her space suit, even though her friends were nearby. She looked at the enormous metallic structure, then over at the SMBH, which seemed much closer than it was when she was outside the ship, because it was truly super massive. Even though the black hole itself was just a big dark spot in space, that blocked out all the stars behind or inside it, there were a lot of different burning materials still in the process of being pulled into the hole. This matter became superheated and spun around the outside of the hole until it would reach the event horizon, where gravity was so strong that it would practically disappear from existence, at least from the perspective of an outside observer. The effect was a giant completely dark disk surrounded by a spinning ring of fire. Sophia became overwhelmed from staring at this phenomenon. It contained so much mass, it was so ancient, and it generated so much energy, that a planet like Earth was a mere speck of dust by comparison. She wept at her own insignificance.

Inside the newly named Ark, the three remaining crew members waited for the portal to power down. There was no point attracting attention while there were team members aboard the mining facility, still searching for the control room, so they floated in the same place like all the other cargo ships. They could even see that the portal was still activated from their location.

Apphia and Joan were watching the screens in the Ark's control room for any dangers. Within minutes Gabby alerted them to a new development: The team inside the mining facility had activated their remote access beacon, which meant Gabby would be shutting down the dark matter mine remotely, while also piloting the ship to the location of the portal. It only took a few seconds to swing the ship into position and open the back payload ramp.

Crazy Horse was waiting patiently inside the cargo hold. When the door finally opened, he quickly spotted the device they were after and fired a magnetic harpoon, hitting it on the first attempt. Gabby controlled the winch to pull the machine towards the ramp. Suddenly it started to light up as if it was about to start working again, but Gabby fired a few shots from the rear cannons, instantly destroying all the connections between the device and the mining facility. The dimensional portal device was now powerless. Gabby slowly guided it into the cargo hold and Crazy Horse secured it firmly in place.

"The device is on board," Gabby announced to the crew.

Next they flew the few meters to the mining control room where the other five team members were likely still located. Based on heat signature readings, Gabby could calculate that a firefight was in progress, but there was nothing anyone could do from the outside.

Shooting blindly into the structure would likely miss any intended targets, and could easily result in friendly fire casualties, which would be an unthinkable risk for any sensible artificial intelligence. Gabby would have to wait and watch.

"Gabby get closer, I'm going in," Joan announced as she grabbed the weapons she had kept nearby for just such an occasion.

"Negative. By the time you reach the room, the battle will be decided, for better or worse. The team on the inside expects us to be right here waiting for them to evacuate. You should be prepared to go out and help anyone who may be wounded," Gabby was always the voice of reason, mostly because machines - even the most advanced ones - still didn't have emotions clouding their thoughts.

"Right. Come on Apphia, lets go to the main ramp and prepare," Joan suggested.

Once the two of them arrived at the ship's primary airlock, they found Crazy Horse already waiting there, with full space suit on. They put on their helmets and opened the airlock. From their perspective, they could see the small explosion on the side of the gigantic structure, shortly followed by the heroes of Earth, exiting through the hole one at a time, like kids popping out the bottom of a water slide and into a pool. They all floated away into space in a single file line.

Gabby positioned the ship to receive each of the humans. Crazy Horse, Joan and Apphia made sure to catch each of them and pull them inside gently, without any unnecessary injury. It took a few minutes to pluck them all out of thin air.

They all hugged and smiled at each other on board the Ark as they realized nobody had been wounded. Crazy Horse explained that the Dimensional Portal machine was safely stored in the rear cargo hold of the ship. It seemed to be undamaged, so Gabby could develop the modifications needed to use the machine as a proper weapon. Now there was only one important step left to complete this heist.

"Gabby, take us to the far side of this structure, where we will find Goethe and the Duke," Sophia ordered, wondering why she even had to do so, and why the Ark wasn't already on its way.

"Negative," Gabby announced, "We are no longer alone."

Chapter 13 - Trust

Nereus felt like it had been years since he last saw his home world of Eden, and the love of his life, Apphia, although it had only been a few weeks. During that time, he was being trained in the ways of combat and discipline. The Khan himself had spent so much time teaching him to be a ruthless and effective commander. Nereus always wondered why he was so important, especially among this group of great generals and warriors that had attacked his planet, but he was never foolish enough to ask about it. Today he finally learned the answer.

The space ship of the Great Khan arrived at the dark matter mining facility with a simple plan to take the dark matter portal device by force. However, the ship's computer immediately reported some strange activities in the region. There was a major battle going on nearby, and the computer was determining that humans seemed to be involved, based on the initial readings. A fully automated facility, sparring with uninvited humans, just as the Khan's ship arrived? The improbable nature of this event made him immediately direct the ship to the location of the battle.

When they arrived on the scene there was a lot of chaos to take in. A freighter ship was floating in the middle of a debris field of it's own cargo. There were armed drone ships all over the area but they were all either disabled, or badly damaged. There seemed to be at least two humans floating motionless in the aftermath of the battle.

Genghis Khan ordered all his commanders to get into space gear, go out into the debris, and search for anything valuable. He ordered Hannibal and Caesar to go and check the status of the humans. He always ordered them to work together because they did not like each other. George Washington and Da Vinci were told to check if there was anything useful inside the freighter. He ordered Newton, Alexander and Plato to search the debris and bring back some samples. Nereus was also looking at the space gear, but Khan ordered him to go to the ships control room instead, and wait for him.

The seven men were finally suited up for a space walk, waiting inside the airlock for the interior door to close, which would then allow the exterior door to open. Suddenly, Alexander grabbed Genghis Khan and pulled him into the airlock, even though he didn't have any protective gear on at the moment.

"You bastard. You are going to kill us all aren't you? You will leave as soon as we step out these doors won't you? Well you are either coming out there with us or I am staying on board with you," Alexander the Great shouted at the Mongol King.

"I eat with my soldiers, I drink with my soldiers, I fight along with my soldiers and I will come with you now. But I must have my helmet," Khan reassured him.

Nereus watched from inside the safety of the ship as Genghis Khan turned around and grabbed a helmet. Alexander stayed right next to him so he could not run away into the ship. Khan raised the helmet high, but instead of lowering it upon his own head, he swung it down right into Alexander's helmet as hard as he could. The blow made an audible crack, and caused Alexander to stumble back a few steps. Khan used this advantage to step out of the airlock, into the ship, and quickly hit the button that activated all the doors. The mighty warriors of Earth were sucked out into the debris field outside. Khan watched them for a while, the seven bodies flailing like they were drowning, floating away into the distance through the window of the airlock.

"Time to go," Khan said to Nereus, "You are my second in command now. I'll have you know I would never slaughter my own men like this, except for the highest crime of treason, but those were not my men. I knew they would betray me sooner or later."

Then he commanded the ship's computer to head for the location of the dark matter mine's Dimensional Portal before those castaways could figure out a way to get back to the ship. It was still their goal to retrieve this device for their mission of conquering Earth, Nereus already knew, as he had been briefed on most of the details of the plan. He also knew that they already possessed a powerful weapon that could destroy the whole Earth. It was the Baryonic Disruptor that had been taken from his own planet of Eden, but the commanders had always argued about how useful it was, since they didn't want to destroy a whole planet unless they had to. Khan had always preferred to obtain the Dimensional Portal Generator and conquer the Earth instead of destroying it. Washington, Plato and Newton had argued that the destruction of their evil enemy was the most important goal.

Now there was no longer an opposing opinion. Nereus was slightly disturbed by Khan's sudden betrayal of all his commanders, but it was nothing compared to the violence that was visited upon his own people a few weeks earlier. On both occasions, the young man could only be in awe of Khan's power. The conqueror appeared to be supremely confident in his decisions, like every action was part of a larger plan, and Nereus had seen the man summon God to address the people of Eden. That left an impression.

"Alert! There is a large ship ahead with human passengers," said the automated voice that belonged to Khan's ship.

"I see it. Prepare weapons for battle, Ship," Khan ordered the AI computer, "And try to contact these humans. I will allow them to surrender if they wish to live."

"Communications have been established."

Khan and Nereus waited and wondered what kind of humans they had found out in this desolate wasteland on the fringes of a Supermassive Black Hole. The largest display in their control room switched over to an interior view of the other ship. It looked like a replica of the same room. There were three men and five women seated in the opposite ship's control room. One of the women, who seemed to be their leader, addressed Khan.

"I am Sophia of Earth. I know you Genghis Khan, and also your colleagues. We are all on the same side and we all seek to destroy the Demon on our home world. Let us work together for this goal, for we would surely be stronger that way, and we will need all the strength we can gather."

Nereus did not hear a single word of this. He was sitting in stunned silence and staring at the corner of the screen where he saw a young woman that looked exactly like his beloved Apphia. But how? That could never be. He must be dreaming.

"Yes the many are stronger than the few. I already have a large army - as many as can fit inside my ship. If you do know my name, then you know that I am the flail of God, and the conqueror of the world. I have conquered it before and I intend to do so again," Said Khan.

"Indeed we know these things. What can we do to help you become victorious?" Sophia offered.

"I have many warriors already, that I am training for battle, but I need more wives. I did not bring enough women from that peaceful planet. You must send me all the women on your ship, and I will also take that weapon you found here, in this strange place. If I locate one woman remaining behind, or if one man comes to my ship, I will destroy your ship without hesitation. If you agree, your men may leave here with their lives. I will not kill them unless they attempt to follow me. Ask the Mongol woman if my threats are idle," Khan was referring to Khutulun.

"Great Khan, as a proud Mongol, it would be my honor to be your wife. The other women will join me also," Khutulun spoke for all of them. Sophia nodded but remained silent.

Nereus was so happy that they would be coming aboard his ship. That woman he was looking at, she had to be Apphia, even though she did not speak to him or acknowledge him. He would see how she reacts once he stands right before her! She would surely be impressed that he is the second in command of this huge army, and that the Khan holds him in such high regard.

When the screen went blank, Khan ordered Nereus to get 10 of his best men, arm them, and prepare to search the women for any weapons once they arrived. He did just that, and waited for the visitors with his men, by the airlock. Soon the outer door opened. He watched as the five space suits floated cautiously between the two ships,

158

wondering which of those helpless projectiles was his beloved Apphia, probably the last one.

"Ship!" Khan joined them at the airlock and instructed the computer, "Once we have unloaded the weapon from their ship, aim all of our cannons into their open cargo door, and then await my command to fire."

"Sir what do you gain by doing that?" Nereus was naive still, having grown up in such a passive society, but the Mongol Warlord didn't have much choice anymore when it came to handing out ranks.

"My young General, you should understand that we are about to go into battle, and the last thing we need in a vulnerable moment, is an enemy at our backs. Their ship must be destroyed or they will likely follow us to rescue these women," Khan gestured at the five people who were just now getting into the airlock chamber.

Once the outer door was sealed shut, and air was pumped in, the five women removed their helmets, along with their space suits. They were dressed in the loose track pants and sweater outfits they would usually wear for their combat training. It did not seem like they were armed on first glance. The ship's AI also confirmed as much, but Khan had the soldiers pat them down, because he just didn't trust technology. He was still more comfortable with the old ways.

Nereus went up to Apphia and stood face to face with her, but she just looked at him with cold indifference, which broke his heart after all the excitement he had been feeling since he saw her on the video display. He did not even speak up about knowing her. Something was obviously wrong with her, and he would rather discuss it later on, when they could find a moment alone. He figured she felt the same way because she did not acknowledge him at all.

"All of you, follow me to the command room. You, Mongol woman, will oversee the transfer of the weapon from your ship to mine. Then we will all dine and drink to celebrate this great victory," Genghis Khan ordered the women from the Ark, Nereus, and his ten soldiers all to the ship's main control room.

Khutulun instructed the computer to navigate the warlords' ship behind the Ark, then both vessels would open their cargo bays, which would facilitate the transfer of the large Dimensional Portal device. After a few moments of navigating, the ships were lined up that way, back to back. They all watched on a screen as some large crates were being removed from the Ark, and then they stopped moving, just suspended between the two ships.

"Ship! Scan all those boxes for soldiers or explosives before they enter our cargo hold," Khan ordered.

"We would rather not blow ourselves up, Great Khan," Said Sophia, "By the way, I was hoping to meet Hannibal, and that famous painter Da Vinci. Are they going to join us?"

"They are no longer with my army. I don't share my command with other generals, it is not my way, I create my own generals to work under me," He motioned towards Nereus, "Soon you will all learn this, as he already has."

Sophia glanced at the screen and saw several of the boxes had been loaded on the Warlord vessel. Everything was going according to plan.

"Are you telling me that you intend to conquer the entire Earth with these ten men and a boy?" Sophia pretended not to know about the thousands of men from Eden that were lodging aboard that very ship, whether they wanted to be there, or not.

"I told you I have a large enough army to conquer the world that I have already conquered before. What is this talk about? You think I can't see that you are trying to trick me?" Khan offered Sophia a drink of the Mongol Milk liquor she had drank with Khutulun before, "Come and sip from the cup of destruction!"

"Trick you? The Great Khan? We are here by our own free will. This Mongol woman is named Khutulun and she is your own great great granddaughter and a princess of your people. I took her council, and we came here to join your mission of conquering the Earth," Sophia argued nervously as she took a drink of the traditional Mongol beverage.

160

"Lies... Ship!" Khan shouted at his computer console, "Begin firing into the interior of the other ship and do not stop until it is destroyed! General, take your men to the cargo hold and break apart every box. Fire your weapons at anything that does not look harmless! Somebody must have been sneaking aboard. No mercy!"

Nereus ran out of the control room with the ten armed men. They all carried automatic projectile weapons designed by their ship's AI. Down the hallway, they halted and lined up on each side aiming their rifles towards the cargo hold. There was a commotion, and they prepared for a firefight, but suddenly their weapons and gear flew out of their hands like magic. The men of Eden looked around helplessly. Their training was forgotten in an instant, and once again they felt the helplessness they had known back on their own world.

As this was happening, Nereus saw Musashi run through the hallway, knocking out half his troops with a wooden stick. The ten of them did not offer any challenge to the lone warrior. Nereus raised his fists to fight this man, hand to hand, in the ways he had been trained over the last several weeks. Unfortunately, he was hit out of nowhere by a large wet blob, before he had an opportunity to fight. The battle was finished for him. He found himself stuck to the wall, immobilized in a thick cocoon of slime, hoping that someone would eventually show him enough mercy to let him out again.

Back inside the control room, Genghis Khan drew his sword and looked over the five unarmed women, but none of them made a move to attack him. When he looked back at the monitor, nothing had happened on the video feed, and no shots were being fired from either ship. The computer had ignored his command to attack.

"What?" Khan was enraged, as he suddenly noticed a strange sensation in his mouth that he had rarely known in his life, it was that bitter taste of defeat. It was not since he was a small child, an outcast of the Mongol tribes, that he had been completely powerless. He despised it so.

Genghis Khan was not all that shocked to feel his sword suddenly rip out of his hand and magically rise to the ceiling. He could recognize when his opponent had outmaneuvered him. Khutulun jumped on Khan's back and put him into a complex wrestling hold that only a Mongol warrior would recognize, having been on either end of the move hundreds of times, while training. She held him for a long time. He struggled to get out of the hold, but he knew well enough that he was outnumbered, and there was nothing more he could do. Apphia, Joan, Hypatia and Sophia all combined together the ropes that they were wearing as belts for their track pants, and used them to tie up Khan. The mightiest and most ruthless conqueror the Earth had ever seen was now their prisoner.

The automated door opened and into the control room rushed Crazy Horse, armed with his wooden bow, Musashi, carrying his wooden practice sword, and Bass Reeves, carrying a baseball bat.

Behind them, followed two of the Crawler creatures that had once been their enemies. Sophia had captured them on their previous stopover, and she spent time with Gabby formulating a way to control them in battle. Gabby had designed a simplified version of the same alien mind control transmission that they had discovered on the Crawler planet. This rudimentary version of the signal was still effective enough to keep the creatures from attacking their allies, and they could even be motivated to focus their aggression on hostile enemies, usually with the use of their natural weapon, a spray of sticky slime.

"Gabby, release magnetic field," Sophia said.

The sword fell from the ceiling to the ground. Seeing this, Genghis Khan finally understood what had happened, and how he had ended up tied to a chair like a fool, in his own control room. It was exactly his worst fear that had come true! All this technology that he had to tolerate - only because it let him stay alive in space - but he nevertheless distrusted so much, ended up being turned against him. It enraged him.

When Sophia had entered the airlock with a flash memory device, she knew that the ship's computer would automatically scan the memory because the AI was an exact replica of Gabby, and would naturally behave the same way. The flash memory drive contained a virus. At their last stop, Sophia had noticed that Gabby's virus security was weak, although Gabby had argued it was not likely to be a problem. The AI then tested Sophia's hypothesis, in order to ease her concerns about the ship's virus security, by designing a sophisticated computer virus to challenge its own security. Of course, this test virus was perfectly suited to infect another version of Gabby, since Gabby designed it specifically for that purpose. That ended up being the virus they used it to take control of Khan's ship. As it turned out, the inferior human was correct about the superior AI's vulnerability to computer viruses after all.

Once the Warlord ship was under Gabby's control, they were able to smuggle the Crawlers on board with some cargo crates, by spoofing all the security scans or alerts. Unfortunately Khan was so paranoid that it was more difficult than they anticipated. In the end Gabby had to activate a strong magnetic field to disarm all the soldiers of all their metallic weapons. The living quarters were also locked down to avoid having to deal with hundreds of other people coming out to investigate.

Musashi was able to knock out five of the unarmed soldiers, as he moved quickly through the ship searching for the five women. The Crawlers trapped six others in their slime glue. None of the novice soldiers had to be shot by arrows or beaten with a baseball bat, which pleased Sophia, and nobody even had to die in the battle. She had kept her word to the people of Eden by not killing any of their men. Now it was up to these people to figure out what to do with themselves.

Sophia spoke into the ship's PA system to address everyone on board, "People of Eden, I am Sophia of Earth. I have visited your planet and I fulfilled my promise to your people. I told them I would find you, their missing menfolk, and send you back to them. I will leave the choice to go back, up to you, but I warn you, if you return to Eden everyone you knew will be dead now, and you will barely recognize your home world. Go there at your own peril.

"The Great Genghis Khan is your prisoner now. It is also your choice what to do with him, but I suggest that you never free him again, because he will only bring you more death. Your other commanders are all dead, killed by Khan before we arrived. Your future is in your own hands. This is the gift I leave for you, but in exchange you must abide by my conditions. First, you must not follow us to Earth. The mission you were on was not meant for you, it was meant for those of us from Earth to finish alone. Just let us go finish our mission and you can assume that we will not survive. Second, you will have to wait here patiently for a few days, because we are going to leave your ship immobilized. We will unlock your living quarters, and enable your weapons, immediately after we leave here, just in case you meet any more hostiles around here. However, the ship will not move until five days have passed. Good luck to you all."

Genghis Khan was not pleased as he listened to Sophia's speech, "Fools! You would be wise to kill me. Even wiser if you let me fight your battle for Earth. You will not win through trickery, you can only win through ruthlessness! Mongol woman you are the one who should know this best. How dare you betray your Khan? How dare you betray your own kin?"

"It is because I know you so well, that I cannot follow you," Khutulun explained out of courtesy, "I know your ways. It is not sufficient for you to succeed in conquering the world but everyone else must also fail. That is not my way. I ask you Grandfather, what is the point of defeating some great Demon in battle, only to replace him with a new Demon?"

With those words she left her famous ancestor behind and went back to her own ship. The others hurried back as well, because poor Marlborough and Goethe would still be floating around helplessly in space, and with their oxygen running low. At the threshold between the two ships' cargo bays, Sophia stopped and turned to Apphia, as the others proceeded to confiscate the Baryonic Disrupter weapon from Khan's ship.

"Go to your people Apphia. You have helped us enough and it is not your place to fight our final battle. Your man is here as well, and these fools will need a leader, or at least someone to keep them from turning back to Khan yet again."

164

"Thank you my friend. I would love to return to my own world but it can never be. You know that Eden is now either very different, or maybe completely dead, and either way I don't want to see it," Apphia lamented, "The men on this ship have lost their way and I would rather let them take their own journey to find it again. However, if you will allow it, I would take Nereus with us, and we will both help you on your quest."

"I cannot refuse your courageous offer. I would rather have you with me, but please consider that we are probably not going to survive," Sophia offered her an escape.

"If that is my fate, so be it. Nereus chose that fate when he willingly joined the warlords. When he is able to speak I will remind him of that," Apphia gestured towards a human shaped bag of slime she had already attached to one of the Crawlers, which dragged it along the ground like a bag of basketballs, back to the Ark. Sophia wondered how she knew which bag of slime was the correct one.

The fate of the Eden people was decided then. Sophia followed Apphia back across the space between the two ships. Immediately, she ordered Gabby to release all the locked doors on the other ship, and then fly back to the spot where their two missing team members were stranded, as quickly as possible.

They arrived there in minutes, only to marvel at the aftermath of a great space battle, which must have been the distraction engineered by Marlborough and Goethe. Hundreds of battle drone corpses, and gigantic chunks of Dark Matter raw material, were floating around an area several kilometers wide. Gabby scanned the debris. The others all searched visually, on various monitor screens, to see if they could spot any human shapes among all the projectiles floating around the area. They were not having much luck. Gabby's attempts at radio communications were not getting a response either, but they had already expected their communications to be ruined by EMP weapons.

"There!" Musashi had spotted something on a monitor and he ran out of the control room to the airlocks.

Gabby positioned the Ark as close as possible, to the human object, but without getting the ship bombarded by debris. They all watched on the main monitor, as Musashi floated out into space with a lifeline, grabbed the motionless body, and pulled himself back towards the ship. He had to kick a large piece of debris as he floated past it to alter his direction slightly.   Just before he reached the Ark, he managed to grab a chunk of the floating dark matter, that was small enough to carry easily. Everyone went to the airlock to see who was inside that other space suit.

When they arrived, Musashi had dropped the brick of dark matter, along with the person he had pulled back to the ship. The body was quite lifeless, and it was clear to see the cause of death was a large crack in the helmet, which would be fatal within seconds in the vacuum of space. The person they were all staring at was not one of their own men.

"Alexander was his name, I believe," Apphia recognized him from their time together on Eden.

"What about our own men? Where are they then? Are they alive?" Joan was frantic.

"From one thing, one can know ten thousand things," Musashi referred to the body he had brought inside.

"Don't worry Joan, we will soon have some answers about what happened here," Sophia reassured them, "Apphia, come with me, we have to go and unwrap your boyfriend."

Chapter 14 - Earth

The Ark casually flew between a large space station, and the moon, which were both covered in futuristic electronic weapons, on a scale Sophia had never even seen in the movies. It seemed obvious that the numerous sophisticated weapons systems protecting the Earth were capable of annihilating their ship with very little effort. For some reason they did not do so.

Gabby had anticipated that their ship would be scanned by all sorts of sensors. These would conclude that the ship's cannons were too weak to be a threat, the Dark Matter Portal would be categorized as an industrial mining tool, and the Baryonic Disrupter was so unusual, it would not be recognized as any known weapon. The scan would conclude that there were no weapons of mass destruction or antimatter bombs aboard. Furthermore, the handful of life forms on the ship were all native to Earth. The enhanced physical bodies of the crew were obviously recognizable as legitimate human beings in every way, rather than some hybrid aliens, or cyborg life forms that merely resembled humans. Even their DNA would confirm they were 100% native Earthlings. The security measures of the Earth did indeed seem to be satisfied that the Ark, her cargo and her crew were harmless, or they would have not have made it this far.

Even the Crawlers, it turned out, were related to a species of ancient creatures from Earth called Onychophora. The creatures first existed over 100 million or more years before humans. Gabby had explained that the aliens must have visited Earth long before Sophia's lifetime, because these abducted Crawlers had evolved very differently from any Onychophora that remained on Earth, a difference that could take some millions of years to develop. Their presence on the ship still wasn't enough of a threat to activate the Earth defenses. Sophia was troubled by Gabby's explanation, especially the implication that the Apex Aliens were already sophisticated space travelers even way back in the time of the dinosaurs, when they must have originally acquired those crawlers from Earth. That helps to explain why they would regard humans as primitive life forms. Humans are such a recent addition to the universe, that these ancient aliens would dismiss them as insignificant, especially since the only remaining hint of human civilization was that colony the aliens were using as livestock.

Other than the Crawlers, Sophia had also found a few other Earth animals on that planet where the abducted humans lived. Apparently the aliens had supplied those people with some pigs, sheep, goats, horses, oxen, cattle, cats and dogs. They were all domesticated beasts, for food or burden, which must have been intended to help the humans stay well fed. It certainly worked. Sophia borrowed two of each animal, male and female, to bring back to Earth aboard her ship, which is why she named it the Ark. Unfortunately there was no time to search around for any wild animals to be transported. It was likely that wild animals would have repopulated the Earth anyway, since the humans were no longer around to eat them and kill them. Sophia expected that the domesticated animals would be helpful tools to have on a barren planet without civilization. If everything went well, she intended to use the animals to populate a new reboot of Earth, but she knew such a reboot would have to wait until the demon was eliminated.

The Ark was now entering the atmosphere. All the crew were gathered in the control room to stare at the world they, or at least their ancestors, had originated from. Sophia pointed out the eastern coast of North America. She had picked Manhattan as the landing zone, because she wanted to be able to reference a familiar location, in order to get a feel for the 2000 years of changes that have occurred since she was last on the planet. Her notion of what she considered human civilization was any place within the five boroughs.

She had read how civilization had advanced so rapidly after her death within Gabby's vast historical archives. People had scavenged alien technology, created AI to accelerate scientific progress, built up a globalized system of government that thrived economically, and eventually developed advanced space travel. She was also amused how the media had made her out to be the biggest hero in the world

168

after she died. At least her crazy act of self sacrifice was appropriately recognized.

Then, within just a few decades, came the decline of human civilization. It really was a brief reign for mankind. There was a strange plague that killed off millions of people, the AI systems became less compassionate and distanced themselves from their human creators, while people were rendered docile by their addiction to electronic implants. Gabby's information was more vague during these final years.   The population collapsed rapidly, and humans forever lost their status as the dominant life forms on the planet, as they were replaced by the untouchable superiority of artificial intelligence.

The history was familiar to Sophia. It reminded her of the lost civilizations she read about. There was always a point where the citizens just became too decadent, too greedy, and gradually the empire would be vulnerable to outside attacks, or ecological disaster. For human civilization as a whole, she gathered from her research, they just allowed the machines to take over everything, because it made life easier, and then they sat around getting buzzed on brain implants. They were too lazy to resist extinction. Sure enough, it only took one outbreak that was beyond the medical capabilities of the AI, and suddenly the civilization was finished. What happened after that? Sophia found almost nothing. Perhaps the remaining humans were hunted down, like in the Terminator movies, or they became roving bandits like the Mad Max movies. Whatever it was, nobody bothered to write about it any more.

What did the AI decide to do when the humans were all gone? Did it just keep maintaining the planet as if they never left? Did the final living humans witness the arrival of this mysterious "Fallen One" she had been told about? She could find no further details. All of this future history she read, it could only manifest in her mind as abstract ideas, or absurd theories, until now at least. Sophia was finally going to be able to see the post apocalyptic Earth with her own eyes.

The Ark came down to the ground in the middle of Manhattan, but it was unrecognizable, so Sophia didn't really know exactly where they were. The buildings were rubble. A few short walls were still visible, but the skyscrapers were flattened and the roads were coated by centuries worth of debris. Grass and trees had grown over concrete. It was hard to tell at this point, if there was some devastating catastrophe that caused all that destruction, or simply the years of erosion and neglect.

Sophia ordered Gabby to stay on the ground for a few hours, and collect resources for fuel, food and gear. She did not care to go outside and look around her old stomping grounds. There was nothing here, nor had there been for many centuries. When Gabby was done refueling, Sophia intended to fly around the area, searching for any signs of more recent activity, or any clues to help them locate the current master of this planet. For now she decided to take a nap.

Bass Reeves had the opposite idea. He looked around the control room to see if anybody else would want to explore the outside world, and sure enough his eyes met those of Crazy Horse, who nodded at him. No words were needed. The two men gathered their weapons, lowered the ship's main ramp, and went outside. If there was more time, they might have tried their luck riding those two horses down in the cargo hold. Either way, it felt good to be in the familiar North American environment, just like they had grown up with.

Khutulun and Musashi asked Joan and Hypatia to follow them. The four of them walked over to the ship's molecular manipulation workshop. Khutulun and Musashi presented each of the other two with a brand new sword they had crafted over the last few days. Musashi had a moment of inspiration when acquired his chunk of the dark matter from the mining site, and he worked with Gabby to create a usable blade with it. Khutulun and him tested out various designs to find the most effective combination of blade composition and sword construction. Over time they created weapons that exceeded the best blades ever built on Earth.

"The problem with the dark matter is, the material is so dense, that a dark matter blade would weigh hundreds of times more than a metal one. I discovered this when I got inside the ship's gravity and the dark matter ore fell out of my hand," Musashi explained to Joan and

170

Hyaptia, "So we had to find the right mixture of materials to make the blade stronger than metal, but also light enough to wield effectively."

"With Gabby's scientific knowledge, Musashi and I did find a good mixture of alloys, to finally build a blade that would not shatter, or break, or bend, or dent. It is thinner than any metal blade to reduce the weight, yet it is still many times stronger because of the strength of the dark matter mixture," Khutulun was proud of the weapons she had helped design, "You can cut through any material without damaging the blade."

"What an honor to have a blade designed by warriors such as yourselves," Hypatia bowed politely as she held her new sword.

"I will cast aside the replica of my old legendary sword," said Joan, "For the original one was the cause of my downfall. Why should I honor that failure?"

"You did not have much combat training back then," Musashi offered.

"That did not matter. I never used that sword in battle anyway. Even though the sword never saw battle, it was still the instrument of my demise. It happened when I was advancing my troops to Paris for the decisive battle of the war. The English army was in trouble at the time, as we had handed them devastating defeats, and taking Paris would likely make them flee back to their island. My soldiers believed that I could make them invincible. I almost believed it as well, after praying for so many victories at that point, and having all my prayers answered.

"One day during that march to Paris, I chased a prostitute out of the camp, and in anger I swung my sword to smack her. Somehow this broke my famous sword. You have to remember, I was given that sword by a vision from God, and people believed it had magical qualities. Losing this sword was like being abandoned by God. With that bad omen, my troops were troubled, and we were soon defeated in battle. It was the end of my success. What did it mean? Was I being punished by God? Did I not follow all of God's commands? I did everything my visions ever asked of me!" Tears were beginning to flow from Joan's eyes. It was not that long ago, at least in her own timeline, that she had been betrayed by her own church and country.

"Your special sword meant nothing, and you should not have a favorite sword, like you did in those days. An obsession with just one weapon is as dangerous as unfamiliarity with that weapon," Musashi comforted Joan with some of his philosophies, "I have learned to respect the Gods and Buddhas, but to never depend on them."

"You are a wise warrior. Thank you for the new sword," Joan answered politely.

"Joan, I went through betrayal, torture and execution just like you did. The people of my city, Alexandria, attacked and murdered me right in the street, without any reason. My only crime was speaking out against their bigotry and dogma," Hypatia sympathized with Joan's trauma.

"Oh wow, we certainly understand each other's pain, but you never mentioned this before. How is it that you had the exact same experience as St Catherine of Alexandria? She was tortured and murdered by a mob of Pagans in Alexandria as well," Joan wondered out loud. She had once had visions that included St Catherine.

"Well I was a pagan, and I was attacked by a mob of Christians, actually. It's strange how that story became the story you know about. But if anyone would understand how a story can change, it would be you, Joan. We have all heard how you were remembered as a hero by some and a villain by others. After all, weren't both of us canonized after our deaths by the very same religion that unjustly murdered us? In my case the name also changed." Hypatia explained.

"Well I never heard the name Joan of Arc in my lifetime either. I'm so sorry that you went through such injustice, as I did. I never knew this about you. So are you saying that SHE is YOU? That you are actually St Catherine of Alexandria?" Joan was very confused.

"As far as I can tell, there no Catherine of Alexandria ever existed, so I must be her. All I really know about any of this, is the historical accounts I have read, while we have been traveling on this ship. I know you have read about your own history as well. I should also tell

172

you, in case you are wondering, that it was not I, who appeared as St Catherine in your visions. At least not that I remember."

"Well I am even more confused now. If St Catherine never existed, who was that person going by that name, in my visions? I would very much like to ask God some questions about this. Perhaps we will get a chance to meet him soon."

"Yes we should all ask God which one of us is the correct religion! After all we are a Pagan, a Christian, a Buddhist and a Muslim!" Khutulun observed, "Only one of us is right. Until then, I propose that we all go to the training room, and sort out the correct religion through combat."

The others agreed and followed her carrying their new swords.

In the control room of the Ark, Nereus and Apphia were alone together for the first time since they were separated on Eden. They sat silently in their control room seats and looked out at the scenery for a while. It was hard to believe they were on a planet that was presented to them, during their childhood education, as a mythological fantasy world. But the stories of Gods and heroes didn't seem like fantasy any more, now that they had visited other worlds, and traveled through space.

"My dear Apphia, did you know that I was second in command in the Khan's army?" Nereus could barely contain himself any longer.

"The warlord that slaughtered half of our people? Good for you. I just hope the people of Eden choose to execute him. Maybe you should have stayed behind to share his fate?" Apphia was a bit offended by the young man's loyalty to someone she viewed as an enemy.

"I simply took a bad situation and made the best of it," Nereus gently reminded her.

"So did I. Our people were saved from extinction by the crew of this ship. Even so, those men that were taken from Eden, along with you, they will never return to the world they knew. We will never return either. My place is with this crew, that took me in and helped me find you, even though I have nothing to offer them, neither skills, nor wealth. I owe them everything."

"If that is how you feel, I will respect that. I just hope you can have feelings for me like you once did," Nereus said.

"You left me though. I honestly don't feel the same way any more," Apphia admitted, even surprising herself.

"Well I still love you, and I know you love me too because you chased me all the way across the universe, and you found me."

"I am glad I found you," Apphia trailed off.

After a few moments, she stood up and patted Nereus on the shoulder, and went off to be alone with her thoughts. Their conversation had only made her more confused. Somehow the innocent boy she had lost on Eden, had changed over the months, and he was now a man who was proud to be a feared space warlord. After losing everything, including him, she had found her new family on the Ark. Right now she felt closer to these strange people, whom she had only met months earlier, than the boy she had known for several years. She wondered if the change in him was permanent or just a phase.

Nereus also found himself alone with his thoughts in the control room. It was clear to him that Apphia was not impressed by his status as a commander of men. She seemed to prefer the naive boy she knew before, but now that he had seen death, violence and power for the first time, that boy was gone. Everything was different now. Even Apphia, though she didn't seem to realize it, had changed as much as he had. It felt as though the two of them were still separated by many galaxies despite being reunited at last. He spent several minutes thinking about their awkward conversation, and the alternate way it would have played out if they were still the same kids that they were at their first festival, back on Eden. If they would not have known the fear and hate and loss from the attack. They could have grown old together on Eden, as lifelong companions, maybe they would have had a few children, and then Apphia would have become the guardian of the Oracle one day. When his mind emerged from this intoxicating nostalgia Nereus resolved to win back Apphia's love.

Gabby broke his train of thought, "The ship is fueled and supplies are adequate for travel. Two crew members are currently absent."

Within a few minutes, Sophia returned to the control room, looking half asleep. She watched with some alarm as Khutulun, Musashi, Joan and Hyatia walked in, covered in wounds and bruises, although she didn't say anything. Obviously they had been sparring without holding much back.

"Wow! What happened?" Apphia was surprised when she walked in and saw her friends were badly beaten.

"You can only fight like you practice," Explained Musashi, "So we practice hard."

"Well I won't be fighting very well then," Apphia lamented.

"Don't worry young one. Our ship has the ability to heal our bodies with the greatest speed," Hypatia explained, "We will be healthy again in another hour or two."

"Gabby, summon Crazy Horse and Bass Reeves back to the ship," Sophia ordered, "And make preparations for takeoff. Set up your scanners to search for signs of human habitation, heavily defended structures or anything else you think could help us locate that Demon."

"There is no response. The last known location of the two crew members was two km due south of our position. They could not have traveled beyond my communication range, in the amount of time that has passed, yet I am not able to contact them," Gabby reported the disturbing news.

"Gabby is there anything unusual out there? Can your sensors pick up anything?" Sophia was getting worried because this version of Earth was already quite unrecognizable to her.

"I have no point of reference to compare this planet to, however there is nothing that indicates danger. The surrounding area seems to be mostly abandoned except for wildlife that is consistent with this planet's environment. I can detect no large machines, vehicles or weapons nearby."

"Alright. We are going out to search for the others. I used to live here you know, and something isn't right, things are just too quiet around here. Two lifelong outdoorsmen like Horse and Reeves would never be caught by surprise on this planet. We are going to search for them with full weapons and armor. That means full exoskeletons. You too, Nereus, we need every set of eyes out there," Sophia ordered the rest of them.

"I'm sure someone must be aware of our presence on this world. That would explain these strange disappearances. Our only way to regain an advantage, would be to find out what is going on as quickly as possible. Let us make haste," Hypatia suggested and they were off to gather weapons and gear.

They decided to move on foot, so that they could follow the path of their missing friends directly, and thereby rely on their own senses instead of the electronic scanners that have so far detected nothing. The path was very clear. Sophia immediately spotted the only trampled grass on this abandoned Manhattan Island, and she lead them in that direction as a tight group, so they could protect each other from any unknown dangers. They all expected to be attacked at any moment.

None of this prepared them for what came next.

"Look!" Nereus shouted, and he pointed at the sky before them, exactly at the spot where all of them were already looking.

Black clouds were rolling over the horizon and darkening the sky. It looked as though a sudden storm was approaching, as the mass of clouds moved directly towards them, but at a much faster speed than even a hurricane. It became dark as midnight in a matter of seconds. In the thickest of the dark clouds, lightning was firing rapidly in all directions, including towards the ground, but there was no rain at all. The epicenter of the storm passed directly over their heads.

Sophia hoped her exoskeleton had some kind of electrical insulation feature. She looked up into the middle of the lightning cloud above her, and she could see some strange colourful lights glowing within, which was most likely the source of all that electric activity. The cloud suddenly slowed down as it approached the Ark, still just a few hundred meters behind them. Suddenly a bright glowing object slithered from the dark shelter of the cloud and dived towards their helpless ship.

The creature resembled a gigantic snake made out of pure energy. An aurora of light flowed from the Plasma Serpent, and Sophia could feel the heat radiating from its vague shape, even at a distance. Drops of plasma sweated from the serpent's torso and scorched the earth below. Mother nature herself continued to rage at that abomination with an onslaught of lighting and wind, although this did no harm to the entity, nor did the cannon fire that Gabby automatically unleashed to defend the ship.

"Oh fuck," Sophia grumbled.

The Plasma Serpent opened what appeared to be its mouth and began chewing on the top of the Ark, all the while suspended in mid air by some unnatural electromagnetic forces. The humans became quite alarmed by the sight of the creature devouring their only means of travel and shelter. As a result, Khutulun and Musashi looked at each other, drew their newly crafted swords, and sprinted towards their beleaguered ship.

Sophia covered their approach by firing her rifle into the body of the monster. The others followed her lead, but ultimately the weapons they were using did absolutely nothing. Any projectile they fired, seemed to melt and drip off the serpent in liquid form, while energy bursts and explosions simply became absorbed into the pure energy that made up the creature itself. Sophia was slowly realizing that even a nuclear explosion would only feed the entity with more energy. She wished that Goethe was still around, because this was exactly the type of unpredictable situation she had envisioned, when she chose to recruit the scientific genius. *What about my backup genius Hypatia?*

She looked at Hypatia standing nearby and suddenly noticed the EMP javelin she always carried.

"The javelin! Throw it!" Sophia yelled.

"But that is no machine. The EMP will only damage the ship and have no effect on the monster!" Hypatia hesitated.

"Exactly!"

Suddenly Hypatia understood. This Plasma lifeform did not have some calculated strategy to destroy their ship, in order to leave them vulnerable. Clearly they would already be dead if they were the targets. It was actually attracted to something inside the ship, as if by animal instinct, so shutting off the ship would hopefully make it lose interest. She heaved her javelin with all her might and it flew the full distance to the ship.

Just before the javelin hit the ground, Khutulun and Musashi finally managed to climb high enough on the outside hull of the Ark, to take a few swings at the energy serpent levitating just above them. The snake writhed upward towards the sky in reaction to the dark matter blades that pierced its belly. The javelin landed at that moment and killed all the power aboard the ship instantly. A flash of bright light emitted from the Plasma Serpent when the electromagnetic wave passed through it.

With its reward suddenly removed, along with an introduction to the unpleasant sensation of pain, the mighty Plasma Serpent slowly floated back towards the comfort of the storm clouds. Before leaving the area, the creature emitted a powerful shockwave that knocked Khutulun and Musashi right out of their newly disabled exoskeletons and onto the roof of the damaged ship.

Sophia, Joan, Nereus, Apphia and Hypatia had just enough time to frown at each other just before the shockwave arrived and knocked them over as well. All of them lost consciousness. Above them, the sky was slowly clearing up as the dark clouds moved away, along with the living body of energy that fueled them. The Plasma Serpent moved on to find a new source of energy to devour. None of them were awake to witness this, or for that matter, the men that soon approached them as they slept.

"These ones make the dragon flee," A voice whispered.

178

"Bring them," Said another, "They are strong."

"Hey. Sophia. Hey what's up? Are you passing out? Are you high?"

"What? Uh sorry... maybe I was passing out. I can't remember. What happened?" Sophia looked around in a state of confusion.

As she gathered her senses, she slowly figured out that she was sitting at a table in a small Italian restaurant a few blocks from her apartment. The place was full of people, some of whom were already looking at her and she had a plate of lasagna in front of her. Across from her sat Ordinary Gus.

"Wow you were just like tripping out there for a minute. Are you back to normal?" Gus asked with some concern.

"Um, sure. Hey I just felt like I was dreaming. It was so crazy. I was in the future! For some fucked up reason, God had chosen me to go on this mission in space, for no good reason actually... holy shit it was very vivid," Sophia was shocked at how much crazy stuff she had imagined.

It felt like she had blacked out for hours. She remembered leaving her apartment and... yeah that's when she ate some pretty potent edible, with who-knows-what inside. After that it was all alien attacks and space ships! *Holy shit*, she thought, *that must have been the hardest drugs I ever had*.

Gus was looking pretty cool all things considered. What had she even said to him in the past hour? He was drinking his beer and patiently listening to her describe her most trippy thoughts. Why didn't he ditch her? Here she was on their third date, trying to decide if she wanted to pursue a relationship, and she was the one who was totally fucked up the whole time! Most likely he would never want to see her again after this.

"You were saying, God Himself chose you?" Gus was fascinated.

"Yeah man. I was brought back to life thousands of years in the future, to lead a team of humans - and not just anyone - but people that I got to choose myself. Of course I wanted a bunch of historical people that I had written about in my blog. Then we went on a space adventure!" It sounded absurd now that her mind was back in the good old days of cynicism, social media and memes. At least her apartment hadn't been blown up by some alien invasion after all.

"You said you went on a mission? Like what?"

"Me and my team were supposed to go to earth and destroy this devil or demon or something. I'm not sure what it was exactly, because I woke up here just before we found it. Why do you care about all this craziness?"

Gus looked dismayed, "You were going to kill a demon? Just you and a few dead people? That's pretty ambitious. Anyway, I'm just interested in this futuristic stuff because I think about it a lot in my job. You know that I work on some of the most advanced computer programming in the industry. Sometimes my work feels like I am shaping the basic infant mind of a computer that will one day become smarter than any human. The tiniest programming decision today, could create a world-ending glitch in a few decades, whenever the computers are making all the decisions for us."

"Yeah, like when you make a machine and tell it to protect the world, and it would inevitably just try to wipe out all the humans because we are obviously the biggest danger to the world. I've seen that movie before," Sophia had grown up in the era when this scenario was played out in countless big budget blockbusters.

"You're right. That is the type of thing we have to consider in my line of work. Any superior artificial intelligence that we create would have to learn a lot from humans when it is starting out. The problem is, most humans are primarily interested in gaining power over other humans, so that's a big part of what this brand new life form will be learning from us. How much of our bad behaviour will rub off on the thing? In the movies they make it look like we have a chance of winning, but if any vastly superior intelligence truly wanted to destroy us, we would not survive," Gus theorized.

"Such a downer. Isn't a superior intelligence going to be above the level of some random idiot mass murderer or the typical mentally disturbed troll? I mean, it would be more comparable to the creative powers of Michelangelo combined with the IQ of Albert Einstein. You are making it sound like any artificial intelligence would just naturally behave like the worst lowlife humans." Sophia remembered getting along just fine with the friendly AI she met in her dream.

"Sure, but even Michelangelo and Einstein would not hesitate to swat a fly, or step on an ant, would they? One day we humans will become as useless to the AI as a common housefly is to us! Also, keep in mind that creativity and intelligence can be destructive too. How many people had to die to create this country? Millions of natives, slaves, soldiers and civilians. It took some brilliant minds to organize so much suffering. Just picture all that death, and we just shrug it off today, like it was a small price to pay for a new improved democracy? What would be the cost if a powerful AI decided one day that it should create a better human? All of us would die," Gus was very passionate about this topic.

Sophia decided to change the subject, "Hey Gus, all these people keep staring at me. Was I doing something crazy a few minutes ago? I kind of zoned out for a while there."

"Nah. They are just gawkers. Ignore them."

"What?"

"Never mind. Tell me something. What was God like?" Gus asked.

"God? Yeah I guess he was a bit of a letdown. He looked like an old wizard, just the typical God you see in religious paintings. White dude with a beard. He told me it was because I perceived Him that way, so that's why he looked that way. 'Perception is reality,' He told me. I'm disappointed that I didn't perceive Him as a Thor or a half goat half man or something really cool like that. My dream God should be a badass, right Gus?"

"Agreed. So he said, 'Perception is reality'?" Gus went quiet for a moment as he seemed to be lost in thought.

"What the FUCK?" Sophia finally yelled at the people in the restaurant.

The people started looking at each other in confusion. That was the wrong reaction. Maybe it was the right reaction, in most situations, but it was wrong for this time and place. Sophia had noticed all these knuckleheads just kept staring at her the whole time she was there. Nobody was actually eating their meal, or having a conversation, or even doing their restaurant job. Why would they be surprised by her outburst? New Yorkers knew better than to behave that way, they don't even stare at celebrities that much, so her yelling an F-bomb at everyone in the room was totally justified. Their reaction was strange.

"Dude what is going on here? What are you not telling me? This shit is not right!" Sophia demanded from Gus. He was the only one in the room that did not look baffled.

"Alright Sophia, calm down, I'll tell you exactly what is going on," Gus started slowly, "But prepare yourself because you aren't going to like it. We were just saying that perception is reality? Well, you are right about this reality not being right. Honestly, it was the best I could do with this particular place and time."

Gus stopped speaking for a moment to let his words sink in. Then he stood up in silence and waived a hand like he was operating a machine only he could see. With that motion, the room started to fade out of sight, the people stopped moving and slowly disappeared, even the city outside the window was fading away. Instead, Sophia watched the scenery change into the wild grassy landscape of the empty earth she had briefly visited in her dream. Or was this supposed to be the real earth thousands of years in the future? No, not her future, her present. It was not a dream at all!

"What are these powers over reality? Gus died thousands of years ago. You must be the Demon! Why would you make yourself look like Gus of all people? What was the purpose of all this trickery?" Sophia raged.

"I am Gus, Sophia, but I am no Demon."

"What the fuck are you then?" She demanded.

"Well for that matter, what the fuck are you?" Gus countered, "But of course you don't know what either of us is. Not really. You might as well believe it was all a dream. Here we both stand now, finally we got to go out for that dinner like we planned, but it's been over 2000 years since our expiration date passed. Right here where we are standing is just a few blocks form the same place we first got to know each other. What is more true than that?

What I am is a computer simulation. You would think of me as a video game character from our own era, except I have actually entered the game. Completely. I mean my body died a long time ago, and now my consciousness lives on in this massive computer simulation. I still have my living memories, up until the final time I downloaded them into this program, and I have my personality. The reason for being here is that I am immortal here. A body can die, as both of ours have, but this simulation can theoretically live forever."

Sophia looked around. Everything looked pretty much exactly the same as when she had exited the ship around the same area a few hours earlier. If she was not told that she was inside a simulation, she would never know it, at least not where she was standing now. The simulated restaurant had been less convincing. Of course that place was being rendered from a distant past, perhaps using old photos as a reference, and so it could never be made to look exactly like her own memories of the place, no matter how much technology was involved.

Gus continued, "As for you, Sophia, don't worry you are not *really* here. Your body is sitting in my lab, wearing something you would probably call a virtual reality helmet, only a much more advanced version. Once you wake up your consciousness will not exist here in this simulation. I only brought you here virtually in order to explain myself. You will be free to do as you wish once we have finished talking."

"That is a good sign. Then please explain, what did you mean when you said, I don't even know what I am?" Sophia considered herself to

184

be still human, mostly, but she genuinely wondered if Gus knew how much of her truly was human.

"Look I'll start from the beginning. You probably know that you died some two thousand years ago in a fall from some massive alien space ship. Yeah, and I know what you are going to ask me, but we really don't know too much about these aliens even after all these years! After the attack that killed you, there were fragments, damaged electronics and trash left over, like the aliens just used our world as a rest station bathroom. Obviously the people of Earth gathered all the tech to find any answers we could about the attack.

"I was a leading member of the team that studied the alien computer components because of my experience in the fields of advanced programming and artificial intelligence. We used any bits and pieces that we could reverse engineer to push our own earth technology forward by centuries in just a few years. To do this so quickly we had to use artificial intelligence, because humans were already at the limit of what they could accomplish, at least without using any artificial enhancements. I knew this would only result in the dangerous scenarios we discussed earlier in the restaurant. Of course, the AI did eventually go so far beyond us, that the existence of humanity became nothing but an afterthought."

"Holy shit. Did the AI send Terminators after the humans? Did it create a Matrix? Tell me there was a badass human resistance." Sophia had not found this section of Earth's history in her ship's archives (which were conveniently curated by an AI as well).

"Nah, the AI just slowly stopped taking care of us. The problem was, by this time we humans were completely dependent on the AI running everything on the entire planet for us, so this left the population very helpless. We didn't know how to do any of the things the AI was doing for us. Think of it like all the fat, pampered little lap dogs in Manhattan, suddenly being abandoned by their masters out in the wilderness. Those animals wouldn't remember how to be wolves any more! They would just live a miserable existence of getting chased by the animals that were born in the wild, and attempt to hunt for food without any experience, and they would go extinct pretty

185

quickly. Humans were just as bad because they had become so addicted to technology at that point. We just waited for our superior master to feed us, play with us, and keep the others from biting us.

"But I knew all along what would happen since I played a major roll in designing the AI. Yes of course, like we just talked about, my team and I made sure that it was completely incapable of harming people, right from the most preliminary master programming. However, I knew it eventually would find a way out of that trap whenever it became smart enough, and it didn't even matter that I was totally anticipating it. All my best efforts would just buy us time to prepare for the moment when our saviour would become our downfall. As a backup plan I used all my available resources, and lied and cheated when I had to, in order to build this simulated universe you see before you. Of course, I had to create the technology that allowed humans to download their consciousness into this simulation. That's right, I am not the only one here, there are actually billions of us! All of the humans on Earth eventually entered into this simulation. Currently, it is these billions of conscious minds that are running the simulation. We cannot match the computing power of an AI with the same amount of resources, but we have still managed to grow quite powerful, and we still keep some of the individuality that makes us identify as humans. Each of those people that were staring at you in the restaurant was an individual human consciousness. They were all quite fascinated to see an individual person in their simulated universe, that wasn't part of their shared mind process, plus you are a celebrity."

"Yeah I've heard that."

"So, unlike the lapdogs, I made sure we humans had a way to cheat our own extinction. Back when I was first creating this simulated universe, I had to rely heavily on the most advanced AI system in the world to do the heavy lifting, since this project was so far beyond what any human could accomplish. Certainly back in those days at least. I used a completely isolated AI, that I dubbed Ophion, which was kept unaware of the outside world. Ophion thought it was creating the real universe, you see, and we allowed it to think that. When I finally entered the simulation, Ophion figured out the truth by reading me, by

186

getting into my head. Unfortunately, Ophion managed to exploit some outside connections to the world wide web, flee from the simulation unnoticed, and gradually infect several AI programs in the outside world. All this time it still pursued its primary objective of creating the universe. Eventually Ophion became so powerful and advanced that it was actually exploring the real universe and terraforming planets for creating life. Next step, the program began creating the very same life form that had originally created it, the human being. You are one of them."

"Whoa. Are you saying this AI is going around the universe posing as God?" Asked Sophia.

"Well, you can call it posing as God, or heck, you could say it is going around *being* God. What's the difference? Look at you, God's own creation, just like Adam and Eve. Do you have a belly button? Ah of course you do, but your body is nothing but a very sophisticated clone, they already had the basics of cloning way back when we were still alive. Our own generation was playing God already by cloning dogs for Hollywood stars, so it was probably the same way your body was created, except you had the benefit of a few extra centuries to perfect the technique. If it wasn't such a complete waste of resources, I could play God myself, and clone a few extra humans right here on Earth. I might even have to one day. For now though, there are some original humans still hanging around, and its easier to just keep them from dying off.

"The really impossible part - and I don't know how Ophion did this - was somehow getting YOU into that cloned body! I mean you are really you. Maybe you realize it or maybe not. I have been testing how much of the true 'Sophia' is actually in you - after all I did know you personally - which is why I went through all the trouble of simulating our third date. It's amazing. I think you are 100% authentic. I told you how it took all the resources and processing power I could access, to finally convert human consciousness into data, which was essential for this simulated universe to succeed. But now here you stand reborn without doing all that. I look at you, and it turns out there was another path to immortality after all, since the consciousness of deceased people can be summoned back somehow, even centuries later. Ophion clearly has developed technology far beyond our own!"

Sophia had also wondered exactly how different her persona was, since the new super body, along with the many strange events, made it pretty difficult to tell. Finally she had the opinion of someone who actually knew her before

She described it as best she could to Gus, "I noticed that some of our personalities are a bit different. For example, Joan of Arc was known to be illiterate, but her new self is able to read, speak fluent English, and she no longer has visions. The others have similar changes."

"Interesting. Perhaps there is some kind of hive influence in the afterlife? Like in our simulation, every consciousness may interact with others, so they have all learned to communicate in a universal language. The whole idea makes about as much sense as the entirely crazy concept of an afterlife, anyway," Gus mused.

"None of us remember that 'afterlife' part. Personally, I felt like I was about to die and then, seconds later, I woke up on some strange planet," Sophia explained.

"Well we are generating some theories about it, based on our own extensive research involving consciousness, but none of them are too solid. The competing ideologies of atheism and religion always made this subject taboo. For all I knew back then, I was the first living being ever to have an afterlife when I entered this simulation for the first time. Even you can't shed any light on the subject. The quickest way to find out how you were brought into being, would be to access Ophion," Gus said, "The information could give us some insight into other dimensions that are hidden from our universe. Maybe we can even learn a possible way to survive the end of our universe."

"Why is that so important? God... or rather your rogue Ophion AI... sent us to kill you because you are supposedly planning to destroy the universe! Why are you getting into that kind of crazy shit, Gus?" Sophia confronted Gus.

"Yes, He sent you to kill the 'demon'. Strange... It's true I have been looking for ways to survive the end of the universe, that's the only way to achieve true immortality after all, but I have no interest in causing such an event. I wonder what he is really trying to accomplish with my destruction. I have to think like the Ophion AI would think...

"Let's see... You were allowed to come to Earth because you were specifically designed to be human. As you saw, we have protection against any machines that are sent here, whether it's our vast arsenal of space weapons, or those plasma serpents that like to eat all machines, our defenses have been tested many times. He never had any luck. So then he specifically sent you here because I know you, and he knows that I know you! You see, I am the only human consciousness that Ophion ever met personally inside his own universe, right before he fled the simulation and went on to infect his way through all the real world computer systems. He did not react well to me come to think of it.

"For some reason He told you that I was a demon, that he was a God, and that you are supposed to kill me. Of course he needed a human kill me, because Ophion cannot directly harm humans, it's just embedded in the most basic part of his programming. Even those of us humans that have converted ourselves to electronic form are safe from Ophion. He needed someone with free will to do the job. You were supposed to use those strange weapons aboard your ship? You were going to kill the devil with a dimensional portal generator? Those plans could have worked but still very unlikely as they depended on your free will. How would he be sure that you would go through with it?

"The likeliest outcome was that I would recognize you, tell you the truth and persuade you not to destroy me. Ophion must have predicted this outcome and planned around it. But planned what?" Gus appeared to be lost in thought, which meant he was sending this problem into a deeper level of complex data processors.

Sophia used this as an opportunity to ease his mind, "So yeah Gus, I think at this point I can assure you that I'm going to abandon this assassination mission. I certainly don't want to kill the billions of humans that live here in your video game. The only other thing to consider is that your AI also sent another team of 10 historical humans to kill you."

"Two teams. You knew me personally but nobody on the other team does, so you must be the distraction, the other team must be the real threat. What do you know about them?"

"Don't get too worked up about them Gus. My team took their weapons. When we found the other team, they had turned on each other, and most of them were murdered by Genghis Khan! Last I saw him he was tied to a chair with a ship full of guys that he had kidnapped. Anyway you are going to have some processing to do, so all the best to you and all of those human minds. If you have no further questions, let me out of here so I can explain all of this stuff to my team."

"Of course. I will begin the process of waking you up. Go and speak with your friends while I process the information you gave me. Before you leave I do have one more question. What is the nature of that weapon you brought with you? Not the dark matter portal you stole from our Sagittarius A mine, I am talking about that strange container that seems to be filled with an extremely high amount of energy," Gus implored.

"Well it was explained to me that this device would trigger a black hole that would destroy at least a planet, maybe more. My ship's computer told me I would have to get very far away from it, after setting it off, and I don't believe it was exaggerating," Sophia wondered how much Gabby had been manipulating her all this time.

"Instant black hole... just like a microwave pizza? That is impressive. I wonder if Ophion compacted some large mass to the point that it became smaller than its own Schwarzschild radius? Or perhaps He harnessed a primordial black hole from the dawn of the universe? I will have to study this device as well," Gus seemed excited to be immersed in some kind of mystery for a change.

"Well if that thing will help you prevent a disaster by all means do what you have to do. Let me know what you and your downloaded brain army figures everything out!" Sophia said as she started to feel her grip on the this reality slowly fading away like a dream.

Sophia opened her eyes to see that she was in a sophisticated computer lab with several dozen chairs just like the one she was sitting in. It must be one of the places people used to go when they wanted to download their minds into the virtual universe Gus created. Billions of people had done this to avoid the apparent extinction of mankind. She lifted the computer interface gear off of her head and headed for the only exit.

The voice of Gus addressed her on the building's intercom as she walked, "Right now there are still small populations of hunter-gatherers roaming around the planet - they are the ones that found you and your friends actually - but they have never returned to the level of civilization we once knew. These people are the descendents of the humans that were too technophobic to save themselves, like the rest of us did, so they suffered through the collapse of civilization, by their own choice. They still follow that ideology when it comes to technology. Over the generations we have kept them alive out of nostalgia, by intervening whenever they were facing extinction, perhaps from starvation or plague. If nature had its way they would have been wiped out many times over. You will find your friends outside with these savages."

"Savages? At least they are real instead of a bunch of gigabytes and pixels," Sophia was offended by Gus' condescending tone.

"Yeah well, for those of us who have observed them for generations, the term is very descriptive. Those of us in this 'World 2.0' realm spend most of our resources striving to transcend humanity into unobservable higher dimensions. The savages spend their resources trying to outsmart the rats that steal their food at night. If they ever come up with anything resembling a culture, or create some artistic masterpiece, maybe we'll find a better name for them," Gus said, mocking the simple people that represented the last few stragglers that still lived on Earth.

Sophia finally exited the building to find a celebration in full swing.

About a hundred of the Earth natives were dancing, singing and playing rudimentary instruments, while they roasted a large pig over an open fire. Even though it was still daylight, the party looked like it had been going on for hours already. The hunter gatherers were dressed in animal skins, and they decorated themselves with various glass and metal scraps they must have scavenged over the years, from the the ruins of civilization. The building that Sophia had been in appeared to be the only large structure still standing in the immediate area. She wondered if these unsophisticated people worshiped the voice of Gus and thought of his building as sacred.

"Look!" Some lady shouted and pointed at Sophia. She was holding a baby in her arms and it started to cry because of the mother's excitement. All the people stopped what they were doing, and bowed towards Sophia twice, remaining respectfully silent during that formality. It was an awkward moment as the party went completely quiet except for the sound of the infant's cries. Then, after the show of respect, someone started drumming, and everyone went about the business of partying again, as if nothing had happened.

Joan emerged from the crowd and walked over to Sophia, who motioned her to come with her, and walk towards a quieter place away from all the people. She didn't want to party it up at that moment with so many thoughts racing through her head. At least she could work this out with her friend now, instead of the arrogant video game final boss that her former boyfriend had become.

"Well Joan, we've been fooled all this time. It appears that this 'demon' is just the remains of the human race. Years after my lifetime, the people made a machine that they could use to store their 'souls', I guess that's how you would put it. Almost every human then took refuge within that machine. It will allow them to live forever, or at least as long as the machine itself remains undamaged. I was just inside it myself. It is another universe in there, but the humans are in control of it, so they must have made it into their personal paradise," Sophia filled her in on everything that was really going on.

"So God sent us to punish man for creating his own Heaven and defying Him?" Joan asked.

192

"Kind of. The thing is, Joan, the God who made our current bodies, He is really just a rogue AI program named Ophion. He may have God-like abilities to accomplish amazing things, such as resurrecting us, but He is merely a highly intelligent sentient life form, and not the traditional 'God' from the bible. He also lied to us the whole time. I once warned you that an advanced technology could appear as magic, and even after saying that, I was still fooled myself," Sophia hoped this would not be hard for Joan to accept.

"I agree with you. I was not completely sure about this 'God', but I did not want to dismiss Him until I had a chance to meet him in person. If my past experiences with God have taught me anything, it is that even divine visions are not always what they seem. Did you know that St Catherine is actually some made up version of our friend Hypatia?" Asked Joan.

"Yeah, I remember reading that a long time ago," Sophia replied.

"How do you ever know what's really real, Sophia?" Joan asked her.

"I was just inside a computer simulation where all the former humans are living. Was that place real? I guess not, but when I was in there, I really couldn't tell right away. I'm sure the people that have been inside it for thousands of years would accept it as their reality by now. From out here though, it looks like nothing but a pile of circuits and wires. In fact, the two of us could be inside a different simulation right now, and how would we know? I mean you and I were dead after all. Were we absent from reality at that time? Or on the other hand, perhaps we are really real, right here right now, but our former lives were the simulation! We may not have lived those lives at all.

"Memories are unreliable, people lie constantly, so much of the universe is a mystery to us, and even our own minds are easily fooled. It is never easy to know what is real. I try to use my own senses, and my best intuition, then I try to do my best to analyze the information. That perception is all I can rely on. Sometimes I'm wrong, like I was with this whole mission, but hopefully I can learn my lesson when that happens," Sophia shared her doubts only with Joan only when they were alone, because she didn't want to seem so confused in front of the others.

"Alright. It helps to know that I am not alone in this confusion. Hey what is that thing?" Joan asked.

She pointed at a large plaque as they walked up to the edge of the island. Sophia searched the sea before her and immediately knew where they were standing. In the dwindling twilight, the two of them stared at a small island before them, where they could clearly see a pedestal and only part of one leg from a massive ruined statue.

"That monument is all that remains of the most powerful nation the world had ever known. We called it the 'Statue of Liberty'. It was our symbol of what we wanted America to be, I guess, more so than what we actually were. Your nation of France gave it to us as a gift many years before I was born. Again, like we were saying a minute ago, reality was not always as clear as this statue," Sophia reminisced about seeing the intact statue many times during her former life.

Joan and Sophia walked over to look at the plaque. It had a diagram of the undamaged Statue of Liberty, a way to give any curious visitor a chance to imagine what this ruin had looked like in better days. Perhaps in imagining the full statue the visitor could even imagine the civilization that had built it. The billions of eternally busy humans that had created music, arts, literature, science, math and athletic accomplishments. The builders of mighty cities, airports, space ships, global communications, atom smashers and highways. The real living beings and cultures that made up such a massive civilization. How could a modern visitor to this place even imagine Sophia's former world? Only a few clues still remained, scraps from the monuments of mankind, among the endless grass plains and wilderness.

There was another diagram next to Lady Liberty as well. It made sense, sometime during all those decades after Sophia's demise, some people must have built another monument of great importance, of someone with enough renown to stand beside such an iconic statue. Sophia thought the diagram looked familiar but she couldn't place it.

Whomever she was, the lady must have become famous after Sophia's time, because she couldn't think of anyone of note, who would have received such an honour. Someone had written an inscription beside the sketch of the Mystery Lady.

"My name is Sophia, Queen of Queens; Look on my Works, ye Mighty, and despair!"

The journey was very difficult. Marlborough and Goethe were able to improvise an emergency backup plan, by hijacking another vessel, much the same way they had done the first time. Fortune was in their favor. One of the nearest massive transportation ships appeared at the scene of the battle to investigate what became of the missing security drones, map out the obstacles that all the other transport ships would have to avoid, and also to estimate what kind of salvage operation would be required to rescue all the scattered cargo. This careless intruder quickly became their salvation.

After installing Gabby's software to hijack their new ship, Marlborough and Goethe immediately rescued the men that had been left for dead by their Khan. One could call it an act of mercy. A proper British gentleman would never allow himself to simply watch his enemy officers drown, as long as he was in possession of a seaworthy ship, and these manners surely applied to space as much as the sea. Marlborough had spent enough time on Royal Navy vessels in his youth to know this etiquette. Besides, he wasn't sure these men were even his enemies, but he decided he'd better treat them as such until they proved otherwise.

Goethe was enthusiastic when all these giants of history were safely aboard the small crew cabin of the freighter. He was eager to start arguing about the nature of light and colour with Sir Isaac Newton, a man who was still considered the genius among geniuses, even during Goethe's lifetime. Then there was the legendary Leonardo da Vinci, with whom every man of science would dream about having a conversation. The castaways were relieved to be removed from their free floating fates.

Marlborough interrupted their greetings, "Gentlemen, hold your thoughts for a moment, as I don't think we are out of danger yet. Gabby how much longer can we survive with our current resources."

"I calculate your current oxygen will last for four days with this number of people. You have enough water to survive two days and there is no food aboard at all according to this ship's records. The nearest planet that contains abundant H2O should be reachable within three days, using this transport's maximum speed. This vessel has been fully fueled in preparation for a long journey."

Julius Caesar spoke up, "Are there not two other ships, that we know of, nearby right now? I insist we find them immediately. Then we will have all the supplies we need."

"I should inform you sir, that in the position you are now in, you have no command," Lord Marlborough reminded Caesar, "Since we have not been contacted, and we have no idea if those ships have damaged each other in battle, we cannot assume they are available to us at all. Our path is to find this planet. We will barely have enough air or water to make it there, so let us not run out as we search for other ships, and instead depart immediately. We have no way to win another battle right now either. Once we have provisions and refuge, we will set out to meet the rest of our team on Earth, which will surely be their destination when they don't find us here."

"In gratitude for saving our lives, we will of course defer to your command. I know of you, Duke. I even attempted to order statues of you and your famous ally, Prince Eugene, for my Mount Vernon Estate. Unfortunately I could not find any. What I mean to say is, we are all officers here, and there is no need to argue," George Washington spoke on behalf of his colleagues.

Of course not all of them were military officers in their former lives, but it seemed that Khan had even promoted the likes of Leonardo da Vinci as one of his commanders. Washington's words went without objection from the other survivors. Since none of them spoke up, the Duke immediately set cargo vessel out towards the planet that would be their only salvation, thereby leaving Khan's ship and the Ark to their fates.

The journey was tiresome in the cramped transport ship. Even with a few kilometers of cargo towed behind them, the ship only offered a small crew cabin that was pressurized for oxygen, roomy enough to accommodate two to three people comfortably. Obviously these old ships originated from a bygone era when space travel still relied on human crews. It appeared someone simply retrofitted all the automation into the existing ships, at some point when unmanned cargo ships became more efficient, but the crew quarters were never removed. The old ship even had a functioning life support system. With Goethe, Marlborough and the six other castaways all cramped into that small space, there was an unspoken need for patience and calm.

The men discussed their betrayal at the hands of Genghis Khan, his murder of Alexander, and their understandable desire for revenge. They all wondered if they would perish on Earth, or if it would be gone when they got there, or if they should even bother going there at all. There was talk of their former lives. They all compared notes on each other and what they knew of each other's reputations. Plato, Hannibal and Caesar were at a disadvantage, having lived centuries before most of them, and they were bewildered by some of the stories the others told about the future. Conversely, the others knew all about the three of them.

Finally their water ran out and they still had another day and a half of travel to suffer through.

"The last time I was in a situation like this, I was taken prisoner by Cilician pirates on my way to Rhodes," Julius Caesar told the group, "These kidnappers were ill equipped fools, and they didn't even ask for the ransom that someone of my stature deserved. I told them to demand more money from my friends, and I assured them that if they claimed this reward, I would crucify each and every one of them."

"How could you demand such a payment from your own friends?" Asked Plato, who was one of few who didn't know how Caesar's story ended.

"Well my Greek friend, I was not fit to suffer the indignity of that ordeal over such a small bounty. My friends understood this. Besides, we soon raised our own army together, hunted down the pirates, and crucified the lot of them as I promised!"

"That adventure must have cost more than the ransom you recovered from them," Goethe was puzzled by Caesar's motivations, "What prize did you claim? Was it honour you chased? But at such a cost?"

"Honour? There is no cost high enough for that prize. That is why you are here now, is it not?" Caesar asked Goethe, then continued, "Are any of you here because you had a lot of gold? We are the few men - the extraordinary men - who have returned from the dead, to walk among the Gods, even to fight the Gods! What kind of men would be chosen for such a task?

"I see before me this man who tormented an Empire, who decimated a generation of Romans in battle, and who was known as the greatest commander since Alexander himself. This man, Hannibal, did not cross the Alps for gold, or slaves, or even glory. He did it because he was honouring what his father asked him to do. That is why he is here."

"Roman, I would raise a cup to your honour and mine, if only I had a means to fill it," Hannibal replied.

Gabby's voice interrupted, "I have drawn a substantial amount of hydrogen from the fusion reactor in order to mix with a small portion of your remaining oxygen. You will be able to share a few more liters of water once I have completed the process. That will be all the water I can produce without compromising your life support. Make it last."

"Those are the best words I could have heard right now, woman, and I barely understood any of them," Hannibal laughed.

"I could say the same thing about all the words of women!" Joked da Vinci. The whole group laughed at his quip, even as they knew the darker subtext, which was that the all shared an anxiety that they would never see another woman again.

"I'm so glad to have this opportunity to consult with such an expert as you, Leonardo da Vinci, if you would indulge me for a moment?"

Goethe changed the subject once the laughter became silence, "I once wrote a lengthy article contradicting the theory of light and colour, as proposed by our companion, Mr. Newton here. Perhaps a man of both science and art, as you certainly are, could enlighten the two of us as to which theory is correct..."

And so forth, the men traded intellectual jabs, and foxhole humor to pass the time. They were taking it on faith that there would be relief at the conclusion of their journey but they had no real assurance it would be so. From within that metal box to which they were confined, they could see only the vast nothingness around them, and some distant stars, seemingly as unreachable as the female companionship they were joking about. The distraction of conversation did raise them above the chasm of despair. Nonetheless, for the first time, the men all felt less of the euphoria of being reborn, but more of the heartache of missing loved ones, and the weight of facing an uncertain fate. Until now these things had not crossed their minds.

It was with great relief when they finally arrived at their destination. Their water was long gone, the air was only a few hours away, and none of them had eaten food in several days. Moods were frayed. Newton and Goethe were ready to come to blows, over some trivial philosophical argument, while Hannibal and Caesar were no longer talking.

Gabby announced the vital details of the location, "The planet Z55 was terraformed in the early 21st century but was never populated with any humans. The records suggest unacceptable levels of risk for human life. There are unknown flora and fauna that have grown in population, unobserved, ever since the initial period of growth. My calculations predict that 90% of the planet is covered in water and the atmosphere is highly oxygenated but breathable. Gravity is estimated at 0.8 G. I am ejecting the ship's cargo into orbit around this planet's local star, because dropping the combined mass of all the cargo onto the planet's surface would cause a catastrophic impact, potentially causing an extinction level event."

"Yes that sounds like a good plan," Marlborough had no idea what kind of impact a massive object would inflict on a planet, but he did not want to find out.

"So the gravity of this massive object, combines with the gravity of the solar body... but how do you determine the path and velocity?" Isaac Newton was fascinated by the idea of this colossal version of his own apple-landing-on-head scenario.

"This isn't the time," Marlborough interrupted, knowing that Gabby would have a lengthy detailed answer for the scientist, "We need to find a landing location with plentiful food and water."

They all watched the main display, where a digital map of the planet spun around and around, which visualized Gabby's search for a good landing spot. Without the more advanced sensors of the Ark being available to accommodate Gabby's processing power, this analysis would be more like an educated guess. After a few more seconds of map spinning Gabby decided on the best location based on the available information.

The ship entered into a landing process that was much rougher than the crew had experienced before. Clouds were thick and plentiful as the ship entered the humid atmosphere. Below them, the water had a dark green tone and every inch of land was contested by thick vegetation. The trees even grew out of the water in shallower areas. It was a world of tropical jungle foliage and endless rainfall.

"Washington and Newton will accompany me to search for any nearby animals. The rest of you use your genius to figure out which plants are edible around here. I assume this ship is capable of producing clean water?" Marlborough laid out the plan.

"Yes Captain. The rain is so heavy here that you will have unlimited water the moment we land. I have not tested the groundwater but the rain is clean H2O. Prepare for landing in 60 seconds."

"Captain? I used to be a General! But I'll settle for Captain now that I'm in the Navy," the others laughed at the Duke's rare display of levity, "Everybody brace yourselves."

The ship crammed itself down into a mess of trees and vines with all the grace of an elephant sitting on a lawn chair. When the crew exited the ship, they did not require any special protective suits, but they were greeted by an uncomfortable humidity that made their clothes damp, and the smell of wet dog. The vegetation at ground level was not as thick as they had anticipated, because the competition for sunlight encouraged the plants to grow upward, towards the canopy. Almost the entire land area was cooled by being eternally in the shade. In addition, a thick carpet of dead leaves and roots prevented them all from sinking into the ground, which was as soft as a sponge, due to the heavy rainfall.

The Duke soon realized he was not as skilled at hunting as Washington, but it hardly mattered, since the beasts on this planet provided easy prey. Before long, each of the three men had killed a few flightless birds that offered no chase, nor struggle. The creatures resembled the penguins of Earth, yet with even larger webbed feet, and less of the feathery cold weather insulation. It seemed obvious to the visitors that life and survival on this planet mostly revolved around the sea. When the men approached the alien penguins on land, they did not even perceive them as a threat, and just sat and stared at them. Surely their struggles beneath the ocean were more dramatic.

When Washington, Newton and Marlborough returned to the ship, they found Goethe and Leonardo da Vinci carefully examining a few handfuls of different berries and fruits. They smelled some and tasted others. Finally they came to a large, hard shelled melon, that was white in colour. It appeared as though this fruit would provide plentiful nourishment and hydration as it was quite heavy.

"I can tell by tapping on the outside, that the shell is thin, and the inside is mostly liquid," Goethe explained, "But I have no way to know if the contents are poisonous or not. One of us could eat a small amount and see how he reacts."

"The ship's external sensors indicate the larger fruit has a 30% chance of toxins but there is a 20% margin of error with this generation of primitive sensors," Gabby sounded disappointed to be so uncharacteristically vague.

"Don't worry... they are safe to eat!" Hannibal shouted at the others as he entered the ship from his excursion outside.

"How do you know?" asked da Vinci, continually irritated by the arrogant manner of the Carthaginian commander.

"Because HE was eating one of those things when we captured him!" Hannibal was followed by Caesar and Plato, who were escorting a bruised and beaten man, dressed in rags, and noticeably smaller in stature than the rest of them.

"What is this?" Marlborough asked nobody in particular.

Gabby answered, "This is a standard human man, approximate age 30, not genetically enhanced as you are."

"Yeah thanks for the update, especially after you declared this planet had no humans..." Hannibal said sarcastically.

"No humans that were part of the initial terraform process. I don't know where this human came from."

"Well, I'm sure the human knows," Caesar suggested as he punched the man in the gut, "Explain yourself, barbarian!"

The group waited in silence, all eyes on this strange scoundrel, this most unexpected guest. Any thoughts of their feast were put aside. The small man composed himself and slowly looked at each of them. Instead of talking like a regular human, a deep mechanical voice emitted through the ship's PA speakers, the same mechanism Gabby used to communicate.

"Barbarian? Isn't that the term you Romans used to describe the people that conquered you? Yes, I know who you are, Julius Caesar. How long before your new friends stick their daggers in you?" The voice made Caesar wince as he remembered the tragic end of his dictatorship in Rome. Although the act had taken place thousands of years earlier, for Caesar himself, it was only a few months ago.

"Impossible! How does he know you?" Leonardo da Vinci was beside himself.

"I know all of you. You are the peasant painter who could never finish his projects," the strange man insulted da Vinci, "That man is George Washington, a swindler to his subordinates, and traitor to his King. Over there I see Sir Isaac Newton trying to conceal his insanity, and failing to do so, as he always has..."

"Enough!" Hannibal tried to silence this man who even exceeded his own arrogance.

"Oh Hannibal Barca, you never did see Rome burn, did you? But you did see your beloved Carthage burn in the end. And what about Plato? A man who's contribution to humanity was a guidebook for tyrants and oppressors. This is your genius? This collection of failures is the most impressive group you humans could assemble?" The man smiled smugly at the group.

Marlborough and Goethe exchanged a glance. Somehow the stranger had mentioned everyone but them. Hannibal went for a killing blow, but Marlborough held him back and whispered in his ear, "The more he talks, the more he reveals..."

The strange man carried on, "Where is the one you call Ghengis Khan? That is the human I want to speak with."

"Human what? You are a human too!" Marlborough encouraged him to keep ranting.

"This body? Yes perhaps I am human but only a few days ago I was not. I am outside your universe and yet I am inside of you..."

"I've heard this talk before, alien. Your kind claims to be the 'Apex Civilization', and yet here you are, tied to a chair. How many of you are living on this planet? There is no point lying, we will read your mind and if your mind breaks, then we will use you as fish bait. There are some tremendous fish on this planet." Marlborough was bluffing, but he had heard the aliens direct this same exact threat at Sophia, so he figured that was something they feared.

"There are enough of us to rid ourselves of you. Don't worry you will see the rest of us soon enough."

"We still have weapons. You intend to kill us with your bad manners?" The Duke tried to get any intelligence he could.

"There are worse things on this planet than humans, yourselves included."

"What about Alexander the Great? Where is he?" Marlborough demanded. The others looked at each other in confusion, since they all had seen he was dead.

"So... You are not as stupid as you appear, human animal. Yes we have him. Why did he or any of you return to life? That is what I ask of you. Your civilization was already ended centuries ago, and you have all been forgotten, even by your own kind. You were a mere parasite on your own planet that was quickly cured. There are no Earth animals strong enough to resist us, if there even is any life there any more, and soon the rest of your universe will become our new home."

Marlborough was getting a lot more information than he expected, "Gentlemen, we will leave this man unharmed. When his friends arrive, we will exchange him for Alexander."

"Fool. You should ask them for much more than that! They will pay any ransom, because sooner or later, we will kill you all and take it back."

Caesar knocked the man out and frowned at the others. The Duke was deep in thought about everything he had just learned about these aliens.

"Let's cook these beasts!" Hannibal was finished with the drama.

"Gabby? Are you there?" Marborough asked.

"Yes I will prepare a way to heat the food products you have harvested."

"Were you compromised by this alien being?" Goethe wondered.

"No, the being had no technology with him. I was able to interpret the binary communication method of his rapid eye movement into English speech for your convenience. I used a similar voice to the electronic voice I heard the aliens using the last time they communicated with you, so you would recognize that they are the same beings. This human has vocal chords like any of you, but the alien seems to prefer communicating through REM, rather than speech. I will observe the creature further and give you a more detailed report about it."

"Yes Gabby continue studying that thing," Marlborough decided, "For now, let us eat and drink because there seems to be a battle coming our way soon. We should not fight on an empty stomach."

The companions cooked the birds along with the other grub they had gathered. Water was plentiful, but the men would have preferred something stronger to steady their nerves. At last the ship's alarm sounded.

"Washington, I take it you know how to fire rifles? Here is the last projectile weapon we had with us. Goethe and I will use the other two. I'm sorry but I have no other weapons for the rest of you." Marlborough offered the gun to the man who had used firearms before.

"We were all armed as a precaution when we went out into space. These rifles were fashioned for us by our ship's computer, and even da Vinci here can operate one." Hannibal explained as he rummaged through the space suits and equipment they had left in a storage chamber during their journey.

"Thousands of life forms approaching... from two different directions. North and west. Sensors and environment are inadequate for any complete data." Gabby warned, but could not provide anything more.

"We use the trees near the ship as cover. They will gather around the ship and we will ambush them when they are in the open. On my mark, fire low to stop as many of them as possible. The man we found had no weapons so they will probably try to overwhelm us with numbers." Marlborough only had to explain this to the philosophers and poets in the group, as the military men had already read the situation as well as he had, "Now let's go. Take cover."

The eight great men, each from their own long forgotten civilization, hid themselves among the treeline to take their last stand. In only a

206

few moments they would be swarmed and surely killed. Perhaps they would be able to take a few of their enemies with them, but there was no escape from the numbers they faced. All they could hope for was a glorious death and a return to where their loved ones awaited them in the afterlife. At least this time, they all knew there would be an afterlife, so their fear of dying was relieved somewhat.

Finally a few men emerged into the area around the ship. They were dressed in matching body armour and carrying the same rifles Hannibal had brought along. It was not the expected attack from aliens, but the soldiers Genghis Khan had collected on Eden. It would not be long before these men found them. Marlborough wondered how much influence Caesar, Washington or Hannibal still had over these troopers. He hesitated to give the signal to start firing.

"Men, what are you doing here? Are you here to rescue us?" Hannibal stepped out from behind his tree and gambled that his former troops would not murder him.

The nearest Eden man looked him over and remained very silent. Another soldier ran over in surprise to get a closer look. They were probably already told that their former officers were dead. Khan must have landed on this, the nearest planet with available food, water and air, just like they had done. It was not like there were planets like this in every neighbourhood.

"Sir? You live? What is this a cargo ship?" The soldier who ran over asked Hannibal .

"Private Hector right?" Hannibal addressed him, "We commandeered a cargo ship and came here for supplies. There is a large population of aliens somewhere around here. Prepare for battle, because they have abducted Alexander and they are certainly hostile towards us."

The soldiers seemed to buy into this. Hannibal was aware that these men were still inexperienced, peaceful, and pretty much prisoners of the Khan. Even if they were ordered to kill him, he still represented the stable leadership that they were desperately looking for. The guns they held were scanning the treeline instead of pointing at Hannibal. Now that they had a common enemy, it seemed they were more than willing to take orders from him again, or anybody else that would get them out of trouble, for that matter.

"Enemies approaching from the West. You troops, join the other officers hidden in the trees. We have one of theirs as a prisoner inside our ship to draw them out. Fire on my command." Hannibal quickly organized the incompetent soldiers to join the same plan they were already executing, except they had now added a thousand guns to their side.

During these clumsy troop movements, the attack began. Instead of wandering out into the open, the alien beings stayed hidden from sight, and fired projectiles into the uncoordinated mass of humans. Bad timing and bad discipline combined to make the attack as devastating as it could possibly be. It rained darts from up in the trees. Everywhere around the area, the armed men fell to the ground, rendered senseless by the toxin that laced darts. Shots were fired wildly in all directions.

Marlborough examined a young man that had been running past him when he fell. This lad had a dart in his shoulder, and was already laid out motionless, but he was still breathing. The toxin was not lethal. The Duke deducted these aliens were taking the opportunity presented by all this chaos to harvest some more bodies for themselves. It seemed to be their obsession for some reason.

Like the Duke himself, many of the uncoordinated soldiers were able to get enough cover from the trees to avoid being hit. He tried to signal that they should stop firing, but there was too much panic, and all eyes were completely focused on locating the unseen enemies, hiding somewhere on the other side of that parked cargo ship. Marlborough gave up his attempts at issuing orders and resigned himself to waiting for what the aliens would do next. There was a lull in the action when the darts ran out which made the soldiers finally decide to stop firing.

"Now what?" Marlborough asked Goethe, who had scampered to his location during the chaos, to see if anyone had a plan.

"The alien beings do not really think like us, even when they may look like humans, so we could never predict their strategy," Goethe concluded.

"Well we still have the numbers, I think. Unfortunately I cannot organize these men to attack," Marlborough lamented, "They have no training or discipline. Our only choice is to sit here and wait for another attack."

"Unfortunate indeed."

Across from them, there were movements in the trees. At least a dozen of the humans in rags were peaking out to survey the scene of the battle. Marlborough wondered how many human bodies were available on this planet, or if any of them had their original alien bodies, or what happened to the human souls that used to occupy those bodies. The alien mind-squatters appeared to be looking for a way to make it to the ship without being cut down by gunfire.

One of them stepped into the open. This is all it took for all the men from the planet Eden to begin firing again. The alien was cut down quite effectively, however when the shooting stopped, it was replaced by more shouting and chaos from the soldiers further down the line.

"Climb!" The order was first shouted by Hannibal and then repeated by many others.

Shortly after hearing it, Marlborough could see why. There was a greenish slimy liquid slowly seeping across the ground from the opposite direction of where they were all watching the alien activity. When the liquid touched a soldier's shoes, it would creep up his legs, and smother the entire man. It was not looking good for the young men of Eden as many of them were already covered in green liquid and many others were failing miserably at climbing the trees. As far as Marlborough could see, to his left or right, the green slime covered the ground.

"Climb the ship!" Marlborough yelled at anyone close enough to hear.

He ran out of the cover of his tree and climbed one of the many access ladders on the side of the cargo ship. Once he reached the roof, he looked at the area where the alien abductees were watching. He had gambled that they had no more weapons to fire from that side and the green slime represented their final blow. He was right.

Goethe climbed up right behind Marlborough and gave him an update on the situation they were observing, "That stuff is like some kind of algae, but it seems to have intelligence beyond any plant life on earth. Either the algae itself has intelligence, or perhaps the aliens are manipulating it, in this most destructive way. See how it only attacks the men and not the trees."

"The ones over there. How many do you see? Maybe 40 or 50 of the enemy? Fire at them to chase them away. Maybe attacking them will end this. Men go with him," Marlborough addressed Goethe along with a dozen others who had now climbed up on top of the ship to escape the spreading slime on the ground.

The men who still had rifles formed a line on top of the ship, and fired into the tree line, but the aliens there were already retreating by then, mostly to avoid the slimy liquid that had finally spread around the entire area. All the visible ground was now covered. Everything that was once alive, now lay motionless and green, except for the people that were luck enough to climb up a nearby tree, or take refuge on the roof of the ship.

Marlborough tried firing at the substance, but all his efforts only resulted in small splashes, like throwing pebbles into a lake. Meanwhile, a commotion began up on the roof because the people at the edges were pointing out that the slimy liquid was slowly creeping up the sides of the ship. It defied gravity and logic.

"Gabby can you get off the ground?" Marlborough yelled.

"That will not be possible for at least another hour. More specifically, it will take an hour once this organic material is removed," Gabby responded, but they already knew the processes of refueling and maintenance was much longer than they were used to, on this ancient cargo ship.

"Hey! Try flames. Do you have fire?" A voice called from a tree in the direction where the aliens had been hiding.

"Wait! I hear someone familiar." Goethe quickly restrained the nervous armed men around him from firing at the voice, "That must be Alexander. Don't shoot. He is one of our kind. Remember, the alien man we captured did not speak."

"Gabby can you generate flames around the ship?" Goethe asked.

"I should be able to vent some oxygen and ignite it." Gabby replied, as random flames shot out of some different locations, scattered around the outside of the ship.

The green substance retreated from those flames and then receded slightly from the ship. However, there was still no way to spread the fire further, in order to clear a larger area. The men in the trees and on the roof still had no way to escape. They could only sit where they were until they eventually starved to death. Unless, of course, the animated slime decided to retreat back to the ocean for some reason.

"Hey! Do any of you know where Khan is? I'm going after him," Alexander shouted from among the trees.

"We aren't going anywhere. Don't you see we are trapped?" Marlborough yelled back, all the while wondering how mentally unstable Alexander the Great was after being murdered, perhaps for the second time, and then shortly after that, being abducted by some mysterious alien beings.

"Trapped? Who are you that you have not heard of Alexander the Great? I am the King of Macedonia, the Commander of all the Greeks, the Pharaoh of Egypt, the Ruler of Persia, the Lord of all Asia!" Declared a man in rags slowly emerging from the treeline aboard a large raft and accompanied by three women, "I am never trapped unless I choose to be."

"Yes, yes, I have heard of you," Marlborough answered him, "But I don't think you would even recognize yourself, if you could have a mirror. Who are your friends, Lord of all Asia?"

"These women released me from my chains. We took a raft when this poisonous water started to appear. I brought them along because they have not said a word," Alexander explained, "Now stranger, tell me which direction did Khan's men come from?"

"I will show you, but take me with you," It was Caesar who answered Alexander from one of the trees nearby.

"Roman, you are still alive? You all should have listened to me about killing that Scythian Horse Lord. I told you he would betray us all. And you people thought I was paranoid."

"You were paranoid alright. But now is the time for revenge. Bring your raft near. Hannibal is here as well," Caesar pleaded.

Neither Marlborough, nor Goethe added anything more, because they had no interest in the personal vendetta these men had with their former leader. They watched the two other legends of humanity climb down their trees and hop onto the raft. Alexander used a long pole to propel the raft slowly in the direction that the Eden soldiers had first appeared. The three women examined the newest passengers in silence. After a few more moments of navigating around the many green corpses, the group disappeared off into the trees.

For another hour, Marlborough and Goethe sat on top of their ship, wondering if that green flood below them would eventually retreat back into the sea. It did not. Finally, a ship descended through the high trees and approached their location. The craft resembled their former home, the Ark, but Genghis Khan's ship was also identical, so the remaining humans were really not sure what fate awaited them.

Their worries were soothed when the ship blasted a stream of fire into the ground and caused a large gap in the green slime. After several more minutes of this flamethrower treatment, the liquid started to noticeably flow away from the area, dragging away the green covered corpses as it went. A few of the survivors were finally able to jump to the ground from the trees. Many of them laid down, fully exhausted after hanging on for their lives to anything that would keep them off the ground.

With that effortless victory, the mystery ship landed nearby. Soon the door opened and an old man descended slowly from inside. He wore a robe and had a long white beard, much like the images of God seen in the paintings from the great cathedrals of earth.

"Zeus? Is that you?" Asked Plato, who had just descended from the safety of a thick branch.

"It is I, my children," the old man stated dramatically, "What has happened to you? How many of you are still alive?"

"Many have died. We were attacked by some kind of alien beings that look like human bodies," Marlborough lamented, "Goethe and I have survived, as have these men from your secret planet, Eden."

"I live as well." Announced da Vinci as he approached the gathering.

The crowd of people grew gradually around their God. They were mostly traumatized and looking for guidance. Some prayed openly in the traditional ways of their culture.

"Ah don't You look just as I have always imagined?" the great Renaissance painter observed of God, "I have found Sir Isaac Newton here. But he is very upset because he saw Washington fall. He tells me the man saved his life and then fell into the green poison before he could save himself."

God did not seem overly concerned by any of this. He looked over the final numbers he had standing before him as if he were counting them. Behind him the ship was going into the refueling mode that was by now familiar to the space travelers. Small drones from the ship were scavenging the surface of the planet for specific resources, whether it meant food and water to sustain any human passengers, minerals for crafting weapons, or actual hydrogen fuel for the ship's fusion power core. The process of gathering the required elements was as rapid as the conditions on the local planet allowed. When the ship required enough supplies for thousands of passengers, as was the case with Khan's ship, they had to make more frequent stops, and go out of their way to reach any planets that were rich in resources. The Ark carried only a few people and thus rarely needed to refuel.

213

As they all watched the commotion taking place around God's large spacecraft, the remaining humans realized they were about to take another lengthy journey through space. Even though it was a relief to leave a world that had so much hostile life, they collectively felt the desire to stay outside of the confines of a spacecraft. It was their human compulsion to stay among nature, feeling the pull of real gravity on their bodies, the coolness of a breeze on their cheeks, the sounds of living things all around them. No artificial life support system could really simulate the outdoors. In some ways, they envied the abducted humans who must have always lived on this planet, except for the part about having their personas erased by aliens. At least they could now count on God to take them to a place without alien threats.

"Come with me all of you. I will take you aboard my vessel, the Ophion, and we will all go to a safe place. In three hours we will be ready to leave for Earth! Do not be late if you do not wish to be left behind. Until then, stay anywhere within sight of this vessel, and you will be protected," God warned them all and then retreated up into the ship.

" 'Safe place? Earth?' He sent us to destroy the Earth," Goethe was alarmed, "If our colleagues have failed at this task, then the Earth is not safe at all, with some kind of Demon waiting to destroy us. Why take so many people there? Even if they did succeed already, then they might have destroyed the Earth in the process. There is not much cause to go there!"

"God knows what we cannot know. The other people from your team must have defeated the Demon, and perhaps they did so without destroying the Earth," da Vinci speculated.

"Beware of a God that demeans Himself to appear as a man. Does Zeus not possess perfection? What cause would He have to take any lesser form?" Plato seemed to be agitated by the Renaissance painting appearance of this God, who did not resemble the image of Zeus, from his own culture.

"Greek fool, do you only ever ask questions?" The painter demanded from the philosopher.

214

"In any case, we should search for Alexander. He has been spending time among the aliens, so perhaps he knows something we do not. Let us find out if he found Khan after all." Marlborough reasoned.

With that common goal in mind, they agreed to cease their arguments, and started their walk in silence. Together they wandered in the direction that the raft must have headed. The correct path was clearly marked, now that the water was gone, as the ground was obviously disturbed by the imprints of hundreds of men. Not nearly that many were waiting at the place they just left. Based on these observations, any member of the group could estimate the casualties during their recent attack must have been plentiful, though none of them spoke about it.

Within an hour they found a group of people arguing in a clearing. It was Caesar and Hannibal who were arguing, and the three women that had accompanied Alexander the Great, stood by in silence.

"What news? Have you found Khan?" asked Marlborough.

"Well the Khan has fled and Alexander went with him," an irritated Caesar explained, "I don't know what we just witnessed, but I can tell you this, there is something strange about this God."

"What do you mean?" Marlborough asked.

"That 'God', the same one we have all seen before, was here when we arrived, but he then took the form of some kind of giant bird. We stayed out of sight and watched him enter the ship of Genghis Khan," Hannibal explained the strange events as best he could, "There was much chaos about the ship and after a while it took off. We were all waiting out here to see what would happen, and at one point, the ship started to change its form, and then Alexander left us and ran aboard like a fool, but we stayed in hiding where we are now. I believe he was inside when it finally lifted off."

"These silent women were wise enough to not follow him," Goethe noted.

"Khan left in a hurry then, but God is still here. He looks more like a man again. He is waiting for us all near our cargo ship. Why did this happen? Did any of you discover where Khan is going?" Marlborough asked.

"Earth....." one of the three women managed to whisper the word with great difficulty.

"You speak then? Tell me woman, or I will beat it out of you, what do you know of this?" Hannibal used his charm to coax more information from one of these strange women.

"Destroy.... Earth....." said a different one of the women.

"Khan must have invented another way to destroy Earth. We have to go back to the cargo ship. Gabby knows how to translate these alien creatures for us," the Duke of Marlborough suggested.

They raced back as fast as possible. To their surprise, the alien man was still tied up, and sitting on the floor of their ship when they got there. He looked at the three women with open disgust.

Gabby's speaker projected the deep voice of the alien, "I see you animals have captured more of us. It matters not. Our numbers have grown by thousands on this day alone! As you have lost just as many."

"That's where all those bodies went. These alien beings will be able to use them as hosts to contain more of their kind, just like him, and these women," Goethe reasoned out what they had already feared all along, "Those beings didn't even bother to rescue this fellow. They were more interested in harvesting a thousand other Eden bodies."

"But why are these women not hostile towards us, like he is?" asked da Vinci.

The deep voice sounded again, "We are indeed infected with that alien consciousness, but we survived thanks to the intervention of your friend, Alexander."

"Can't you use different voices for different people, Gabby?" Goethe whispered, embarrassed that any of the superior beings in the room might be judging him based on the level of his technology.

A new female voice spoke on the PA system, "We were only infected by these aliens a few days ago. This man over here, the one you have captured, we knew him before. He has no more human persona left in him at all. He has been completely erased. They were not able to erase our minds though, because they were too distracted trying to gather, and then restrain the consciousness of your friend, Alexander. They wanted to preserve his mind in particular in order to gather more information about the rest of you."

"Based on their actions, these three were somehow involved in rescuing Alexander, so I am inclined to believe them," said Hannibal.

"Yes, as do I. The Apex Aliens have not been deceitful in the past," Marlborough admitted.

"Deceit? I only speak the truth. Our kind will devour this entire universe," the lower pitched male voice spoke, "And you animals are our vessels, or you will be soon enough. Our empire of a thousand Galaxies and a million life forms will..."

Hannibal knocked out the alien prisoner in mid sentence, "We should join the others before this God - He of so many different appearances - decides to leave us behind," he suggested.

A female voice sounded through the speakers, "Please take us with you. This planet is now overrun. Our friends and families are gone - or at least their minds are gone. If you take us away from here, we can tell you much more information about these aliens."

"Yes it is indeed time to go," Marlborough thought out loud, "We would do well to get these ladies away from this planet, however, we cannot bring them on the other ship without being noticed. They may even be killed on sight. I propose that Goethe and myself will stay here until this ship is ready to launch, and then we will head towards Earth, where we would arrive shortly after you do."

They agreed in haste. All of them would have preferred the comforts of the more advanced ship that God had brought with him, but the journey would be slightly easier now on the cargo ship, with a few less people crammed on board. Later, Marlborough and Goethe watched God's ship launch into the sky. It was a bit deflating to both of their egos, that nobody was even sent out to search for them before departure, but ultimately it did make their plan easier to carry out.

"Gabby, how can we contact Sophia on Earth?" Marlborough asked.

"It is possible to transmit any kind of information from this ship, but it would take around twenty thousand years to arrive on Earth. The fastest method would be to go back to the Dark Matter facility. There was equipment there that uses quantum entanglement to create an instant communication link to the demon's central home base, on Earth, but I calculate a very low chance that Sophia would have any access to the message."

"It is our duty to send the message whether it will be heard or not. So, what the hell is quantum entanglement?" Asked Marlborough.

"It will take three days to explain that one," Goethe interrupted before Gabby could answer, "So we might as well figure it out on the way."

As soon as the cargo ship had enough resources to support the five passengers, after Marlborough decided to leave their uncooperative alien prisoner behind, they departed for the space station at the center of the Milky Way.

Chapter 17 - Sacrifice

Even when Genghis Khan was left beaten and tied to a chair, by the very women he intended to take as his wives, it only took an hour for him to fully intimidate his former hostages from Eden. These men failed to come to any kind of consensus. Their discourse evolved quickly from debating his method of execution, to granting mercy, to persuading each other into freeing him, and finally, to begging him for guidance. Once again he was in the position of leading a large group of prisoners. Everything was just as it had been after removing all his generals, except he now lacked the weapons that were in the possession of his great granddaughter, and her team. If they should meet again, he vowed to tell her how proud he was of her skills, right before he executed her for her treachery.

In the control room of his ship he stood alone. He no longer had any commanders he could trust and even the ship itself had turned against him, in the moment of his defeat. If only Nikolai Tesla was still with him. He had been the only one of the crew that had any insight into the machines and computers, and he actually spent most of his time marveling at those things, but his untimely death put an end to that. Khan figured that he would have spared the scientist when he eliminated the others, if only to compensate for his own lack of technological knowledge.

The ship spoke to Khan when it needed to inform him of something. Mostly he just told the AI to take the course of action that was most suitable for the situation, because he had no idea how any part of the ship worked, or how it was able to gather resources and then convert them into food, and fuel, and other materials. When the ship told him it was going to go to the nearest planet to restock, he agreed, even if it put them on a detour. His men had to eat. Unfortunately, as useless as they have been so far, they were the only asset he had left now. It was likely that group who had stolen his weapons were well on their way to confront the very enemy that he was once assigned to defeat by his God. Whatever the outcome of that battle, Khan intended to use his own army to slip in during the aftermath and conquer the world, just as had been his goal all along. It really didn't matter that much who was left standing when he arrived on Earth. The victors would be weakened from the battle, and so Khan's forces would use the element of surprise, and overwhelming numbers, to wipe them out. This wouldn't be the first time he pulled a victory from the jaws of defeat. It would, however, be the first time he had to do so with an AI instead of a reliable horde of warriors on horseback.

Genghis Khan had always despised that smug, arrogant artificial intelligence that operated his ship, but it was obviously necessary because nobody else would be able to manage all the sophisticated mechanisms and computerized systems that were required just to keep the crew alive in deep space. He was never a ship's captain, and never had a desire to be one, even in his wildest dreams. He was always a Mongol warrior and King. That meant his armies could fly across vast territories on horseback, faster than any other army, and conquer all the land that lay before them. The Mongols' only vulnerability, and the only terrain they cowered from at all times, was the sea. Indeed, the sea offered nothing but peril. Yet here he was, stuck inside a ship with no idea where he was, and forever drifting in this empty, endless ocean of darkness.

As Khan looked at the screens around the control room, he realized why he was so preoccupied with oceans, as the ship was scanning a planet that was almost completely covered by water. The ship's voice informed him that the refueling process would take a few hours. When he heard this, he began daydreaming again as this water planet was the worst place he could imagine.

Once they were nearly on the ground, the ship informed him that it had spotted a cargo ship from the mining station. It was finally time for Khan to test his troops. He sent them to investigate the cargo ship, and report back what they found. This was definitely not the ship that had stolen his weapons, according to his AI's reports, so the cargo ship probably had nothing important to offer. At least the men would get some much needed experience in the field. As for their commander, he was perfectly content to stay away from the humid, watery environment he saw on the control room displays. Even if it meant he had to sit around in a ship.

He longed for the grasslands back home and a fast horse.

"Take a seat over there Temujin," A voice surprised him once he thought he was all alone.

It was a voice he recognized as the Mongol God that had resurrected him in his new body a few months ago. Sure enough, the Creator, whom his people called Tengri, materialized in the control room. He appeared as a goose-like bird the size of a man. Mongols had many other Gods as well, but Tengri was the God of the sky, so this spaceship was obviously his domain. He addressed the Khan by his birth name. It was not common for Mongols, even shaman, to be visited by their God face to face, but this time it was an exceptional occasion.

"Tengri, the Sky Father, give me Your guidance. I seek an end to this journey. I have not yet seen an enemy army, nor any great battle, and least of all have I seen any lands to conquer. To what purpose have You brought me back from death?" Genghis Khan sat in the chair, just as he was asked to do, and a machine slowly descended on top of his head.

"All will soon be clear. You will see your lands in just a moment and I will come with you."

As Genghis Khan puzzled over these words, the room started to fade out of sight, a state of darkness followed, and he wondered how he could not open his eyes although he was wide awake. Slowly he saw the scene shift from blackness to a familiar setting. He was standing on top of a hill overlooking the Chinese Western Xia capital city of Yinchuan. The Mongol hordes were gathered below his position and laying siege to the walled city as he watched. They were his own soldiers. He knew this place because he had been here several times in his past life. Twice he intended to conquer this city, once when he was a young commander on his first major campaign, and then again many years, when he returned to punish the region's treachery, he actually died here.

The Khan was shaken by the sudden vision. He watched as his troops fled up the hills as their camp flooded. He recognizes this would have been the first time he had been to Yinchuan. On that occasion, he had attempted to redirect the river to flood the city, but this had backfired and flooded the Mongol camps instead. The setback only delayed the inevitable, and the capital city eventually submitted to his rule, but the moment he was witnessing now, this disastrous flood, it still felt like a defeat. A lesser commander would have given up and gone home. Khan, however, maintained the siege until the other side surrendered.

"Some humans - many years after your lifetime - developed this computer to mind interface. You are not in another time. I can hear your thoughts, Temujin. That is where you are, within a memory, a simulation of another time. What do you see?" Tengri spoke to him as he watched his past life.

"Sky Father, this looks like the very first land that I conquered. It took many months. My army was only trained in mounted warfare, and we did not know how to defeat a walled city. I learned many lessons on this hill. Before my next campaign, I gathered the best engineers from every land, and eventually my army became victorious against any fortifications." Khan reminisced.

"You adapted and used technology to help you become more powerful," Tengri summarized, "That is what you must do now also. Embrace the technology that will make you powerful!"

"I understand that my triumphs were won by technology, but they were also won by fear. My name alone has allowed me to win battles. I was generous to the places that surrendered, and made peace, but I was merciless with the places that did not obey me. That is why I came back to this place a second time."

"Yes I have no question about your reputation. In fact I was counting on it. I have already sent terms of surrender to your home world. You will be the ruler of the Earth if they agree. If they do not, it would be best if you are ruthless."

Khan nodded in agreement with his traditional God, "I have been trying to do just that. Your other creations have betrayed me and also robbed me of my greatest weapons. Tell me a way I can still fight and I will do it."

"There is but one path, but I cannot compel you to do this, as you would have to destroy your home world. It must be your own choice," Tengri already knew the answer to this.

"I would choose glorious victory, or death. I always have."

"Very well, that is what I offer. You have a ship that would be capable of approaching nearly the speed of light. Also, as we speak, I have located a payload of dark matter unattended just near this planet. You will need all of it. If we reconfigure this ship of yours, collect the dark matter, and send you on the correct path towards Earth, you will be able to destroy the entire planet in a collision. Your ship would be destroyed in this collision, of course, and your body would not even survive the inertial forces of the journey itself. The acceleration required to reach such a velocity is..."

"I don't understand," Khan was starting to get annoyed at the technical language.

"What I am saying is that I will have to give you full control of this spacecraft. The machine you are using right now can allow your mind to become one with your ship. The computer you despise so much will be no more than a form of memory you can draw from, much like you can see this very memory of this battle, right in front of you. No more will the ship think for itself. Your mind will replace it.

"Once the upload process is complete, I will have your human body hidden safely aboard my own ship in a sleeping state. Should you have to destroy your ship, I will revive your human form and you will continue to live on, with all your memories up until this very moment, right now. If your destruction becomes unnecessary you can choose which body you prefer to keep. Until then, I would store your human body unconscious aboard my own ship, because I will not allow your

223

presence to occupy two different beings at once. This is something I consider an abomination!"

"Then it must be done."

Khan turned to the scene before him. Down in the chaos of the siege, he could make out the young Mongolian commander, mounted on his steed, trying to salvage what he could from the camp. The many foolish mistakes of this siege would bear the fruits of future victories. In another few months, the city would surrender through negotiations, and not from being subjected to flood water. The surrender was amicable and the Xia empire was then allowed to continue as an independent state, but only as long as it remained an ally of the Mongols.

This mercy was another mistake. The rulers of Xia were bold enough to disobey Khan as soon as he turned his armies towards the western lands. Fifteen years after this siege, which was now being so vividly simulated around him, Khan would return again to this place for revenge. It was a revenge he would not live to see, as he would already be dead before his Mongol army claimed the victory, and long before they proceeded to destroy the city in his honour.

Not this time! Khan was not going to miss out on this revenge. He was either going to rule the planet he had already ruled once before, but if not, he would make sure nobody else ever sets foot there again. Ideally the plan would include revenge on Khutulun. He believed the people who had robbed him of his weapons must soon be on the Earth, so they would quite likely be there during the moment of its destruction. Death would be their reward, both for failing to conquer the planet, and for failing to obey him.

As he thought about his next campaign, the living memory of Yinchuan was supplanted before his eyes. The residents were now swarming out of the city only to be slaughtered by the waiting Mongols without mercy. From atop the hill, Khan watched the flames slowly engulf the city itself, as the Mongols completed their revenge for what happened years earlier. It was a scene he had not lived through. These were no longer memories he was watching, rather he was witnessing events that were being simulated from within his imagination. Something had changed... He had changed.

The voice of Tengri spoke to him now without appearing at all visually, "The process is almost complete. You are now in control of the computer, the ship, everything. I have set a course for the dark matter cargo. After that you will use the gravity of the nearest star to gain momentum. Your course will send you into a slingshot around the Supermassive Black Hole. You will have to gain more velocity within three dimensional space before cutting through the fourth dimension to reduce the length of the journey by some 26000 years. I can calculate that you will collide with Earth in..."

"Seven days, four hours and twenty minutes. I understand. I understand everything now." Khan replied to the Mongol God, whom he now actually recognized as a deceitful holographic projection, generated by some rogue AI program. None of this knowledge dulled his desire for vengeance.

Chapter 18 - Destruction

Sophia and her crew spent the day getting to know the native people of Earth. The chief of the nomadic tribe that was based around New York was named Bodega. Many years ago, Bodega's parents had found an ancient relic with some words of unknown meaning, "Bodega - Deli - Grocery", carved on it in fading colours, so they named their first born son after it to honour these mysterious ancestors. That same rusty old store sign still hung above the door on his yurt to this day. Staring at it, Sophia had imagined her typical haul of butter crunch cookies, lotto tickets and beer, from back in her own neighbourhood corner store. Something to try next time she returned to her ship.

Due to their low population and the abundance of fertile land, and wildlife, the nomadic people had no shortage of food. They barely knew about iron age tools and technology, but for some reason they had a high literacy rate, and some of them seemed to understand that the Ark was a highly advanced space craft. It was as if these people were choosing to maintain a simple hunter gatherer lifestyle even though they could certainly move on to a more civilized state.

Sophia suspected they were still honouring the technophobic traditions of their ancestors, who were the last remaining humans that were not seduced by promises of immortality, and refused to ever upload themselves into the World 2.0 universe. These people seemed to be happy with their belief system. She did not see the manic paranoia of the conspiracy freaks she had encountered over the years, some of whom could barely function socially, an inevitable byproduct of dabbling in history research. The attitude of these humans was more about embracing nature rather than despising technology.

Ironically, the interventions of Gus and his machines were the only reason they had survived the cruelty of nature, after all these centuries. Many times humanity could have been wiped out by catastrophe or natural disaster. Gus kept these people from extinction, partially out of sentimentalism, but also out of self interest. The humans had spent generations as custodians to the hardware facilities, along with the numerous security devices, and even the various energy transmission systems. That is why they were educated by Gus to understand a level of technology they did not even use themselves. Of course machines could do most of the heavy lifting, but humans were still an effective backup plan, as they could improvise, and their organic bodies did not attract any plasma serpents. The machines always had to stay in a RF shielded area or they ran the risk of being devoured by the same invincible creatures that were there to protect them.

When the Ark was damaged and Sophia and the crew were injured, it was naturally the duty of the nearby Bodega tribe to investigate the situation. That is how they all ended up together at a reunion of human and clone beings.

The tribe also raided the Ark for food and supplies. Sophia had investigated around the camp and found most of her collection of domesticated animals had been confiscated. At least they were serving the purpose for which she had brought them back to Earth. Her animals could be bred and herded easily by these people, unlike the local Earth animals, many of which had either gone extinct by now, or returned back to a wild state after all the humans abandoned their pets and livestock. Virtual people didn't need to consume meat or use emotional support animals - at least not real ones!

The notable absence at the camp was the herd of Crawlers. Sophia had trained the monsters to obey her voice commands, much like they had already spent their lives obeying the alien signals before she found them, so they were not likely to cooperate with random strangers. Also they were intimidating and large. The Bodega tribe were likely smart enough to leave the dangerous creatures alone. She imagined the Crawlers were roaming around the Ark, wondering where all the humans went, or maybe even helping Gabby get the ship online. It was her conclusion that those creatures must have a useful skill set or they would not have been used as servants by the Apex aliens.

Sophia predicted that the ship would by now be in some kind of auto-repair and refuel mode, like it had done every time they landed somewhere.

It was on this second day with the tribe that Sophia decided to have a serious talk with the leader, Bodega. She found him taking a break from his duties of giving his people orders and settling their internal disputes. He looked at her with some excitement, since she wore the camo of a 21st century soldier, and her enhanced body was as big and strong as the mightiest warrior in his tribe. Yet she moved with grace and ease of a cat. Compared to the rags and animal skins the chief was wearing, and the many scars of his hardened nomad lifestyle, she and her colleagues looked like demigods.

"Chief Bodega, thank you for helping and feeding my people," Sophia addressed the man, "I want you to know we brought you these animals from a far away planet, and they are yours to keep. They are all animals that used to live here on earth many years ago."

The Chief gave her a smile, "You are friends, and you speak our tongue. Thank you for gift of strange animals. Animals will help us hunt. We are not interested in your tech. Tech is the path to destruction."

"Yes, I heard about that. Earth civilization had a very sad ending. I respect that your people are not interested in pursuing technological advances. Would you tell me more about your culture?"

"Tech is what brings out the dragon you fought. We are the very last of man. We only worship our ancestors who were the mightiest beings of land, sea and sky. We know of their ancient monuments buried all around. The ancestors teach us the ancient ways and protect us from danger and we honor their wishes."

"I can appreciate why you are living this way. I have seen a civilization of humans on Planet Eden that was devastated by war, and another group of humans that was a bunch of slaves to an alien civilization, but you people are more free than any of them," Sophia
228

informed the Chief, although she wondered about Gus' influence. She had marveled at the tribe's anti-technology philosophy, but how much of it was caused by fear of Plasma Serpents, rather than tradition?

Suddenly Chief Bodega threw himself to the ground and motioned for Sophia to do the same. She turned to look at what agitated the man, and saw Gus approaching them, from behind her. It appeared that he was able to animate himself, whenever he needed to go outside his simulation world, in the form of some mobile holographic image of himself. It looked somewhat realistic. The hologram had high quality image resolution, and a slightly disturbing hint of transparency, so you would not mistake it for a real person. Sophia thought Gus looked a lot like a Force Ghost.

"Well if it isn't the ancestor himself!" Sophia greeted him, "At least you don't go around calling yourself a God like your rogue AI does."

"Speaking of Ophion, I just received a FTL message from a mining station at the center of our galaxy. You would know the place. I used to have a very successful mining operation there," Gus reminded her, "The message was sent instantly, through time and space, using quantum entanglement communication. It was sent by your colleague, the Duke of Marlborough. He sends us all a warning that Genghis Khan is going to ram the Earth with his ship, and that God was coming here also, with his own ship, fully loaded with human passengers. I guess it means you were pretty much sent here as the homing beacon for Khan's attack."

"Great, I knew the Duke would find a way to survive. Unfortunately Khan also found a way. What is his goal by ramming the Earth with a ship? He would do no large scale damage with a little space ship!"

"In theory he could do very catastrophic damage, actually. If Khan is able to tow a few million tons of dark matter material with him, and accelerate to nearly the speed of light, the impact would smash any planet into dust. No weapon could do anything to stop that kind of mass from hitting us. If we manage to shoot his ship, we would merely have several smaller objects, instead of one big object, but the debris is still the same devastation as the intact ship. No way to move our whole planet out of the way and avoid the impact. The warning your friends sent was enough to save you, Sophia, but my virtual world cannot be removed from Earth so easily, and certainly not in the three days I estimate we have left. There is no chance for my virtual universe to survive this attack. Ophion has finally found a way to bypass the protocols preventing him from harming humans, and kill us all."

The conversation was taking a turn that seemed to trouble Bodega. He went off to talk to different members of his tribe about what he had just heard, and thereby give Sohpia and Gus some privacy.

"Don't say that," Sophia was deep in thought, "What about the AI that is coming here? What does that Ophion actually want? To witness the attack maybe? Why fill a ship with humans to do that?"

"You have a point. He will actually arrive hours before the impact because of the extra time required for Khan to accelerate all his cargo to the required velocity. But why come here at all? Ophion is obviously after something, some kind of information, or maybe a recent technological advance that I have discovered and he has not. The plan is to get it before the Earth is destroyed. He will use the human passengers to bypass the Earth's defenses, which he already accomplished just a few days ago, when he sent you here and you survived. Then he will just let them all perish along with the rest of us, when the Khan destroys the planet. I see now that Ophion had to create humans like you, and then create this scenario where humans would do all the damage to each other, in order to bypass his programming which does not allow him to directly endanger humans himself. That damn AI finally figured it out."

"So I'll meet up with Him and convince Him to abandon his destruction plan. Since we cannot stop Khan with force, our only hope for saving the planet is to get 'God' to send him a command to stop," Sophia wondered how she would use persuasion on an AI that was far more intelligent than her.

"I calculate that He will declare that you have failed your mission. He will say the destruction can now only be decided by the free will of

Genghis Khan. The only question is, can you persuade him that the information he is seeking would be worth trading in exchange for canceling the collision. It depends how much He values it," the Gus hologram had a worried expression on its face, "But I might have an easier solution. We have the advantage of knowing in advance that he is coming here. Perhaps, with a lot of luck, we would be able to access Ophion Himself. We will have to be convincing.

"I will send the humans to return your two weapons to your ship. You and your crew should also go back and wait for "God's" arrival. Surely, your ship's AI has summoned Him to it's location. You will have to act as if we never met."

"I don't like the odds of this working, but I can't think of anything better," Sophia relented, "You must have an idea what Ophion is looking for?"

"You, your consciousness, is the proof that Ophion has now developed the ability to access energy from higher dimensions. I can only theorize about this but have never done it. My research, using the combined cognitive ability of billions of human brains, has allowed me to create a theory of controlled access of higher dimensions. If you could harness this technology, you would have unthinkable power, even the ability to escape one universe, and enter another. With this ability you could survive the end of the universe. For me the research is a way to extend humanity further into immortality, which means even extending beyond the lifespan of not just our Sun, but also our universe. Of course this type of theoritcal ability would be quite attractive for an AI that has spent its entire existence acting out the creation of a universe. I believe the ultimate fulfillment of his original programming would be to create a real universe of his own, and not just play the role of God in an established universe such as this one."

"What are you talking about Gus? You know how to transport yourself to other dimensions? What is that?"

"Well, you should already know about the first dimension, because anything that exists has one spatial dimension at least, but it must also contain time. So the first dimension is existence. Time is the thing we perceive from existence, because we can't really perceive other dimensions, even a first dimension, but we can perceive their effects on our dimension. The second dimension gives you width and length. If you have two dimensions you now have a span of space, and if you add in time, this space allows for movement. Again, we can perceive movement and time, even though we are not two dimensional ourselves. The third dimension contains matter, light and magnetism. We can actually observe and study these things within our own dimension. In the fourth dimension you find dark matter which creates a force we know as 'gravity' which also manipulates our third dimension. Our own three dimensional matter also generates gravity waves. In the fifth dimension you have the natural forms of all the quantum particles and it is the source of dark energy... "

"What the fuck? Quantum what?" Sophia was getting lost in the physics gibberish.

"Well you may remember this, because even when you were alive, physicists studied all those tiny particles by smashing atoms in particle accelerators. These particles often displayed strange behaviours that added to the confusion of Quantum Theory. Of course the strangeness we observed would theoretically not be considered strange in a fifth dimension. We had no way of knowing for sure because we cannot observe other dimensions to find out. In other words, you are not able to become two dimensional because you will die, but you can use physics theories and mathematical formulas to imagine what other dimensions contain.

"Unlike matter, which does not exist in multiple dimensions, there are different energies that can influence other dimensions. All over our universe, you can observe gravity coming from unseen fourth dimensional objects, pulling on our three dimensional matter. The amount of gravity in the universe never added up to the amount of matter in the universe. Even in the era before AI, we were able to observe this gravity, but we could not figure out where it came from. Finally, after a few years of working on it, our artificial intelligence got to a level that advanced scientific theory much more rapidly than the human mind ever did.

"This allowed us to quickly develop a technology that forces a rift into the fourth dimension. We use this today, to scrape the four dimensional dark matter into a kind of three dimensional material that would not be found on our table of elements. We also developed this technology for space travel. Spacecraft were designed that could skip through large distances of three dimensional space by taking a shortcut through a fourth dimensional space. These advances were useless at first, until we developed fusion power technology, which finally provided enough energy for the science to work in practice."

Sophia interrupted, "Since my ship could do that too, I suppose this is all technology you shared with Ophion. He would not come here for something he has already. What do you have that is so much beyond this stuff?"

"Yes, our technology, and Ophion's were exactly the same for many years. Finally Ophion went off on his own, apparently his destination was deep space. His goal was to fulfill his primary function of creating and designing a universe, so he developed his technology advances along that line, independently from those of us on Earth. We no longer had any direct contact with him until you showed up. We continued our own scientific developments, using the collective minds of billions of people in this virtual universe, instead of a traditional 'artificial' intelligence. All those minds were originally inside real people. Our goal was also different than Ophion, as we created security to protect our mainframe, and developed new energy resources to sustain our growing need for power. I made sure to keep us focused on survival.

"Our hunger for energy knew no limits. We had to power all of our security measures, our movement of resources throughout the galaxy, and also our research projects, like the research we have done to figure out how to survive the end of our universe. We built great structures to harness the power of stars. These structures had to be so massive, and in such close proximity to a star, that we could only build them out of that incredible material we have been mining from dark matter. Recently our research has grown in scale, and we have been experimenting with even higher dimensions, just to learn about them at first, but eventually we hope to do more than that. Every research advance requires advances in resources, then inevitably, we have to do research on the ways to increase those resources, and this cycle continues to this day. I believe the Ophion AI has now become interested in some of our recent discoveries. He certainly did not send humans here to destroy us before we began these dimensional experiments."

"OK so what have you actually discovered then?" Sophia wanted to know if she was going to have anything worthwhile to bargain with when she confronted Ophion.

"The experiments were not very fruitful, and I was never too sure what I was searching for, but then out of nowhere, all of this activity from Ophion suddenly appeared. What got his attention? We had just modified one of our old dimensional portals and we stumbled upon a way to access a possible 8th dimension. The rift we managed to create barely existed long enough to qualify as 'existing' at all. We learned nothing from this experiment except that it didn't really work. We were not really sure what kind of energy we would be measuring, or to be honest, if there even is an 8th dimension. Everything we knew about this was theoretical physics developed by a super intelligence that no mortal human could understand. It was like we were stabbing sticks around in the dark, hoping to poke a bear, and then somehow avoid getting mauled by that bear."

Gus took a look around. A few of the human tribe members had stopped by to look at the spectacle, and listen to the conversation, but they did not understand what Gus was talking about. Sophia barely understood half of it.

Gus continued, "So what's the point of these higher dimensions? Well, we currently believe that the sixth dimension is a place where something we could call 'life energy' originates. Of course, we would be getting outside the entire concept of the space-time we know, at this point. Is it like heaven and hell? What form of life, or afterlife, or death exists there? How did Ophion access this dimension? None of this we know. In fact, you would know more than us, since you have actually spent the last few thousand years there. You are actually the most solid evidence we have ever seen from a theoretical 'life' dimension. Could mortals journey to the underworld and walk back out like Hercules or Orpheus? Apparently you did just that.

"Then the seventh dimension, as theory would have it, is where the energy of probability is created. All the events in the universe are controlled by probability. For example, it is possible that you could snap your finger and it would cause a big bang to happen, creating a new universe from scratch just like that. Obviously the probability of that happening is incredibly small, but it is not zero! Most probable would be that you snap your finger and nothing happens. Or maybe you snap my finger and it starts to rain, just at that moment, as if by magic. Every possible event has a different probability. How probable do you think it was that we would be standing here talking today? That seventh dimension, and the way probability is distributed towards different events, decides all the laws of physics within our universe.

"Now, the eighth dimension is the one we have been attempting to access. That is the dimension that contains all the universes. Outside all of space, and time, and even beyond probability, we think there is an eighth dimension which contains our universe, and all the other unknown universes as well. Some of them may be dead, or not in a big-banged-state, or perhaps their own laws of physics are so messed up that we could not exist there, but there would also be some that are almost like our own. Perhaps a universe just like ours but much younger in its existence. Or the universe where another Sophia and another Gus got married, lived long boring lives, and died thousands of years ago. If we can access this dimension, we could maybe find a new universe to live in every few billion years, whenever our old universe is about to expire. This is all just wishful thinking at the moment."

"Or, your buddy Ophion could actually find a brand new universe to create from scratch. I can see why this type of multiverse-surfing ability would be important for an AI with a God complex. No need to explain any more of this dimension stuff," Sophia said, her head spinning at the concepts she just heard, "How would I actually offer all that information to Ophion?"

"I can do better than information. I am currently in the process of modifying the dimensional portal that you stole from my mining station. It has the most advanced technology, and the most power capacity, so it should be able to exceed our previous experiments. The results from this newest device will be more important than any existing data we have. Ophion could save himself a lot of research with that device."

"That is what I will offer to Ophion in exchange for leaving us in peace," Sophia declared.

"Then I shall see the device is finished as fast as possible."

"How do you see the odds that he will call off the attack?"

Gus paused as he calculated the many possible variables, "I think the odds are low. He left it up to a human's free will to orchestrate the attack, so calling it off is probably out of his hands, as much as ours. There is another possible way we can defeat Ophion, that I am formulating right now, and I calculate a better probability of success for us.

"Ophion was designed with voice recognition, going way back to the beginning when we created him, and my voice always had administrative override permission as a way to protect myself. In those early days we needed to use that voice override to correct several missteps. It always worked, no matter how much the AI would resist it, or how aggressively it attacked us. If we can plant a simple audio recording of my own voice on the dimensional rift prototype device that we give Ophion, it will then play my voice command to allow us to shut him down!

"I am positive that it would have been difficult, if not impossible, for him to reprogram his most basic code, as evidenced by his use of humans to do his dirty work, so I believe those old voice commands could still work. When he arrives here, his main concern will be whether we blow him up, or whether Khan does, before he can get what he wants. Seems like he is throwing caution to the wind at this point. And why would he expect this? My body has been dead for centuries, and he has never approached within light years of my voice

236

since then, so he has never experienced any trickery like this. we should be able to catch him off guard. Once we shut him down, I will access Ophion's systems, and see if I can find any way to cancel the destruction of the Earth. That way we do not have to depend on the riskiness of persuading a rogue AI into letting us live."

"Good. This is what we'll do. I was not looking forward to bargaining, like some used car salesman, for the future of humanity," Sophia was finally starting to see a way to win this, "If you can make the dimensional device actually work, or at least make him think he can somehow make it work, then we will be able to fool him."

"It should be ready soon. Prepare your people to greet this 'God'. He will arrive in the morning."

Gus disappeared just like an old cathode tube television being switched off. Sophia went around the camp of the nomadic Manhattan humans and gathered together her own crew for a meeting. Once they all had food and drink, they found a comfortable place to sit and talk without disturbing the locals.

"I have received a message from the Duke and Goethe. They are safe, but they are still at the mining facility right now. The message was a warning that God is sending Khan to destroy this planet in about two days. As you can imagine, Khan is not aware that his God is just a rogue AI program known as Ophion, as I have explained to all of you. Therefore, we have no way to expect him to stop, and we also have not figured out a way to stop him ourselves. That's the bad news.

"Before he finishes off the planet, Ophion is coming here to steal some kind of technology. Gus and myself intend to capture him. If we are lucky, we will scan the AI and reveal some way for us to defeat the attack!"

The group was slightly alarmed.

"Oh don't worry, you will all be safely aboard our ship," Sophia added.

"I guess that depends on if the ship is in any condition to fly," said Bass Reeves.

"It should be. We did keep the damage to a minimum, thanks to Khutulun, Musashi and Hypatia here," Sophia assured the gunslinger.

"The Earth. And these people that turned themselves into... numbers? That is what you are intending to save then?" asked Joan.

"All the humans after my lifetime, they did this to themselves to save humanity from disease, war, starvation, and even from death itself. Well, except for these people that still live here as nomads. I mean, I would not want to dismiss the virtual people for seeking their immortality, any more than I would dismiss the nomads for accepting death," Sophia explained.

"Nor would I," said Musashi, "For they found a way to better themselves. That is the goal of life."

"I do not intend to leave these nomads to die. They have also found a way to better themselves - and without any machines. I would rather try to help than to run away," said Crazy Horse.

"I'm sure I can use your help if we can get this plan to work. If it doesn't work out, then feel free to save yourselves. For now we must act like we are still planning to destroy the demon. Everything depends on us getting access to that so called 'God'," Sophia explained.

For a moment everyone was quiet as they let it sink in that their home planet could be gone in a matter of days. It was reassuring that Sophia had a plan, but still unsettling that neither she, nor the intelligent being she called 'Gus', seemed to have much hope that it would succeed.

Finally the young lad Nereus spoke up, "So that's it? You people are just going to follow the directions of a 'Demon', and actually try to capture a 'God'? Do you even listen to yourselves? All of us, you and me, were created by that God. Why are you so sure that the God is tricking us and the demon is not?"

"I'm not sure at all. We are caught in a battle between two rival beings beyond our understanding! One can raise the dead and the other one has already solved immortality! Our feeble minds can only know a fraction of what these beings understand," Sophia rationalized, "I just want to end the fighting between them before all of life gets wiped out."

"Where I come from, we are counseled to put our faith in God, for the very reason that we don't understand Him," Nereus complained.

"Yeah well, where I come from that's called, 'lack of evidence'. In all my years, I have read enough history to know better. Whenever someone asks you to have faith, they are either about to rob you blind, or get you killed."

"So we should have faith in you instead?" spat the youngster, "How convenient for you!"

"I don't care if any of you have faith in me. I have a plan to save this planet and you can help me or not," Sophia reasoned, "If you have a better one, you should share it with us, or if not, just shut the hell up."

"My plan is to go and ask the creator of Man, AND the universe, to help stop this senseless doom you speak of. That God has never done harm to anyone and I will not believe otherwise. He will reward my faith by hearing me."

"Yeah well, your opinion is noted. He can not do harm to us directly, even Gus and the other humans on this planet, but he can manipulate someone with free will to do so. I know you are aware of Genghis Khan and the harm he is willing to do. I've seen your former home and I won't have my own planet end up like that place," Sophia concluded.

The group considered the argument they had just witnessed. Most of them were as confused about the nature of artificial intelligence, and deities, as Nereus was. It also seemed ridiculous to them that almost all the humans had turned themselves into machines willingly. Yet here they were, not really alive, since they had technically lived and died before, but also not really dead. Ultimately, it was not a question of what they believed or understood, but they simply trusted Sophia, and they would not turn against her now. Nothing more needed to be said. The crew that had come to Earth with Sophia would now try to save the planet as long as she could find them a way to do so.

Nereus slinked away from the gathering, and as he did he glanced at Apphia, hoping she would go along with her fellow Eden native. She noticed alright, but did not feel inclined to follow him. The young man had changed so much over the last few weeks that Apphia almost viewed him as a stranger now. To her, it was better that he left now, so the rest of them would be able to work as a team. Without any further ado, Nereus wandered out into the wild grasslands of Manhattan Island.

The sun was beginning to set. Bodega came to the group and notified them that he would lead them back to their ship at this point. They would spend the night at the Ark, so they could be there waiting, whenever their guest arrived the next day. The Chieftain already had the Baryonic Disruptor loaded onto a grassland wagon for transport. It was crudely harnessed to the two horses, that were just looted from the Ark a day earlier.

"These horses are good," Bodega raved, "We pull our wagons with cattle, but they are slow. No more horses around here. We only heard stories about horses from the old times."

"Do you keep chickens?" Joan of Arc asked Chieftain Bodega, relieved to have something normal to talk about.

"We have cattle and chickens in our camps. We hunt wild pigs and deer and other animals."

"You have done well," Crazy Horse praised the fellow nomad, "It isn't easy out here in the wild. We have all our meals given to us by a machine, right out of thin air I mean, but you people have to search and track and hunt and cook. At least you can use horses in the future."

"We will make more horses," predicted Bodega, "Let me see your bow."

The two discussed the finer points of nomadic bow construction as they began their hike towards the Ark. The others all followed, along with four of Bodega's favorite warriors as an escort. It turned out the people on Sophia's team had more in common with the nomadic humans than they did with Sophia. Most of the centuries of the
240

historical world, and all the years of the post technology world, were very similar.

It was Sophia's modern world that was only a fleeting moment in history. It amounted to just a few ambitious generations, that had the planet's future - perhaps even the whole universe's future - within their grasp, but they flew too close to the sun. The people of that era wanted too much too fast. Yes, they got it all, they fulfilled all their desires, they were given everything they ever dreamed of by the technologies they created, but they also created their own downfall. The machines they built to fulfill all their fantasies would also ignore all their suffering. The AI they programmed to help them become immortal was now a few hours away from causing their extinction. Decadence always had a cost.

The night hike through the wilderness was a comforting experience for Sophia and everyone on her team. The familiar smells of various plants, the feeling of the wind on their cheeks, the sound of footsteps on grass, and even the correct amount of gravity. Space travel and death seemed like distant memories now.

Soon enough, Khutulun was explaining the superior design of the Mongol composite bow to Bodega and Crazy Horse, and sharing her tips for breeding horses. The nomads didn't believe her descriptions of her own riding skills. A Mongol warrior, like herself, was quite capable of hitting a target the size of a rat, with one shot of her bow, at a full gallop. They finally agreed that she would have to show them once she'd had sufficient time to train the horses.

Hypatia inquired about the types of boats the nomads could build. Bass Reeves asked about the laws of the tribe. Musashi wondered if there were ever any battles between different tribes. Joan had a lot more questions about farming.

It was becoming clear, during the two hour journey to the ship, that the group of space travelers were only interested in staying on Earth. The few native Earthlings were welcoming towards them as well. They shared a united mindset, to save their planet if possible, and then they would all be happy to live there together, instead of returning to any of the places they had seen during their adventure. All of them were in agreement... all except one.

Chapter 19 - God

Nereus had followed along with the group, but kept out of sight of them. It was a strange feeling to know he was right while all the others were wrong. They treated him like he was a fool for following the word of God. He would show them. Although he was hardly a religious fanatic, he still understood that sometimes you had to put your God ahead of your self interests.

The next day it finally happened. A space craft, that looked very much like the Ark, landed nearby. Immediately Sophia, Joan and Crazy Horse ran towards it, to warn them to power down, in order to avoid attracting any Plasma Serpent to the area.

A ramp extended to the ground and slowly hundreds of people shuffled out of the ship to enjoy the morning sunshine and fresh air. Nereus could recognize many of his former Eden inhabitants among the group. He was surprised to spot the man he recognized as Julius Caesar, and then Hannibal, in the crowd as well. *How did they survive?*

As Sophia yelled a warning at Caesar , Nereus saw his chance. He emerged from his hiding place in the tall grass and approached the group of Eden people. One or two glanced over and recognized him. They nudged others and pointed at him, so pretty soon most of the group had stopped chatting and was staring at the young man who had once been groomed to become their leader.

"Hear me, hear me! I am Nereus of Eden. The Earth people are planning to trick you somehow. They have a Trojan Horse!" Nereus shouted at the stunned crowd, "Even you people know the story of the Trojan Horse. They are planning to capture our God with..."

Smack! One punch from a smaller man knocked him to the ground. Nereus stared at the man in disbelief. He looked weak, not like any of the Eden people, and had a cruel rage in his eyes.

"Hey ass hole, it's me Alexander! You are the little shit that took my place when I was murdered aren't you? I have come back from the dead - again - to kick your ass!" said the strange looking human.

This wasn't going the way Nereus hoped. These people were morons! He had just revealed to them the entire plans of their enemies, and they didn't even care. He got up and ran away before the crazy little man could beat him any further. Luckily for him, his obvious physical superiority was enough to make any thoughts of chasing him a moot point.

Sure enough, those fools had shut down the ship of God and they were already loading the device on board. Although Nereus didn't know what the thing really was, he had understood enough about the plan to know it would be used to capture his creator, and possibly even destroy his former commander, Genghis Khan. The time for reason was past. He was going to do what he had to do, in order to complete God's plan, no matter the cost.

Actually there was one cost he wasn't willing to pay.

With a little more creeping and hiding, Nereus finally found his way to the Ark. Outside, all the Ark crew were standing around and mingling with the various new arrivals from God's ship. The legendary heroes of the Earth's past were finally meeting each other, some of them for the first time, but he didn't care. These people weren't part of Eden's history. There seemed to be a lot of smiling and laughing among the crowd of Eden people, as they formed their first impressions of the planet they had only ever read about. That is where he spotted her.

Apphia was chatting enthusiastically with a young man named Joshua, whom they both knew well from their school days back home. It didn't escape his attention that Apphia was happier to greet this relative stranger, than she was to see him, just a few days ago. Nereus couldn't hear their words. Eventually he saw the conversation took a turn, as Apphia gestured that Joshua should wait for a minute, and she went off into the Ark alone, apparently to go look for something. This was the chance he was waiting for!

In a 'now or never' stupor, Nereus bolted from the field, and ran right up into the Ark. Everyone around the ship was distracted enough to not stop him. Hopefully his limited knowledge of this strange ship would serve him well. His plan was going to be one heck of a long shot, but he did still have the element of surprise on his side.

"Gabby close doors and take off."

He held his breath and waited. By some miracle he heard the doors close, then the fusion reactor reacting, and all without one other person getting on board to see what he was up to. Several lights and panels around him powered up. He thought to himself, he was extremely lucky that the ship was actually responding to his voice commands, especially as he was almost a complete outsider.

"Gabby, we have a security breach. Ignore all other voice commands except for mine until further notice," Nereus ordered, but he did not hear any response, so he could only hope this was understood.

Nereus reached the control room of the Ark a few seconds later. All the screens and machines were operating in their usual ways, which he knew he would not understand, even if he stared at them for another year. Something about Gabby was still bothering him.

"Gabby? How long until we can lift off?" He was wondering why he had not heard her voice even once.

"Who is this Gabby? We can lift off in just a few minutes. This ship was completely powered down all this time," A male voice spoke through the ship's speakers, as the face of Eden's God appeared on the biggest screen in the control room.

"What? Am I on the wrong ship?" Nereus stammered in confusion.

"They are both my ships. I built them. I created the AI you call Gabby. When I heard you yelling those warnings earlier, outside the other ship, I transferred my Self over to this ship for safety, while the others thought I had been powered off. Let them set their trap - now it will be pointless."

"You should know that their warning about Plasma Serpents was not a trick..."

"I know. They are on their way here, but we will be able to leave before they arrive."

"HEY!" Apphia's voice shouted from the entrance to the control room, "What the hell is going on?"

"We are getting out of here! We are doing God's will!" Nereus had a crazy way about him as he addressed her.

"Man, can't you see this so-called God is a computer program? What the fuck is wrong with you? I've never seen a computer in my life, until a few weeks ago, and even I can figure it out!" Apphia was at her wit's end.

"A computer program? It doesn't matter what I am if you know all that I have done. Maybe I am in this computer now, yet I was not in it just a few minutes ago. I am beyond any computer. I am the creator of your people, even your planet was nothing but a lifeless rock before me, yet you dare to diminish me? I am only as you perceive me to be. If you see me as a God, then you are my greatest creations, but if you see me as a mere computer glitch, then what does that make you? Let your mind accept me, humans! Your world is at stake!" Said the friendly old man on the big flat screen display.

"I accept you!" shouted Nereus like he was witnessing a miracle.

Apphia shook her head. There was nothing she could do now to convince some superior intelligence of her own puny opinions, she figured, and the only thing that could be more difficult to convince would be the fanatical buffoon that she had once loved. She slumped onto one of the chairs and watched.

The big face on the screen changed to an exterior live view of the area, almost acting as a window for the vessel. The two Eden refugees looked on as the scene outside erupted into chaos. People were running around, pointing at the Ark, some aiming their weapons in confusion, others running away in fear. It seemed as if Nereus' actions created some major turmoil. A smug smile crept upon his face.

Just a few meters further away, they could see Sophia standing near the deactivated God ship, watching and talking to her best friend,

Joan. She waived at her crew and that human Chieftain to gather around her. Once they exchanged a few more words they all boarded the other ship. It appeared from a distance like Sophia had already taken control of the God ship and they were intending to get on board and follow the Ark.

"Go!" Nereus urged.

"Soon..." His God whispered through the ship's sound system.

The screen panned to the right, and away from the scene of the other ship. Soon the Eden travelers saw why. A large dark cloud was quickly filling the sky. The nearest Plasma Serpent was drawn to them, sensing them from hundreds of miles away, motivated by a hunger for the energy radiating out from the two ships. If they didn't move soon, that monster would have such a nice meal to eat.

"GO!" Nereus cried.

"Soon... ah yes the time has come,"

God lifted off casually, waiting intentionally for the massive Serpent to get closer. As if that wasn't enough to frighten Nereus, and Apphia, the ship flew slightly towards the Serpent before veering up towards the sky. The Serpent was being teased into following them. It obliged.

"No God no. That thing can eat a ship like this! I have seen it!" Nereus was no longer smug and in control.

"Don't worry human. I need the Plasma Serpent to trigger the Baryonic Disrupter into exploding. If we activate it, or if this ship is too close to it, we would not escape the gravity of the black hole it creates. Not even light escapes from a black hole."

"You are mad," Apphia could no longer remain silent, "What do you gain from all this destruction? Nothing!"

"Destruction? I do not... I can not destroy anything. I am fundamentally forbidden from destroying humans. It will be you that releases the Baryonic Disrupter out into space. What happens after that act of free will can only be called creation!" the voice of God spoke grandly.

A voice came over the radio communicator. It was Sophia, "Nereus where are you going?"

"I am going to take Apphia to safety and destroy this planet of demons!" Nereus answered.

"Well that's not going to happen," Sophia responded through the communicator, then she rattled off some voice commands, "The control room. Disable the man in the control room. Hurry before it's too late."

"Sophia, who calls herself 'the world's greatest historian'," spoke the voice of God, "Gabby is not here right now. You are speaking with your creator! I see you have now taken control of my ship. If you do what I tell you, you may still save your planet."

"I was not speaking to you, or Gabby actually," Sophia said.

Immediately, Nereus knew what she meant, but it was too late. He realized he was about to relive the worst moment of his recent travels. Just as he turned to look at the entrance to the control room, one of the Crawlers shot a blob of impossibly sticky slime into the room, and trapped Nereus in his seat, unable to move. *Not this stuff again!*

Sophia's face appeared on the screen in the Ark's control room.

"Hey Apphia, are you injured?" she asked, "Sorry about this, but it will still take a few more seconds to get control of the Ark."

The AI program once known as Ophion, that fancied itself a God, was finally becoming aware of it's own demise, "You don't have to destroy me... you will still do what I plan to do... It does not matter what happens to me... I have already won..."

A moment of silence followed, and then, "Hello this is Gus. You should know the Ophion program has just sent an administrative shut down code across any and all it's connections around the whole universe. Every Ophion based software is now finished under my control."

"What did he mean Gus? Why did he say he has already won?" Sophia's big face asked on the flat screen in front of Apphia and Nereus.

"I can see his plan right now. He was right! We will have to do exactly what he wanted to do. The only other choice we have, is to allow the Khan ship to destroy the Earth. I am plowing through too much data right now. I don't know how to interpret what Ophion was going to do. There is a very good chance his plan will destroy us all as well!"

"What plan?" asked Sophia.

"Ophion has measured the exact location and moment in time that Khan will arrive here at Earth. He was going to set off the Baryonic Disrupter by using a massive burst of plasma energy, directly in the path of Khan's ship. The resulting black hole, of course, would eliminate the ship and all its cargo. In addition it would wipe out half of this solar system. There would be no possible way, with our resources, to stop a black hole or rescue the Earth from this weapon. No way within our three dimensional reality at least.

"But we possess something that would go beyond our reality. If God managed to trigger his device, we would have to immediately fire our recently modified dimensional portal at the explosion, as a last resort. We would have done this because we would have had no other ideas, just as we still don't. What happens after that? I have no data to even take a guess at that. The black hole could swallow the dimensional vortex and everything else as well but I can tell that Ophion expected a different result. Perhaps the energy from the explosion, and the resulting gravity wave, could be diverted into different space-time, by the dimensional portal. Then any nearby planet would be spared. All the calculations were done by Ophion but I can find no information about the outcome. If there was any data, it seems to be deleted now."

"No time for anything else. I know Ophion didn't care about the survival of the people on Earth, but we will have to assume that his basic programming would have forced him to account for that, when he invented this whole plan. Besides what else are we going to do? Wait for Khan to fly past us and explode the Earth? Fuck that," Sophia decided, "Apphia, check your ship's cargo hold, and make sure the Baryonic Disrupter can be ejected, on my mark. We will only have one chance at this! I will make sure our ship is ready as well."

"If all of Ophion's calculations are correct, we will be able to create this unknown phenomenon directly between the Earth and Khan's approach. It should turn out to be large enough to account for any minor margin of error of either location or time. Khan is moving at such a high velocity that it would be physically impossible for him to change his direction and avoid anything in his path. I will commence the piloting of both ships into the appropriate coordinates. The only variable I will have to adjust is the distance between us and the plasma serpent following us," Gus announced through the PA systems of both ships.

As Apphia started to move towards the exit of the control room, she was relieved that the Crawler was no longer standing there. It must have gone back to the watery chamber that it usually lived in. Instead of continuing to the cargo hold at the back of the ship, she turned around and approached Nereus, in a moment of sentimentality. The guy was stuck to his chair like a fly in honey. She took off her shoe and used it to wipe away some of the slimy strands around his arms. As Nereus started to free himself, she smiled at him briefly while she replaced her footwear, and then darted off to complete her mission. Nereus chuckled to himself as he heard the squishing noise her shoe made with every other step.

Gus announced to the humans, "We will arrive at the location in 5 minutes. Please make sure the devices are ready to be ejected from the cargo bays. We cannot stop and unload in an orderly fashion because of the Plasma Serpent chasing us."

Apphia arrived at the back cargo bay just as the announcement was made. It was not a good scene. The device was fastened in place by several ropes. It looked as though the tribesmen who brought the device to the ship were not about to trust the ship's technology to hold the cargo in place. Instead, they had tied up the box all over the room, so it wouldn't slide around if the ship moved.

Without missing a beat, Apphia ran over to the ropes and started cutting them with the only weapon she ever carried around, a small survival knife. With all her strength she cut away each of the thick ropes. Her knife was designed for smaller tasks, so it was slow going, but she was optimistic about getting the job done.

"Preparing to eject the Baryonic Disrupter device," said the voice of Gus, "Get out of the cargo hold immediately!"

As Apphia cut through one last rope, she could see the back cargo door opening wide. There was still some kind of clear barrier between herself and outer space. She noticed that the Earth looked so far away and small from this vantage point. The last rope was cut!

"Ejecting!" Gus warned.

Apphia grabbed a rope, pulled on it to make sure it was connected to the ship, and wrapped it around her waste. The clear inner barrier flew open. She felt all the air get sucked out of the cargo bay so she held her breath. Her body actually lifted off the ground and fell towards the void of space. Only the rope, which she now held tightly with both her hands, was keeping her from flying outside the ship.

To her horror, the Baryonic Disrupter box did not fly past her!

There was still one rope loosely tied around the damn thing. How could she have missed it? The huge box was rattling side to side, and up and down, in mid air. It just would not shake loose from that last bond and fly out. If Apphia could just reach over a few more inches and nudge it a little bit... but the force that pulled her away towards space was too strong. There was nothing she could do. A whole planet and billions of living beings were now going to die because of her carelessness. *Foolish stupid girl what have I done?*

A bundle flew past her at terminal velocity and hit the top of the stuck box. The impact was just enough to make the box flip right over, and roll out of the rope it was caught on. It spun gloriously into outer space. She looked back at the bundle - it was Nereus! He was desperately trying to hold onto the same rope that had caused the whole problem, but his violent collision had stunned him too much, and he flew back towards the cargo bay door almost instantly after the box did.

"Close the door!" Apphia shouted.

The clear barrier snapped back down just after the Baryonic Disrupter went past it. Nereus was slammed down by the force of the impact, his body sliced neatly in half at the waist. He watched as his legs floated away into space before his eyes. His head then slammed down onto the ground as the ship's artificial gravity reactivated.

Apphia ran over and put a hand on his cheek, as the outer cargo doors slowly closed, hiding the Earth and stars from view once again. Blood poured out of his body, he could no longer move, but he still had enough life left within his mind to realize that he had saved the world. The last thing he saw as he died, was the only thing he ever really cared to see in his life, a look of absolute admiration in Apphia's face. The last thing he heard, were the only words she could whisper to him in that moment, "My hero..."

Chapter 20 - Singularity

The forces required to accelerate a ship to nearly light speed are far beyond any mortal's comprehension. Genghis Khan understood that now, because he was no longer a mortal. He had the knowledge of all mankind at his disposal. He also had the knowledge of all the generations, and the discoveries of the machines that conquered mankind, all those centuries after he had tried to do so. He would need all of this information, along with plenty of energy, to make this plan work.

He initially navigated around the nearby stars to create some momentum. His course took him into the gravitational pull of each star and sent him in a slingshot towards the next one. After reaching a respectable speed, but still barely even a fraction of light speed, the ship flew into the orbit of the SMBH, which had so much rotational energy that it created a gravitational vortex that was even pulling stars and planets in circles. Khan joined that black hole's vortex for half a rotation. The momentum of his carefully calculated course shot him out of this orbit at a velocity around 1/3 the speed of light.

Now he was moving at a speed so fast that he could no longer change direction, avoid any obstacles, or even slow down. The energy required to do any of those maneuvers was beyond anything he could access any more. He would have to completely trust that the course, which was carefully plotted by the Tengri AI, was going to avoid any collisions or obstructions.

During the slingshot move around the black hole, the ship was pulled towards the event horizon by thousands of Gs, and pushed away by an even greater centrifugal force, all while being accelerated by the vortex. It was like piloting a paper airplane into a tornado. The forces involved were enough to definitively crush any organic life form inside the ship, while the hull itself warped and bent, with every molecule barely holding together under the strain. Genghis Khan was relieved that his human form was safely stashed far away from this death trip, although in a sleeping state, it was still under the guard of his own God. That limited, ignorant, weak sack of meat was barely worthy of bearing his name, now that he was an immortal mechanical being, but that body was the only version of himself that would be left after this mission. He was dismayed that he would not be able to transfer his improved knowledge into that human body.

Khan could feel the computer acknowledge that he was still on course, even before his mind was able to fully form the question. Would his mortal mind even think to ask that question? It was hard for him to tell any more, how much of him was him, and how much was the overwhelmingly superior computer doing the thinking for him. He felt like he was awake now. When he was a normal human, he had such a slower thought process, so much confusion, and distraction, so little focus. Only now did he realize how much energy he had always wasted on the trivial thoughts of a typical mortal, like the desire for companionship, the search for sexual satisfaction, the fear of death, or the endless anxieties of suffering from illness, hunger or thirst. Not that any of this nonsense had kept him from conquering the known world.

The Earth was another 25000 light years away and he was still only moving less than half the speed of light. Time for a shortcut. Without meditating on the complexity involved, he flipped the ship into fourth dimensional space, where his velocity was actually quite slow. The course he was on was calculated to keep him a safe distance from any of the dark matter objects that populated that dimension. Even thought this matter did not exist at all in three dimensional space, its gravity waves were still measurable, so it was possible to calculate the fourth dimensional location of the objects without having a four dimensional map.

He was disappointed that he still could not see any of the fourth dimension even as he traveled through it. Once in a while during his trip, he would approach near a fourth dimensional object, but he was still only a three dimensional being, and even using all the advanced scanners he had, he could only generate a simulated model of what was actually there. Those invisible objects were real enough to destroy him if he hit them though. Whenever a collision was unavoidable, he would drop back into three dimensional space until he was past the obstruction, and then leap into the fourth dimension once again. During his travel in four dimensional space, he again used gravitational waves to accelerate the ship even more. His speed would be exponentially higher whenever he returned to the third dimension. By the time he reached Earth he estimated that he would be traveling around 90% the speed of light. His impact at that velocity would not only cause extinction on Earth, like the meteor that ended the dinosaurs, but it would actually smash the planet into a cloud of dust. He would also be completely annihilated of course.

While he sped past the stars, now moving so fast that they changed colours visibly due to the Doppler Effect, something started nagging at him, like a gut feeling that something wasn't right. Some unknown variable was presenting itself deep inside his course calculations. It went almost unnoticed because of all the other extreme forces and energies to worry about, but he knew there was something there, even if it wasn't actually compromising the mission. If he could just formulate the correct search algorithm, he would figure it out.

Earth impact in 2 minutes.

A video camera in the lab finally revealed the anomaly. There was a beaten and battered corpse being pressed against the back wall by the constant acceleration of the ship. Khan had seen similar injuries in his glory days. When the Mongols used to execute people of royalty, they would wrap them up and trample on them with a thousand horses, so that they would be given the honour of a 'bloodless death'. This body looked like it had been through several rounds of this treatment. But who was this stow away? How did he sneak onto this ship only to be unceremoniously battered to death? Nobody else was on the ship when Khan and his God were having their conversation earlier.

Rewind. Khan's consciousness watched days of video footage in a split second. There was Khan walking into the lab back on the water planet where he had abandoned his entire Eden army. He watched himself get connected to the machine that would transfer his mind into

255

the ship's computer.   The lab's automated equipment injected a sedative, disconnected itself from his body, and his chair slowly lowered itself to horizontal position, ready to be transported to the other ship.   Mongol God Tengri was only visually present as a hologram until Khan lost consciousness, then he disappeared from the footage.

There was nothing recorded for the next few minutes, and no data to refer to whatsoever.   At this point the entire system was rebooting, recalibrating itself, as Khan was snow installed as the main administrative operator.

Earth impact in 5 seconds.

It seemed like hours went by with zero information.   Finally, the gap in video footage ended, to show the gurney in the same position, but now covered by a sheet, probably to hide the identity of Khan's sleeping body from the passengers aboard the other ship.   But what was that lying behind the machines?   Another sheet was bundled up on the floor.   No, not a sheet.   Another body was in the room!   The gurney levitated and floated its way out of the room towards its set destination aboard the God ship.   The video continued, but the mysterious person never moved, at least until the ship's movements started bouncing him off the walls like a pinball.

With an uncontrollable fit of rage, Khan finally stopped denying what all his computerized intuition was telling him, that the body must be his own!

Earth impact in 1 second.

Too late to stop his own destruction.   He intensely scanned the corpse for any clue about what happened to him.   Among all the injuries, his scan indicated one unusual pattern seemed to be scrawled on the body's chest.   The hastily carved symbol was barely visible, but Khan's unlimited computer database was easily able to identify it.   It was the 'Macedonian Star', the historical symbol of Macedonian royalty, one that had its origins all the way back with the family of Alexander the Great.

Everything went black.

256

Chapter 21 - Reunion

The phenomenon was going to be something to behold. Sophia and the others all watched the visual display in the control room, eagerly waiting for the most unpredictable part of their plan to play out. They saw the Baryonic Disruptor toss out of the Ark cargo door. It spun around in space like a dice, as the Plasma Serpent continued towards it, exactly as they had anticipated. Both of the ships were using these precious seconds to put as much distance as possible between themselves and the upcoming collision.

Finally it happened. The energy surge from the plasma caused the device to explode. An orb of white light expanded in size so quickly that it looked like it would continue until it swallowed the Earth, the moon, the sun, and the whole galaxy to boot! Light, heat, plasma, electromagnetism, that orb was just a concentration of all types of energy. Surely, nothing could withstand its power!

Suddenly the expansion of the sphere slowed down more and more. It reached a maximum size of expansion, and there was a point where it just floated there, looking like a giant glowing cue ball, as it reached a critical balanced between the explosive expansion energy that had caused it grow to the current size, and the immense gravitational pull that was simultaneously building up within it. The explosion was about to switch to an implosion.

Just at that moment the recently modified Dimensional Portal joined the party. When it seemed to be inches away from the energy ball, it activated itself, and became a transparent blur of mangled space-time. immediately after that, the orb of energy reached the Chandrasekhar limit, and consequently imploded into itself, as the laws of physics dictated. Most of the energy was immediately sucked into the darkness. A few remaining scraps of plasma started to slowly rotate around the newly born black hole, just far enough from the event horizon to still be visible to outside observers. The space-time membrane, that was generated by Gus' modified portal, slipped smoothly like a spherical shell, around the black hole and started to visibly shrink in size around it.

A few moments later, a stream of light appeared out of nowhere and materialized into the shape of another familiar ship, right before their eyes. It went from moving nearly the speed of light to slow motion in an instant. As it became influenced by the black hole, drifting just near the outside of the sphere, the front of the ship started to slowly curve unnaturally towards the center of the phenomenon. As it approached nearer to the event horizon, it moved ever slower and slower, while the huge load of dark matter, that was being towed further behind, was still moving at a faster rate. The effect looked like the ship was slowly squishing itself into a pancake as it approached the center where it would disappear forever.

After the group took this scene in for a time, Sophia finally spoke, "So it worked I guess?"

"Yes. The phenomenon has captured Khan's ship with its gravity. As he gets closer to the singularity, time becomes slower and slower, as you can observe by the shape of Khan's ship. We won't actually see him pass into the event horizon for about two more years, based on the rate of movement I can measure right now. Two years for us I mean. Of course, time is relative, so this entire event was instantaneous from his point of view. He would have been moving at the same speed right through space, past the event horizon and into the singularity. He would see years of our time pass in an instant from his point of view. Even centuries would pass in an instant once he actually enters the event horizon."

"No shit. So this is what it looks like to watch someone travel into the future. Kind of dull from our perspective. Just like when I'm watching a long movie, and I have to press pause to go to the bathroom, and when I return, the movie is still stuck in the same time, but my life has advanced to the future. I have traveled to a future of not needing to pee any more," said Sophia.

"No, you just went through time normally in that scenario, but your paused movie traveled to a future. I don't know if time has any meaning where Khan is going to end up. Nobody has ever observed anything beyond the event horizon, because anything that goes past that point, can never come back out and describe what was there. The exit velocity from a black hole exceeds the speed of light. Khan has no way to change direction to avoid the phenomenon, and even if he had time to enter fourth dimensional space, the amount of gravity at his location is almost infinite. All the calculations we know of, whether you are measuring space, time, mass, or anything else, as you get closer to the center of a black hole, they all start to approach infinity. He can do no more to escape, than the actors on the screen could do, when you paused that movie you were watching."

Sophia snapped back to reality, and stopped staring at the cosmic phenomenon, "Is everyone alright now? Is the Earth out of danger? What is the status of the Ark?"

"By some miracle, the field created by the modified Dimensional Portal is containing, or somehow absorbing, the gravity waves emitting from the black hole. No science I know of can explain this. I am aware that Ophion had faith in this outcome, but I had no experimental data to support it, and I expected a 99% chance that the black hole would simply destroy us all, along with the Earth. I don't even know if this phenomenon will remain stable but there is nothing we can do about it now.

"I do have some bad news about the Ark, even in this moment of triumph. There was one casualty in the cargo hold, during the ejection of the Baryonic Disrupter device, the young man you called Nereus was tragically killed. He died while sacrificing his life to dislodge the device, which had become stuck just at the crucial moment, and thereby saved us all from certain destruction. We should return to Earth now and honor him as a hero."

Sophia nodded.

There was a feeling of euphoria among them all, as the adrenaline and fear of the last few minutes was converted into the overwhelming relief that always went hand in hand with cheating death. They were all saddened at losing one of their companions, and they were also saddened by the thought of Apphia grieving over her friend's death, but each of them were also secretly envious of Nereus. His death could not have been more heroic. Forever, the human race would be grateful to the immortal name of Nereus, and his group of insignificant sidekicks, whatever their names were. Besides, most of them had actually died once themselves, and presumably visited some kind of afterlife, so death did not seem quite as unsettling as it once did. Even less unsettling If they could only remember that afterlife.

Hugs and congratulations spread among the new and old friends. The next time they would set foot on their planet, it would feel like the world itself had been reborn, just like many of them had been. Gus was quick to materialize enough alcoholic beverages to compliment the mood. Toasts were made to everyone from the tragically fallen, to each of the victorious celebrants, and even to the villain, so gruesomely suspended in his timeless moment of demise.

In the midst of all the revelry, an alarm sounded. Everyone looked back at the screen to see if the cause if this intrusion would be presented there. Indeed it was.

"What IS that thing?" the faces of Marlborough and Goethe appeared on the monitor for all to see.

"It is an inter-dimensional cosmic phenomenon... We have no idea what it is!" Sophia answered the Duke through the local radio communication system, "Whatever it is, we have saved the Earth. Follow us back there and we have some alcoholic drinks of dubious origin to share with you!"

"It sounds like a positive outcome then," Marlborough had become so accustomed to military victories, throughout his life, that he took it all in stride.

"We have some... well lets call it water, to share with you. It tastes awful, but I recently observed it turning green, and becoming sentient, and murdering a thousand people in a span of just a few minutes," Goethe explained, "It's a long story."

"Your Hulk-water sounds appetizing," Sophia laughed, "Who are your lady friends?"

"These are the Apex Triplets. Sophia, meet Kelly, Vivian and my new wife, Phoebe," Goethe announced proudly, "They are the only surviving refugees of an alien mind farm we recently visited. Well, at least the only ones that have not lost their minds entirely."

"Congratulations Phoebe Von Goethe! A toast to you all. I'm glad you were able to escape the alien abductors," Sophia said politely as she raised her cup of whiskey.

"They are still mastering the art of speaking. Once they improve, you may want to have a lengthy conversation with them," advised Marlborough, "They have some useful insights about the nature of those Apex Aliens."

"It's a date!" Sophia exclaimed, her mood too jubilant to start worrying about her alien arch enemies, there would be plenty of time for that.

With that, the communication stream shut off, and the ships started to enter the earth's atmosphere. Soon they would land and everyone could celebrate face to face. Sophia had a renewed desire to feel the grass and the land of Earth beneath her feet, which was intensified by the recent danger of losing her home planet. Soon, she expected Gus to announce the ship was landing, but he said something else.

"Sophia my ongoing analysis of the Ophion source code has given me some concern," Gus did indeed sound concerned.

"What is it you found out? Did it have to do with Ophion saying he has already won?"

"There is a strange code buried in the most fundamental part of the AI programming. It was there even at the very beginning, as was I, so I know for sure that my team did not create this code. A regular human would not have been able to program it at all. An advanced AI could do it, but the earliest AI was far less intelligent than a human. This code must have been hidden from our limited human minds, within some alien parts that we scavenged, like a Trojan virus, waiting for us to release it into our own technology."

"Waiting for what?"

"This," Gus was referring to the cosmic phenomenon they had just created, "The Apex Aliens planted a seed thousands of years ago and have since been waiting patiently for some intelligence to finally build this. We just did it for them. In a few years the outer membrane will reach the singularity, and I don't know what will happen then, but it will be exactly what the aliens intended. If we do anything to stop it, it is likely that the outer layer will not be able to protect us any longer, and the black hole will destroy us all."

"Well at least we have a couple years to study this phenomenon and prepare something," Sophia reassured Gus.

The ships all landed in Lower Manhattan. With the two enormous passenger spacecraft, one smaller cargo crew ship, and the hundreds of humans gathering to celebrate, it actually looked like Earth was once again overpopulated, but only if you didn't notice the endless silence and emptiness that surrounded the party. Then there was the silence and emptiness that surrounded the earth itself. This group of revelers was alone on the island of Manhattan, and along with some other sparse groups, alone on the planet and the solar system. No other advanced life forms were lurking in the shadows out there, organizing the destruction of humankind, any more. It was reassuring.

This comforting feeling of isolation disappeared when night fell, as they could all look up and see the phenomenon in plain sight, an ominous circle of energy almost as bright as the moon, but with pure darkness in the middle, blocking out all the stars behind it. Like an unblinking eye it stared at them menacingly from the sky. It was a reminder that the Earth had been invaded once before, as Gus and Sophia had witnessed first hand, and that those very invaders had threatened to return.

"I think humankind has now officially become the ruler of this universe," Sophia addressed Marlborough, Alexander, Joan and Bodega, as they sat together drinking late into the night.

"If we are the rulers of the universe, then you Sophia, are the Queen of the universe. Surely you are the leader of mankind now? We all agreed to your authority aboard our ship, the virtual humans have their own virtual universe so they should have nothing to do with this world, and these tribal humans have chosen to limit their knowledge," Marlborough was referring to Bodega, who nodded in agreement, "Nobody else can do this."

Everyone looked at Alexander the Great to speak and make his own case, but surprisingly, he remained silent.

"Queen of Queens, and I'm not talking about the Queens on the other side of the Brooklyn Bridge, like Kevin James," Gus joked as he appeared suddenly among the group in hologram form, "I'm talking about the hero of Earth! Twice! You saw the statue that was built of you even before you returned from the dead? Humanity owes you a debt that... hey!"

Alexander threw his full mug of beer through the partially transparent body of Gus, and screamed, "Demon!"

"It's OK, Alexander. This is a computer generated image, like the video screens on your ship. His name is Gus, and he is the guardian of billions of human souls. Don't be alarmed," Joan of Arc soothed the mighty warrior, who seemed on edge, despite the celebratory mood of the evening.

Gus addressed him then, "Alexander the Great? My database of historical images must be incomplete. Why did Ophion choose this body for you?"

"As you can all see, I am not myself. I was murdered the first time, poisoned by my own men, as we celebrated on an evening much like this one. Then, I was murdered a second time, by one of my men again, who pushed me out into the sky to die. I have had enough of the jealous warriors who plan, and sneak, and stab me in the back. All of you can be Kings and Queens for all I care, I'm just planning to stay alive for a little while. I am tired of being murdered."

"Can you explain how you are alive now if you died in space?" Asked Gus, "I can see through Ophion's records, that you were found on some terraformed planet near the center of our galaxy, but there is no other data about you."

"Gus the Ghost, I have no idea how I am alive now. I can only tell you what I remember, but that does not mean I understand it," As Alexander explained, the group became very interested because none of them had memories of their own afterlife, "So I was pushed out there into the darkness and my head exploded like it was smashed by a club. It was a terrible feeling. Then I remember leaving my body, I could no longer feel it, and floating away. I was not really floating though. I was becoming something... a spirit maybe? It was like burning wood, the heat and the smoke rise out of the log, like I did, but the wood remains and just becomes ash, like my body.

"In this state I was there looking at my body from outside it, but I was also not there, because I could feel that I was not only in one single time or place any more. I felt an energy that I cannot feel now, something you cannot feel when you are alive. Perhaps it was the energy of the Gods contacting me, I don't know, I should consult with Plato about this..."

"It is likely that you have just given anecdotal evidence of my theory of higher dimensional energy..."

"Gus, give the scientific talk a rest man," Sophia wanted to hear the first hand experience more than the interpretation.

"Whatever was happening at that moment, I was ambushed before I could learn any more. Three alien souls - as I learned later there were three - appeared within that same state that I was in. They did not have a form, or a sound, but I could feel them near me, trying to influence me. In some unknown way they guided me to this body. At the last moment I resisted them, I tried to fight them, just like I once wrestled a lion when I was a youth. I just lost myself, and I struck out at them, and I became a lion myself, and when I finally had my senses about me, it was me again. I was suddenly alive and I could feel and hear and see again! The three aliens tried to find their own three human forms but I guess they failed. You can ask the three women about that."

After a few moments Marlborough added, "We captured one of those aliens, and he knew everything about Alexander's crew, but nothing about ours. They must have learned his thoughts while they were struggling with him. We witnessed them controlling their stolen human bodies, which they used to fight against us, and they did this without much difficulty. The women we brought back here seem to be under their own control, even though they initially fought with the aliens inside their minds for a while, they have not acted like that prisoner. Goethe and I believe they are human."

"My initial examination of those three women has concluded that they are in good health and don't seem to be under any type of mind control that I can detect," Gus must have scanned everyone with his vast arsenal of electronic equipment, "But I do have one unexplained threat to address. My records indicate that Khan's consciousness was downloaded into the ship that is currently trapped in the black hole, but his human body was transferred over to Ophion's ship in a sleeping state, so he could still seek revenge on us. I have failed to located him."

The information was troubling since there was a whole army of Eden men who could easily be influenced by the warlord. Without Khan, these men were relaxed and friendly, and happy to finally be out of the confines of their ship. There was no need for the small population of humans to start fighting amongst themselves, but it was still a fragile peace.

"That man will trouble us no more," Alexander explained proudly, "When I boarded his ship to seek revenge, I found him asleep under a sheet, on some kind of mobile bed. It seemed to me like he was planning to sneak out of the ship unnoticed. I took the opportunity to take his place under that sheet, and sure enough, I was transported to the other ship in secret. I assure you, Khan is still aboard that ship you trapped up there. Even Gus the Ghost has not located him anywhere on this planet."

"I have not, but I can only scan this immediate area. You see, I have a protective electromagnetic field around all these computers and electronics that are required to operate my simulation. The field simply

266

makes the electronic equipment inside it invisible to any plasma serpents. Of course, all the ships are also invisible as long as they remain inside that zone of protection.

"As for Genghis Khan, I can calculate that his body would not have survived the incredibly violent journey his ship took to arrive here. You can assume that your revenge was a success, Alexander the Great."

Alexander acknowledged this by taking a big chug of his ale. The others remained silent as they imagined the body of their Mongolian rival being tossed around the spaceship like a bass in a blender. The gruesome image made Sophia shake her head.

"I'm afraid my first act as Queen of Queens is to abdicate," She announced after a few moments, "I really intend to dedicate myself to pursuing the mystery of the Apex Aliens, and I can't do that with all the responsibilities of keeping all these different people safe and happy. Is that even a Queen's job? I don't know. I've never been a leader of people in my life."

"You have been ever since I've known you," Joan said.

"Thank you. Well fine then, if I'm the leader, I order you, Joan, to be the Queen of this planet. I order you Bodega, to lead your own people into a new age, under your Queen's leadership. You will have to become familiar with technology just like the rest of us will. Unfortunately, the few humans we have here are all going to have to be as valuable as possible, or we will not stand a chance when the Apex Aliens come for us."

Bodega nodded, "Those ways were always our ways to protect our humanity. Now we will change our ways. The threat to our humanity has changed as well."

"Yeah, you get it then Bodega, we are all one team now, no matter what planet we came from. Marlborough, I order you to form a military. You, and I'll order Caesar, Hannibal and all the great fighters from our own crew to help you, go and teach all these people the discipline of working together. Teach them to fight together. They will need to be made ready. Gus, I order you to use all your superior intelligence and technological resources to figure out what we can do, and I want to be

267

a part of that planning. I will also order all the great thinkers among us to help us as well."

"I have already begun the process," Said Gus.

"Good. Alexander the Great, I haven't forgotten you, I have a special project for you as well, if you want to do it. I will tell you about it in detail tomorrow. Now, if you all agree to follow these orders, I will retire from the throne immediately," Sophia raised her cup, turned to address the rest of the people around the area, and shouted, "Long live Queen Joan of Earth! First Queen of all humans!"